Passage

Jim Poling Sr.

Passage

ISBN: 978-1-7779087-8-2 (paperback)
ISBN: 978-1-7779087-9-9 (e-book)

Cover & Interior Design by Legacy Book Publishing
Cover photo of Jim Poling Sr. by Ron Poling

Printed in Canada
A Legacy Book

Legacy Book Publishing
TORONTO - CANADA

DEDICATION

This book is dedicated to Stuart Robertson, media lawyer, editor, advisor and friend. Stuart dedicated his life to journalism. He helped journalists and other writers to tell important stories factually and fairly. He had an interest in all types of storytelling and it was he who encouraged me to tell this one.

CONTENTS

CHAPTER 1

Cloudburst

THE CLOUDBURST WAS a premonition.

It started as a deep, eerie darkness looming on the northeastern horizon, before falling across the Sydney Harbour Bridge. Lightning flashes and exploding thunder warned of dangers ahead.

The cloud bottom gave way like a rotted wooden ship deck no longer able to hold the weight of its cargo. The rain roared out, plunging anxiously to join the harbour waters below.

The storm ended the bon voyage festivities, untying and scattering knots of people clustered on Sydney's departure pier.

Green, gold and red crêpe streamers, flimsy connections between the ship's decks and dockside well-wishers below, sagged and fell in fragments onto the brass band beating out a spirited version of *Waltzing Matilda*.

The musicians tried wiping wet clumps of streamers from their instruments, but gave up the fight, stopped playing and reached for their instrument cases. Fat raindrops thumping black-skinned umbrellas replaced the band's brassy beat.

Celia was secretly thankful for the downpour. It shortened an awkward and artificial goodbye, relieving her and Bertie from a strained happy family veneer put up for anyone taking notice.

"I must run," Bertie shouted into the wind trying to tear from his hand the umbrella he held over their heads.

"Celia, take good care of our little girl," he said, turning away quickly to give Nancy a kiss and a bear hug that snapped one of the yellow and orange Bird of Paradise stems he had presented to his daughter.

No hug nor kiss for Celia, but she had not expected any displays of love or affection. The relationship between her and her husband now was one based on practicality, not love.

Still, it hurt. Wetness filled her eyes as she told herself it was the rain.

"Be sure to write, darling child," Bertie bellowed against the hammering rain. "Indeed cable. Damn the expense. You're already bankrupting me."

"Good voyage. Good fun!" he waved, turning to follow his umbrella into the sideways rain.

As the dock area cleared, deck crews, stooped under weighty rubber rain slickers, tossed off mooring ropes and RMS Strathaird, dazzling white-hulled pride of the Peninsular and Oriental Line, shuddered with the first calls for power. Three deep-throated blasts, followed by the whine of the ship's steam-powered electric turbines, signalled crew members to set their work pace at full speed.

The six-week voyage to the other side of the world officially was under way. Across the Indian Ocean into the Red Sea, through the Suez Canal to the Mediterranean, then through the Strait of Gibraltar into the Atlantic and up to England.

A long journey. Tedious and tense considering the effort needed to chaperone an intractable nineteen-year-old daughter. But an important one.

Celia had survived the shouting matches with Bertie in which she argued that the trip was important. It would be a coming-of-age tour to help Nancy grow up and get focussed on adult life.

He argued that coming-of-age tours for young women were archaic thinking. There was nothing wrong with Nancy. Sure, she was impetuous and rebellious but those were signs of a developing strong personality.

Bertie eventually tired of the arguing and agreed to the trip. It certainly wouldn't hurt Nancy to experience life beyond Australia. Also, it would put space between he and Celia and free him, at least temporarily, to pursue the life he really wanted.

CHAPTER 2

Umbrellas

T HE WEEK BEFORE Celia and Nancy sailed, a wet gloom descended on Sydney, smothering the harbour and downtown with a grey gauze dome. Most days, Bertie Coulson could stand at his fifth-floor office window and look out to the blue harbour he described as a dance floor for sunbeams.

Today, steel-gray rain dropped from the heavy cloud blanket over the harbour, obscuring most everything, including the tops of the tallest buildings. He scarcely could make out the Gothic façade of the nearby Grace Building, obscured alternately by driving rain and grey mist.

Black umbrellas waggled and bobbed along the grey sidewalks below, looking like ink blots on the wet concrete. A splash of red appeared at the inside edge of the blots, stayed still a few seconds, then moved into the flow of pedestrians, right hands clinging to umbrella stems, left hands firmly planted on hats straining to take off into the wet wind.

The burst of colour on the drab canvass was Nancy in her new coat as she stepped from the building's front entrance. She had left his office a few minutes earlier after stopping in to show him the coat.

She hadn't needed another coat but said it would be perfect for the wet weather. He had paid for the coat, and smiled when he thought about it. Bloody rich, but she loved it and he loved spoiling her.

She had come to the city with her mother, a rare occurrence. They had come by train and the terminal was only a short walk to the office but Celia had chosen not to stop by.

He would have been shocked if she had. He was already shocked enough to learn that she had come to the city. She almost never left home but Nancy said she was fussed up about getting gramophone records for the voyage. Records that apparently could be bought only at a Sydney record shop.

"Why she needs more records is beyond me," Nancy told her father after arriving at his office.

"They must be new and just released to entice her into the city," said Bertie. "You asked her to come up?"

"Yes, but she said she didn't have time. She's in a panic to go right back."

Bertie frowned. "It's not good to have her wandering around alone. She gets mixed up sometimes. I'm concerned about this long trip she is insisting upon."

"She still insists on doing everything by herself," said Nancy." You know what she's like. Stubborn as a bandicoot."

"Now, now. You need to try to get along with her. Don't be giving her gip. Remember: Patience is bitter, but its fruit is sweet."

Nancy threw back her head and laughed: "You never exercise much of that."

"I'm too old to learn. You are not. Besides running this business leaves me little time to be patient, especially with all this war talk."

"Well, it's all talk isn't it?"

"The Germans keep pushing their agendas but nothing will happen for a year or so. The Pommies continue to placate them. But it's a boomer for business. The government keeps calling us for more and more supplies in case there is a war."

Bertie kissed her forehead and gave her a huge hug before sending her on her way.

Now he watched from above as she struggled impatiently to open her umbrella on the sidewalk below. Impetuous, he smiled to himself. A genuine hoyden. The apple fallen not far from the tree.

Nancy was aggressive and boisterous like himself, but totally different physically. She was tall, well proportioned, even athletic looking compared to his short stocky frame. She was a fully developed woman who looked older than nineteen. Her hair was a full, rich chestnut, in contrast to his thinning mousy gray-reddish-brown, and she had started wearing it long, which was now the fashion.

Bertie liked long hair on women. It projected strength and vigour.

She needs strength to get along with her mother, he thought. They were the like ends of magnets, always pushing each other apart. Whenever their opposite ends drew them together, they clashed.

Celia saw Nancy as being adrift. Not focussed on growing up and becoming what Celia expected her to be. Unlike her brother Neil, who although younger, had known exactly what he wanted in life, but sadly would never achieve it.

Celia had enrolled Nancy in a private finishing school where she would learn to manage her future household, plus develop the skills needed to become a polished hostess.

Nancy did not polish well. She skipped classes and spent her time playing and partying at the beaches, which made Celia as happy as a cut snake.

Bertie himself had been a beach bum partier but had outgrown that and believed Nancy would also. She eventually would meet someone like himself who would marry her and take an upwardly mobile position in the company. Perhaps a position that had been planned for her brother Neil.

Thoughts of Neil telegraphed a sharp pain to his stomach, but he wished it away as quickly as it came. Bertie Coulson never allowed himself to dwell on the past.

The jangle from his desk telephone turned him from the window, so he missed seeing the collision on the street below.

CHAPTER 3

Collision

Two steps into the human flow outside her father's building Nancy crashed full on into another pedestrian. Her umbrella fell; she lost her balance then found herself with both hands clutching the trench coat chest of an older, but strikingly attractive man.

"A collision at sea can ruin your whole day," he smiled, steadying her, then bending to retrieve her umbrella. He straightened and gave the brolly a quizzical look. "I'm afraid a rib or two is bent. It's easily righted if we get out of the rain. There's a restaurant across the way, dry and warm."

Nancy, uncharacteristically flustered and unable to respond quickly, found herself guided gently but firmly across the street and into Cahill's Restaurant, near empty after having served the breakfast crowd. The man guided her to a seat near a window and under a light, then slipped on half-glass readers to examine the damage.

"There, let's see what we can do about this brolly. I'm terribly sorry. I wasn't paying attention to where I was going."

"No, it was definitely my fault," Nancy said watching him twiddle the umbrella. He pushed and pulled gently some of the spokes, looking up periodically over his half glasses.

The stranger was slim, apparently robust and projected a commanding demeanour. Obviously, a person who spoke and you followed without questioning. She guessed he was about her father's age. Silver gray temples accenting quiet eyes that were either grey or pale green depending on how the light struck them. The eyes transmitted trustworthiness and that, Nancy thought, is likely why I am sitting here with an older man I have never seen until colliding with him on the wet street.

"I'm Nancy," she said extending her gloved hand. "Nancy Coulson. I'm a bit rattled. I wasn't watching where I was going." She glanced nervously at her watch and saw it was nearing the time she agreed to meet her mother for the return trip home.

"Niles," he said, reaching around the table to hand her the mended umbrella, "Niles Langer. Your brolly is not much worse for wear."

A waiter approached and Langer ordered tea and biscuits. Nancy disliked tea, preferred coffee, and was not particularly fond of biscuits. She was outside her character in not objecting to the order, or the fact that this man had ordered without asking her. He had a domineering kindness that dulled her aggressive edge. They fell into easy conversation, something odd for two strangers, especially strangers with a twenty-year age spread.

Langer was an attentive conversationalist, smiling often with both his wide mouth and studying eyes. He tilted his head when he smiled, crinkling the skin at the corners of his eyes, and creating the image of a face that was always questioning. He had a small nose and narrow chin but a broad forehead that suggested a significant amount of grey matter occupied the space below his receding hairline. His face was smooth and mildly tanned. It was the face of someone honest and outgoing, but someone who never revealed all about himself.

"I hope your collision at sea comment is not prescient," Nancy laughed. "I'm leaving next week on the Strathaird sailing to Europe."

"That's a huge adventure for someone your age," Langer said, pausing to pour the tea. "The continent is becoming a bit unsettled."

"My mother worries about it. She's coming, of course. I want to go on my own but we have the most ridiculous travel and passport laws for women."

She sipped her tea, then added: "I won't have to bother about them soon," dropping a hint that she was nearing the age of majority, which was more than a year off. "My mother is a Nervous Nelly. But my father says nothing much will develop very soon. He says our businesses will benefit if war does come."

"War can be good for business," Langer smiled. "Some businesses. What business does your father have?"

"We have a variety of interests," Nancy said, emphasis on the 'we.' "Some involve supplying munitions, and other soldiering gear. Much of it is quite secret actually."

'Really," Langer laughed. "We must keep a good lookout then for any spies within earshot."

"This is downtown Sydney, so that's not likely," said Nancy with the authority of someone much experienced in such things. "You've been to Europe?" she added, anxious to tell him more about her trip.

"Of course. I'm English. I'm in Australia visiting my sister."

"She lives here in Sydney?"

"No. Off in the outer reaches. She has a small farm on the upper North Shore. I'm just in seeing the city sights. Not much to see that isn't wet this week."

"We live outside as well," said Nancy. "Wahroonga."

"Ah, yes. I know of it. I went to a church outing in nearby Waitara a couple of times with my sister. She goes sometimes to the church there – Our Lady of something or other. Interesting history. There's a large foundling home there, I understand."

"Our Lady of the Rosary. My mother goes there all the time. She's fanatically religious."

She gave the word 'fanatically' extra punch. She delighted in overstating any of her mother's characteristics that she considered negative. "You're not religious too?" she asked with an exaggerated frown.

"Oh, not at all. Spiritual, however. At any rate, I was at the Waitara church just to accompany my sister. For me organized religion is a template. Too much tribalism. Prevents people from doing their own thinking."

Nancy's face lit up with delight. "That's exactly how I feel! I'm sure my mother will want to drag me through every cathedral in Europe."

"What places do you intend to visit?" Langer asked.

"France of course. We get off the ship in Marseille. Then a rail trip over to Italy. She wants to go to that Lourdes religious site in southern France but I hope not."

"Switzerland?" Langer's head tilted as he looked up from his teacup. Nancy noticed he did that when he asked a question. She thought it cute. "Lovely villages and good hiking. Spectacular mountains, of course."

"Really. I thought it was a depressing place. We had to study a book about it in school. About sick people and hospitals in the mountains. It was an awful book. Thicker than a brick."

"Oh, it was probably *The Magic Mountain*. It is taught in English schools as well. It's all about the meaning of life and death. You have to be older to understand it."

Nancy paused, smarting inwardly from the comment about needing to be older.

"I can't imagine anyone building a hospital on top of the mountains," she said. "That's too far-fetched. Why wouldn't they have hospitals down below where everyone could go to them easily?"

"They are not actually built on a mountain peak," Langer laughed. "One that I was at was in a village surrounded by mountains but quite accessible."

"In a hospital there? You were ill?"

The smile crinkles vanished from Langer's face. Switzerland had slipped from his lips only as a suggested tour destination but perhaps his subconscious had forced it from him.

"I wasn't. My wife was. It was a place where they treat lung illness. The mountain air . . . healthy and all that . . . ."

The word wife jolted Nancy. She was so used to being around young bachelors that it did not occur to her than this interesting and exciting stranger would have a wife.

"So, the mountain air helped her?"

Langer looked away, watching the umbrellas passing by the restaurant windows. It took a minute for him to answer, and when he did there was a catch in his voice. "No, unfortunately. She passed away there."

"I'm sorry," Nancy said lowering her head and reaching out to touch his hand. She was not one to reach out to anyone but the sudden disclosure of his wife's illness and death knocked her for six. She did not know what to say or do.

Langer continued to stare out the window. Then he brightened, turning his gaze to Nancy.

"So, I decided to spend time with my sister. Good therapy. I must return soon. In fact, I should get along now."

Nancy did not want the tea break to end. Langer enthralled her. He was fascinating, erudite. A mature, worldly man unlike the young men of her school years, or the silly pups she knew at the beach and the tennis club.

The lilt in his speech, the dance in his wise eyes, excited her. The tilted smile made her feel she was the only person in the restaurant. The only girl in Sydney. She could imagine the envious looks of her girlfriends if she walked into the tennis club lounge with this man on her arm.

They finished their tea and he escorted her to the street. They shook hands, he apologizing once more about her umbrella, Nancy saying she hoped they might meet again.

"You never know," he said. "Life takes strange turns."

She considered kissing him on the cheek but he let go of her hand and waved as he crossed the street. She glanced anxiously at her watch, then hurried off to find her mother, who would be pacing furiously because her never-on-time daughter was now twenty minutes late.

Langer paused across the street to watch her disappear among the shifting sidewalk canopy of umbrellas. A spirited and beautiful young woman. Enthusiastic. Somewhat self-absorbed. There was an ambiguity about her. She was one thing, then perhaps another. He shrugged mentally. Maybe that's the way young women are these days. Certainly, she had talked enough about herself and her family to give him useable information.

He raised his umbrella and set off quickly for the office of MacDonald, Hamilton and Co., ticket agents for the P and O Line, owners of the Europe-bound Strathaird.

CHAPTER 4

The Meeting

A LONG THE PASSAGEWAYS and inside the cabins, porters and maids scurried to prepare passengers' sea-going living spaces. There was much to unpack and organize for a voyage that would last nearly six weeks.

It was a big ship to get organized. It eight passenger decks held 1,100-plus passengers served by a crew of 490.

Departure always saw hive-like activity, but today was more frenetic than usual because the fog and heavy rain had delayed departure and all passenger quarters had to be made comfortable before evening dinner services.

Celia fretted about having the suite she was sharing with her daughter fully comfortable before dinner. She disliked being late and glanced anxiously at the clock on the dresser. Almost 5:00. Their sitting was at 6:30.

"We've little time to get all this put away," she fussed, folding sweaters and tucking them neatly in a dresser drawer. "Dinner is at half past six and we shouldn't be strolling in late."

"Why not mother?" answered Nancy, buttoning her rain jacket and straightening her rain hat. "Late entrances are fashionable. Arrive late and get noticed. That's what the film stars say."

"Well, we are not film stars. Peacocks are fashionable and get noticed. And they get shot for their feathers."

"There's time enough. Weeks. I'm off to the decks to catch the scenes."

She was out the cabin door before Celia could protest.

"Impetuous and headstrong," Celia muttered and slammed shut a dresser drawer.

The trip was not yet fully begun and she could see problems already. Weeks of petty barneys over makeup, what to wear, where to go and what to see, and of course, Nancy's queenly attitude.

There were expectations that weeks away together and seeing some of the world's most fascinating sights would melt tensions between the two. Celia had her doubts now. In fact, she had them from the beginning, but she needed the trip. Needed time to think, and to do it away from Australia.

She opened a box of books and gramophone records for sorting. They were weighty items to lug halfway around the world, but she cherished time alone reading and listening to music. She had asked and was told that the ship had a music room with gramophone. She looked forward to the solitude of that room, playing her favourites, most of which were tangos.

She arranged a few more things then sat with a sigh. She should at least go out on deck to watch the ship steam away from the shore she had never left before. She hesitated at the cabin door, thinking about putting on a coat, then decided not to because she would be outside for only a quick peek.

The wet decks were empty. Few people remained at the rails even though the rain had weakened to drizzle. She was too late to hear the cheers rise into the wet skies as the ship's tip passed beneath the dripping steel web of the Sydney Harbour Bridge.

Celebrating a ship's passage beneath the bridge had become a tradition - a rite of passage - despite its relative newness to the Sydney horizon. It was just seven years old – built in 1932, the year of the Strathaird's maiden voyage – and was a wonder as the world's largest single-arch bridge. Locals called it The Coathanger for its shape and strength to carry a giant's overcoat.

The decks had held shoulder-to-shoulder, belly-to-back crowds a few minutes earlier when the Strathaird glided beneath The Coathanger, igniting an explosion of cheering. Then the celebrants, laughing and shouting, fought each other playfully for quick entrance into the passageways and the warm, dry hospitality of the Verandah Café. They shook off the wet, lit fresh cigarettes, topped up their whiskies and gins and exchanged views on the bridge's wonders and the adventures ahead.

No doubt Nancy was among them, Celia brooded.

She leaned against the deck rail and watched the drizzle and mist swallow The Coathanger. Once it was fully out of sight, the ship would turn at the South Head cliffs and head into the Tasman Sea. It was bound for scheduled stops along the Australian coast, then Ceylon, Egypt and Marseille, a voyage of forty-one days or more depending on weather.

To most people, the Sydney bridge was a marvel. A brilliant piece of engineering, a symbol of human ingenuity and imagination. It brought people closer together and improved their lives. Not for Celia. She wished it would disappear completely and forever, or better still never have been built.

It had changed many lives in New South Wales. Before its construction, the road from her home village of Wahroonga seemed an impossibly long twenty-five kilometres that ended across the bay from downtown Sydney. Anyone going into the city needed to board a water ferry or private boat.

Lives lived on each side of the water were separate and different. The North Shore was high and peaceful in forested hills, bright meadows and clear air. The homes and their gardens and the surrounding orchards formed a heaven above the grimy congestion and confusion and social ugliness of urban Sydney, just now dragging itself from the dirty years of the Depression.

The bridge shortened the distance and blurred the separation between countryside and city. It was a permanent link allowing city and country living to blend, with city life inexorably gaining dominance.

Celia's husband, Havard Albert Coulson— everyone called him Bertie – held an opposite view. To him the bridge was an example of mankind overcoming the obstacles thrown up by nature to hold back progress. He was a city person, preferring his business life on the Sydney side of The Coathanger where living was faster and looser, with its mahogany-panelled offices, dinners and lunches with associates, the club and evening amusements.

The bridge made it easier for him to transfer between that city life and Wahroonga, which Celia called Bertie's vacation spot with its cricket matches, golf, social club functions.

His split life was not unusual in Wahroonga, which had become the home choice for business people whose work life was in Sydney. Business families began moving from Sydney's urban core in the 1890s, populating Wahroonga's leafy neighbourhoods, which they saw as refuges from the city's pollution, poverty and crime; places where their families could grow, be seriously educated and soak themselves in the cultural mores necessary to succeed as members of the business class.

Celia had lived in Sydney for a while after marrying Bertie, all the time missing the freshness and freedoms of the North Shore. The birth of Nancy, followed by Neil, helped push back the yearning to return, but when Bertie's business flourished she pestered him to move. He agreed on the condition they build an estate home like the other successful entrepreneurs putting down family roots in Wahroonga.

On return, Celia found her village overpopulated with more of everything, most of it not needed. It was inflicted with citification that brought too many shops, too many people and too much bustle. She saw local values customs and values being lost.

A consolation was that the Outback was nearby with its farms and orchards and bushlands of wild forest, rugged hills and hidden streams.

Bushwalking had been the favoured pastime of her parents and she tried nurturing an interest in her own family. Bertie was not interested except for the occasional outing to keep his wife happy. Nancy took to the outings as a younger child then followed her father's judgment that nature was boring compared with the amusements of populated areas.

Neil was ardent and he and Celia hiked often together. The outings built a strong mother-son bond, while Bertie and Nancy bonded just as firmly during their social activities in Wahroonga and Sydney.

For Celia, bushwalks were like stepping on a cloud and floating above the changing society she increasingly disliked. Above the complications developing in her family life.

Maybe this voyage would make the complications disappear, she thought, as distance made The Coathanger grow tinier. She bent over the rail, stared down becoming mesmerized by the water churned by the ship's hull.

There is something mystical about a ship just under way that can keep some people at the deck rails, no matter how foul the weather. Enthralled, they alternately stare off into the flat horizon, then straight below where the hull churns blue-gray sea into milky froth.

The ship's engine rhythm quickened and its glide toward the outer harbour became noticeably faster against the incoming swell. Celia raised her head and saw ghostlike shores, appearing and disappearing as the ship moved through the mist. The eucalyptus thickets were dark smudges in the grayness. No fishermen or strollers, often seen in large numbers during fine weather, were out in the rain and chill.

She studied the gray clouds that appeared lighter and relieved after having dropped their heaviest loads. They rode an updraft that was moving them on, much like a freed kite loose in the wind.

The breeze pushed wet air into her face and she realized that she was on deck without a coat. Her black pencil skirt and white silk blouse, open at the neck, provided little protection. Raindrops puddled on the deck below her skirt hems, slowly growing wider and deeper and dampening her feet. She scolded herself for not bringing a coat but had not planned to be on deck for long.

The drizzle had turned her uncovered hair the colour of dark brick. A couple of strands plastered her right cheek, hiding the right edge of her thin lips, now drawn downward by some secret sadness. Her cheeks were damp, perhaps from the rain, perhaps from tears.

From a distance she was a petite woman, slim and wiry. Her face more the creation of a chisel than a mold. It reflected the outdoors; forehead, cheekbones, nose and chin all prominent enough to have been carved by the wind. Earth tone eyes and bronze tan hinted at an aborigine background. She had no aborigine blood, although nature and bush outings once had been a happy element of her life. Now, they were dark, painful memories to be buried through hours of digging, planting and pruning in her gardens.

Busy hands creating beauty dissolve the problems of the present, as well as the memories of the past, she said to herself. Beauty, bad memories and problems. Such contradictions. An unreasonable thought, she reflected, but one that mirrored the contradictions in her life.

Her moods of late were much like the Sydney weather, one minute sunny, then with little more notice than a frown, dark and damp for days. Today's Sydney weather did little to dispel her despondency.

"The mist will make it disappear," said a voice behind her. It was a cultured English voice, easily distinguishable from everyday Australian. Despite being soft and smooth, the voice caused her to jump back from the rail. She turned to face its source, a man whose smile dissolved with the realization that he had intruded on some deep reflection.

"Pardon me?" Celia snapped. "How could you possibly know what I was thinking?"

"I'm sorry. I didn't. I . . . just . . .," he stumbled. "I was just observing that the mist is thickening and it will soon hide the bridge. Shame. I hear it's a wonderful sight sailing out on a clear evening. My apologies. I didn't realize you were so deep in thought."

The trench coat with the collar turned up and the fedora with the brim turned down made it difficult for Celia to see to whom she was talking. He could have been one of those American movie stars who played gangsters in films. Perhaps even Humphrey Bogart. She was not impressed and turned abruptly, disappearing through the passageway door.

He watched her leave, then lit a cigarette and leaned against the deck rail. Obviously, he had approached her at the wrong time. She was not the same bright and sunny person he had seen chatting and gesturing gaily in a churchyard a couple weeks before.

She had not seen him but he had watched her from a distance that day and had been intrigued. Why he was not sure. She was attractive, personable and seemed outgoing. Many women are, but she seemed different. Mysterious and guarded.

He planned to get to know her, and her attractive daughter, much better.

CHAPTER 5

Table Eleven

WALKING INTO THE Strathaird's first-class dining room on F deck was like stepping outside into bright sunlight.

"Wow," a wide-eyed Nancy blurted as she and her mother stepped through the mahogany-trimmed cut glass doors.

Large flush-to-ceiling disk lights flooded the room with whiteness that reflected off octagonal mirrored columns, white cane dining chairs and starched white table cloths covering elegantly set tables for six.

The table settings accentuated the elegance. Cut crystal vases containing red roses, twinkling silverware and Royal Doulton plates, cups and saucers affirmed that this was a first-class dining room. Missing only were bright bursts from exploding flash bulbs of press photographers.

The Coulson women were arriving late, so many of the diners paused their chatter to watch them pass through to their table, Number Eleven. They were an attractive pair, hard not to notice. They might be taken for a young woman accompanied by a young aunt. Or, a young woman accompanied by her older sister.

They would not be immediately seen as mother and daughter because there was little resemblance. Celia, was average height, blue-eyed and auburn haired; Nancy much taller and darker, almond-eyed. More the child of her father in appearance, certainly in temperament.

Celia wore a simple off-white ankle-length gown that complimented her slimness. Her hair was shaped in the latest fashion, grown just below the ears and brushed sideways with a soft wave over one eye. It was the lived-in look of the times, less stark and more feminine than the short shingle bobs and finger waves of the 1920s. She was a woman in her prime, far from going to seed.

Nancy had dressed to catch attention. Her high-waisted silk gown with fitted sleeves and padded shoulders exaggerated her tallness. The silk, in bright claret, caught the light and accented her long dark hair and dark eyes. The gown's low neckline and high hem were daring for the times and raised a few eyebrows.

Nancy's choice of dress set off a heated discussion with her mother twenty minutes earlier. Low necklines and hems above the knee send wrong messages about a young woman, Celia said.

"It is not so much about modesty as it is about attracting unnecessary attention. Trouble never has difficulty finding anybody, so why make it easier?"

For Celia, the shadows at the edge of the spotlight offered shelter.

"Nonsense," said Nancy, whose personality demanded centre stage and a spotlight.

"Showing less leaves people intrigued," said Celia.

"I'm proud of my body and I don't intend to hide it," Nancy retorted. "Unlike old ladies, I don't have anything to cover up."

"Bodies are bodies. Everyone has one. Character – good character – is what gives people something to be proud of."

"Really mother. Must you always be such a wowser?"

The wrangling over the dress was a side dispute, on the surface just one of those common differences between mothers and daughters. The underlying issue of their bickering went deeper and was more serious. It had grown over months, even years, and now was large enough not be hidden.

An impartial observer viewing the pair over time might conclude that they had developed a mutual dislike for each other. The kind of dislike that occurs when a child becomes an adult and the parent realizes this is someone he or she would not prefer as a friend.

Young women often see their mothers as aged and old-fashioned. Certainly that is what Nancy saw in her mother. It was not what others saw, however. Celia was quiet and content to live within herself. She was contemplative but socially outgoing among company she enjoyed or respected and in fact could cut up a bit if the circumstances were right.

Also, most people viewed Nancy as bubbly and adventurous. Perhaps a bit too outgoing and outspoken. Celia saw it as more than that. She felt her daughter was becoming increasingly narcissistic. Nancy was a yakker who talked not to convey something, but to attract attention. She treated others as if they existed to serve her needs.

Neither mother nor daughter gave any hint of their disagreement as they approached their table. A steward in trim black tuxedo, who had guided them to their assigned places, drew chairs for them. Three people already were seated and chatting.

The Coulsons introduced themselves to their table companions, with whom they would share meals on the entire trip. Mrs. Beatrice Cross, a dowager returning to England after visiting her son in Australia. Mrs. and

Mrs. Tom Carlisle, Bostonians doing an around the world adventure. The last empty seat was reserved for Charles Crawford, a British civil servant posted to Australia and returning home for his retirement.

The group fell into easy conversation, mainly about the splendour of the ship, and the disappointment of not sailing beneath the Harbour Bridge on a brilliantly sunny day. The women, outnumbering Carlisle four to one, excitedly discussed the Strathaird's décor and modern comforts. They noted how the dining room was so sparklingly modern with hexagon tables draped in exquisite white linen cloths. Staff had folded napkins to resemble swans.

Hexagon pillars, hexagon ceiling light fixtures, black and buff carpets with their bold geometric circles and squares and the white-washed Rattan dining chairs all complimented each other to give the large room its eclectic look.

"It's all so elegant," said Mrs. Cross as her eyes swept the room.

"Sleek and so non-traditional," said Mrs. Carlisle.

The art deco look was chosen by P&O to create an atmosphere of sophistication and wealth. It certainly succeeded in creating that atmosphere, although it was somewhat out of place now following the vicious Depression from which the world was just beginning to recover.

The fuss about décor made Carlisle, lanky in physique and cranky in disposition, impatient. He ignored the conversation and scanned the room in hope of seeing the missing male table mate arrive. He was eager to discuss the ship's more important features, like the fact that it was built less than six years earlier and that it could make twenty knots, in spite of its 22,540 tonnage.

"I wonder what's happened to our sixth," Carlisle asked. "Can't be seasick. Smooth as a newborn's bottom, out there," he added with a chuckling meant to emphasize the cleverness of his wit.

The steward's approach spared the others having to laugh. He guided an aristocratic-looking gentleman to the empty seat at their table.

"Ah, delightful. Here's our man," Carlisle said, rising with an extended hand. "You must be Crawford. Great to see you."

"Actually this is not Mr. Crawford," said the steward. "The seating got somewhat confused. This gentlemen will join your table for the voyage."

Carlisle looked confused and before he could seek clarification, the steward went off on his duties. Nancy, who had been chatting with Mrs. Cross, turned to greet the newcomer. Her eyes widened. Her jaw dropped.

"Mr. Langer! What are you doing here? What a splendid shock!"

"Hello again," said Langer taking her hand while scanning the table. "You never know where I will pop up."

Then turning to Celia: "This must be your mother. I'm Niles Langer. Delighted to meet you Mrs. Coulson. I've met your daughter, and I can see she is excited to tell that story."

Celia took his hand and smiled warmly. She did not recognize him immediately as the man in the trench coat who had spoken to her briefly on deck. He had been bundled up against the weather; she occupied with her thoughts.

Before anyone could say anything else, Nancy leaped in with the story of how colliding with him on a rainy Sydney street turned into a wonderful luncheon the week before. It was obvious from her enthusiasm that the man had captivated her and she now was overwhelmed by this sudden re-appearance.

It must be destiny, she thought. His knowledge and sophistication were beyond anything she had encountered in Wahroonga, or Sydney. His stories of world travel had left her spellbound. He was dashing and funny and the most interesting and most intelligent person she had ever met.

He was certainly older but young in spirit, handsome and knew how to make a girl feel like a woman.

"What a splendid coincidence," said Mrs. Cross, a large, joyful woman in a much too floral dress. "I'm a great believer that coincidences lead to wonderful things."

Carlisle started to speak but Nancy interrupted. "This is truly exciting," she gushed. "It must have been predestined that you join our voyage. You didn't tell me the other day that you were planning to leave. I thought you were staying with your sister for longer."

"It was a spur-of-the-moment decision," Langer replied. "I needed to get back to England sooner than I thought."

Carlisle looked confused.

"Peculiar," he muttered half to himself. "I checked with the head steward this afternoon and there had been no change. Always good to know who you'll be breaking bread with, right?"

He was disappointed not to be able to chat to Crawford about his posting in Australia. He had checked and learned that the Coulson woman and her daughter were Australians but he was more interested in getting a man's take on the place.

"I hope you won't mind," Langer said to Carlisle. "I'm not such a bad sort and promise to behave myself."

The ladies laughed and immediately began fussing over him. Langer had won them over before his buttocks touched the chair seat.

Carlisle, the ultimate alpha male, mentally circled and sniffed the air to get the measure of this newcomer. He knew from the man's voice and bearing that he was British, well-bred and obviously social. What he needed to find out was whether he would be "a good fit" for the present company. The quick way to discover that was to draw out his views on the two big topics. A fast read of religion and politics showed where a person stood in society.

Since it was Saturday evening, Carlisle asked the table what shipboard church services everyone planned to attend in the morning. After all the ladies had answered, Celia Coulson on behalf of her daughter, who leaned back and rolled her eyes, Langer remained silent. His silence prompted all eyes to focus on him.

Finally, "I don't attend services," he said. "Prefer to do my meditating alone."

"Ah, a non-believer," said Carlisle with a sense of victory.

"I don't think I said that, did I?"

Langer quickly developed a dislike of this puffed up man. He was the worst of Americans. Those few who treasured their country's revolution against Britain but who, when abroad, tried to sound and act British, perhaps because they felt it made them appear more sophisticated.

"Well, I assumed that if you did not go to church, you did not believe in God," Carlisle persisted.

The ladies shifted in their seats. Doreen Carlisle tried to say something conciliatory, but Langer headed her off. The soft, jovial demeanour he had brought to the table, hardened.

"I haven't decided yet whether I believe there is a God. His, or Her existence cannot be proven, or disproven. I do know that if there is a God, his or her plan I'm sure is to leave us to work through our own problems."

He paused and looked directly at Carlisle, smiling without showing his teeth.

"In other words, if there is a God I think he minds his business and leaves us to mind ours."

Carlisle's head snapped back and his face reddened. Langer decided not to let the slap to Carlisle's ego linger and smiled at Celia.

"Your daughter tells me you attend Sunday services at Waitara. I've been there with my sister. I believe I've seen you there. Or certainly someone who looks like you."

"I don't recall seeing you. I thought you said you don't attend church," Celia replied.

"I don't normally. Organized religion does not question so many things that need questioning. At any rate, I went to Waitara a couple of times to accompany my sister. She was keen to show me the church and the area. Lovely setting and wonderful work being done there at the foundling home."

Celia told briefly of her parents' involvement with the home.

"It was my father's job but of course it became life's work for both of them. It provided foundlings with some chance for a future."

Nancy squirmed impatiently, waiting for a pause in the conversation so she could squeeze in and distance herself from her mother's connections to church and other matters in which they did not agree.

"My mother is obsessed with the church and religion," she broadcast to the table, and anyone else within ear shot. "It's so old-fashioned," she laughed. "There are so many government agencies that can look after social needs now days. There's really no need any more for religious groups to be involved."

"My daughter has a very narrow view of religion," Celia said quickly. "She thinks it is just about churches and priests. It is of course about helping to find answers to the big questions of life – where did we come from? What happens to us after death?"

"We simply evolved, mother. Spots in the ocean developed legs and crawled onto land, etc. It all seems quite simple and reasonable."

"What nonsense," said Carlisle. "The Bible is the source of all human knowledge. It is clear that God created the world. They convicted that lunatic Scopes in Tennessee for teaching that men evolved from monkeys. Should have hanged him."

"His conviction was overturned by the appeal court," Langer said.

Carlisle glowered and did not reply and the table remained silent.

Celia broke the quiet, resuming the debate with her daughter.

"When you say we all evolved from a particle in the ocean Nancy, that might be correct. But then you have to question where did the ocean come from. And if the world began with one tiny particle, where did it come from? Who or what created the particle?"

Not knowing what to reply, Nancy turned to Langer. "What do you think, Mr. Langer?"

"I'm neither a firm believer nor a firm non-believer," Langer replied. "When there are no irrefutable facts it is a good course to keep all options open."

"There will be no options left if these Nazis get their way," said Carlisle, changing the subject to the second big topic. "They are out to destroy all religions."

"I'm not sure that is accurate," said Langer. "They talk a lot about creating a new, positive Christianity, in which the Bible would be purged of all its Jewish content."

"I think it's accurate," Carlisle shot back with a belligerence strengthened by two stiff Scotches and now the dinner wine. "And you Brits will be at war soon again if the Germans continue their nonsense."

Langer considered that while he chewed on a piece of grilled saltwater cod, the main course. War was a possibility but he believed that a bit of cool intelligence exercised in the right places could avoid an extensive conflict.

"There's little reason for a long and expanded war," said Langer. "After all the Germans do have some legitimate grievances stemming from the last war. Helping to resolve them might dampen the war talk."

"Legitimate grievances?" Carlisle sputtered. "Do you mean to say that you would try to appease these Fascists? They want to rule the world!"

Carlisle's voice became louder as his face became redder from emotion and the gulps of white wine between bites of cod.

"I think they want to try to recover what they believe was a better past," Langer answered calmly. "Fascism is a reflection of a strong desire for change. And God knows there are incompetent political systems and governments around the world that could use change."

"Surely, to God you don't favour Nazism," sputtered Carlisle, boozy-wide eyes darting from Langer to the ladies and back to Langer.

"What I favour is change. We have incompetent bureaucracies, politicians who do not see the difference between doing the right thing and expediency, and a world economy shattered by Depression."

"We have German spies in Australia," Mrs. Crawford informed the table. "I read it in the newspaper. There are branches of the Nazi party in Tanunda and Adelaide."

"My father says there is a Nazi in his club in Sydney," Nancy offered. "He always refers to him as 'that Nazi bastard.'"

That remark caused Langer to smile, but left the ladies stone faced. They were not used to hearing a young woman using barroom language. Mrs. Carlisle, uncomfortable with war and spies talk, steered the conversation into more comfortable territory.

"Well, that's enough of Nazis and war. We need to make dessert selections. Has everyone noticed the beautiful artwork on the menu?"

She held up the front of the menu on which a figurehead maiden was clinging to garlands against the backdrop of a giant clamshell.

The dinner table broke up quickly after dessert. Carlisle, wife in tow, left without a word. Langer exchanged pleasantries with all the ladies, adding to the Coulsons that he hoped he would see them in the morning. Nancy jumped on that.

"I hope so," she said quickly. "There are so many activities aboard. I'm hoping to learn archery for one thing."

Langer offered a lesson.

"I'm told the archery range on one of the stern decks is excellent," he said. They agreed to meet after breakfast the next day for the lesson.

• • •

Everyone had their reflections on the evening, some regarding Langer who was mysterious enough to be exciting, or in Carlisle's view, sinister.

"Nazis," he muttered as he and his wife strolled the promenade deck after the dinner. "Look at that."

He had spotted Langer and a short blond man locked in serious conversion beside the aft rail. A wave of hair fell up and down the blond man's forehead as he punched his words with much animation. Carlisle could not pick up the conversation but he told his wife they were speaking German.

"Oh, Tom, don't be silly," said his wife. "You can't hear what they are speaking. They are just two passengers having cigarettes and a conversation."

Carlisle searched for the key to their cabin as they turned into the passageway leading off the deck.

"There's something ominous about that man. I think he arranged to trade places with the Charles Crawford who was supposed to sit at our table. I don't know why but I can feel it."

Doreen Carlisle rolled her eyes and no more was said about the mysterious Mr. Langer.

Much was said, or at least thought, about Langer as Celia and Nancy strolled the other side of the ship.

"Don't you think he's the most exciting person you've ever met, mother?"

"I don't know about exciting," Celia replied. "Interesting, yes. He certainly has firm views."

Celia had observed Langer closely during the meal. More closely than she would have observed the average table mate. He was an unsettling presence when she put together the coincidences that came with him. He said he had seen her at the church in Waitara recently. Then he had bumped into Nancy in downtown Sydney. Now he had shown up at a seat at their table, a seat originally assigned to someone else.

Definitely an unsettling presence, yet charismatic and physically attractive, Celia thought. His eyes drew her just as easily as if he placed a hand on the small of her back and pulled her into him. They were the colour of a clear late autumn sky, Arctic blue but not cold, and their shade and texture shifted just like an autumn sky is changed by strips of fast-moving cloud pushed by the change-of-season wind. Their colour shifted from winter blue to cloudy grey depending on what fast-moving thoughts were moving across them.

They were deeply expressive eyes, much of the time carrying a hint of amusement. The crow's feet at their corners amplified that sense of amusement but helped create an impression of attractiveness and intelligence. When he spoke he often turned his face slightly, as if to avoid confrontation, while upturned eyebrows created an image of a man who is always questioning.

During the course of one dinner conversation, he had questioned the prevailing views on Nazi Germany and possible war, plus organized religion. His questioning was not bombastic or shallow and appeared anchored in research. He was a charming talker but unlike many good talkers appeared to carry substance behind his talk.

She smiled and thought of Bertie who she often said could charm his way off the gallows. He was an oily manipulator who usually won his way without producing any real evidence to substantiate what he said.

Langer appeared open-minded in his views rather than driven by bedrock beliefs but maybe that was just a first impression. He is not an uncomplicated person, Celia concluded. Certainly not straight forward nor easy to understand.

Nancy did not see all that, Celia thought as they walked back to their stateroom. Her daughter had yet to develop any critical thinking. She saw Langer's surface but the quick, heated thinking of youth got in the way of seeing any deeper.

"You are just put off by his attitude on religion," Nancy said. "He is right. Organized religion is stuffy and stiff. Too many rules about how you can live."

"Yes, I imagine he is one not too concerned about rules. He is divorced, I assume. Or says he is."

"Actually he is a widower. He told me that in Sydney."

"That's what he tells you."

"I don't believe in God," Nancy blurted, then smiled. She meant for the statement to shock. It didn't.

Celia had not heard it directly from her daughter before, but the fact that it was never spoken did not mean it did not exist.

"I'm glad they taught us Darwin's evolution in school. It makes so much more sense than religious mumbo jumbo."

"It's hard to argue against evolution," Celia sighed impatiently. "The world evolved from a speck of dust. Organisms in the ocean developed and crawled onto shore. Species of animals evolved, including apes from which humans evolved. All easy enough to follow. Like I said before, one question remains unanswered: Who made the speck of dust?"

While Nancy considered what to say next, Celia changed the subject. The conversation about religion was bait to lure her into an argument, and there was no winning an argument with Nancy.

"I thought you would be bored with the dinner table talk and more interested in that young man sitting three tables over. He seemed to be the life of the table."

"I didn't notice him," Nancy sniffed. "A lot of those fellows are much the same. Stallion brawn and chicken brains. Boring. Mr. Langer is so alive with knowledge about everything."

Celia walked to the deck rail and gazed over the slate grey waters turning indigo as they swallowed the last of the submerging sun. She felt a fresh breeze on her face. It was an ocean breeze, freed of mainland scents, and tasted clean and saline. Then she found herself staring at her daughter.

"Why are you looking at me like that?" Nancy asked sharply.

"It's nothing. Just staring and thinking. It's time to go in."

Their stateroom had yet to feel like a comfortable home. It would, presumably, over the course of forty days. It was a large single room with a separate bathroom. Confining, yet spacious enough to allow someone to erect an invisible privacy wall. An ample writing desk of Ceylon satinwood separated two double beds. There was a mirrored double door closet at end of the stateroom, the doorway into the bathroom at the other. Against the wall opposite the beds and writing desk were two satinwood dressers separated by a dressing table below a large mirror. Off in a corner were a settee, matching bamboo chairs and a coffee table.

Celia, pre-occupied with removing her gloves, did not notice the rose. Nancy did.

"Look! A rose on my bed."

"Someone on the staff must favour you," Celia smiled.

Nancy lifted the rose to her nose and breathed in deeply. The fragrance was heady, almost rebellious. Nancy smiled the knowing smile of someone guarding a secret. She knew who sent the rose; and it was not the ship's staff.

• • •

Langer did not return to his stateroom immediately. He took a couple turns around the deck, smoking and stopping for rail side chats with one or two other passengers.

The Strathaird had left the clouds and rain clinging to the coast and was nosing through choppy seas under clear skies. They likely would have smooth sailing once well away from the Australian coast. No storms had been forecast for the trip but certainly with flat seas would come the stifling heat as they approached the Indian sub-continent and their port stop at Ceylon.

He thought about the dinner conversations and his fellow diners. He had immediately pegged Carlisle as an ass. His wife seemed to be pleasant enough despite the burden she had to bear. Beatrice Cross was a bit vacant but she was bubbly and seemed to enjoy some fun.

The Coulson women were pleasant, well-spoken and both attractive. He sensed in them a lack of what he considered typical mother-daughter friendship. They was a tension between the two, an irritation. The girl wore an effervescent personality, but not far beneath that there was an insecurity that demanded acceptance and much attention.

The mother displayed a sharp intellect that she chose not to display. She was a self-contained thinker who kept her thoughts to herself for fear that letting them spill out might bring unpleasant consequences. A person who preferred keeping a bright light under a basket. There was much on her mind that she needed to examine, sort and deal with. She was a troubled woman seeking change but uncertain about what kind of change, and worried about how change might affect her life.

What was it the French author André Gide had said?

"Man cannot discover new oceans unless he has the courage to lose sight of the shore."

The shore is fading into the distance. We'll see what new oceans Celia Coulson might be willing to discover, Langer thought to himself.

CHAPTER 6

A rchery

NANCY WOKE WITH a start. She sat straight up in bed, disoriented and confused. The stateroom was still and quiet, but for the murmuring from the ship's engines several decks below.

She glanced to the bedside table where the alarm clock sat wearily, its alarm spring limp after ringing a full two minutes without reaction from the room. Its black spider leg hands read five past eight and reminded her that breakfast was served only until eight forty-five.

No matter. She had no yearning for food. The previous night's wine at dinner had left her stomach acidic and her head logy.

Besides, Langer did not take breakfast. He said that he never ate before noon, so Nancy felt no urge to join the breakfast table without him being there.

No doubt her mother was there listening to that boring ass Carlisle. And, his wife and that Mrs. Crawford who were both female fogeys who added nothing interesting to the table talk.

"Imagine, German spies in Australia," Nancy muttered recalling Mrs. Crawford's dinner comment. She rolled herself from bed, stretched and yawned.

A cut glass vase with the single red rose stood on the dresser top. Nancy leaned over it and inhaled the fragrance. It had not lost any of its intoxicating power overnight.

Her mother had said the rose was placed by ship's staff, an elegant touch to help justify the cost of the capacious stateroom made pretty with the latest art deco fashions.

Nancy knew better. Langer probably arranged the rose with the suite maid, then swore her to secrecy with a much-appreciated gratuity.

She washed and preened while wondering whether Langer had booked this voyage because of her. It was too much of a coincidence; the luncheon at Cahill's, then showing up on the ship. And of course, arranging a seat at their dining table.

It was not unreasonable to believe that these were not coincidences, Nancy thought.

It was not unreasonable to believe that an older man would be interested in a woman so much younger. He was younger in looks and in spirit than other people his age. She was more mature in looks and more sophisticated than other girls her age. There were cases spotted through history of older men marrying younger women and many of them resulted in long, happy, successful partnerships. They were not just the typical dime store novel examples of a younger woman chasing a man for his money. Or an older man chasing a younger woman for her body.

What she had expected to be a tortuous voyage now promised excitement, even romance. There was only so much a girl could do on board for almost a month and half. Reading and swimming and listening to the old ladies cackle in their deck chairs.

The nights might have been interesting if there were dances and some young men aboard. Now, the presence of Langer stimulated her.

She stretched again lazily then remembered she had agreed to meet Vera at nine o'clock and they were to go off together exploring the ship.

"Damn," she muttered. Vera was her best friend. They had started school together. Grown up together, sharing their dreams and secrets. Or at least sharing Nancy's dreams and secrets. Vera Fenwick was an acquiescent, who yielded softly to Nancy's domineering personality. She saw Nancy's faults but accepted them as only a true friend can.

Vera's mother Cora was a good friend to Celia. They had known each other since school days but went their separate ways as young adults, keeping in touch occasionally. They grew closer again when Celia learned that Cora's husband John had lost work during the Depression and the family experienced hard times. Celia asked Bertie to find John work in one of his businesses, which he did.

When Celia told Cora about the coming out trip to Europe, Cora thought it was a splendid idea and that perhaps she and Vera would book the same passage and would spend time with relatives in England. She secured a cabin on the same sailing, although in tourist class on a lower deck.

Nancy glanced at the clock again. There was not much time to prepare and dress for the archery date, so she would catch up with Vera later. Vera would understand Nancy skipping their date when she heard Nancy's excited recounting of the intriguing older man she had met.

She searched her steamer trunk for an outfit appropriate for archery. She had ignored her mother's suggestion that she empty the trunk so that the clothes could be hung to avoid wrinkles. She had been too occupied with departure partying for that and now hoped she could find something not needing ironing.

She wanted to wear something bold, but not outrageously daring. She settled on a white tennis dress that was the latest fashion back home. It was a short skirt effort with bloomer, a zipper front and a tie belt. And, it did not need ironing.

Langer was waiting at the archery range, a roped off area on the poop deck. It had a large round target made of compressed straw and covered with linen on which was painted a red, white and blue bull's eye. It was large enough so that even a beginning archer would find it difficult to miss. However, any arrows that did miss completely would sail over the stern railings and into the sea.

Langer wore grey trousers and an off-white V-neck cable knit tennis sweater that looked warm even for an early spring morning. He wore no shirt beneath and the open V showed a luxuriant bush of brown-black chest hair splashed with traces of grey.

Nancy viewed him appreciatively, noting the exposed greying chest hair as a sign of virility, not age.

"Good morning, Niles. I'm ready to learn how to play Cupid."

"Good morning, Miss Coulson," he said, offering his hand. "Did the rocking of the seas help you to sleep well?"

"Yes, indeed. As did the rose. It has a wonderful calming fragrance. Thank you."

Langer looked at her quizzically. He began a reply, but Nancy's exuberance cut him off.

"I'm so excited. I've never held a bow and arrow before. Just seen it in the movies. Just like Robin Hood!"

"Well let's get at it, then. The first thing you need to know is that it is possible to become quite accurate reasonably quickly in archery, once you know the basics."

He showed her how to hold the bow in the palm of one hand and draw the bowstring back with two fingers of the other hand. Nancy initially was confused about what hand to assign what chore. She discovered she was more comfortable holding the bow with her right and pulling the string back with her left.

"See how the arrow has a notch in its back end?" Langer instructed. "You push that notch into the string and place the arrow body on the lip of the bow handle."

He put his arms around her and helped her pull back the bow string.

"You push the bow with your palm, pointing the bow downward to get better leverage. Pull the string back like this as you push downward, then raise the bow up to sight. You do it all in one smooth motion."

He held her closely and put his cheek beside hers, instructing her how to aim and how to release the bowstring and the arrow. The first shot hit the centre of the target.

"Oh my God, I hit the bull's-eye," Nancy cried, lowering the bow and wrapping it and her arms around Langer.

Celia arrived just in time to catch the scene.

"He's made me into an archer, mother. He is a natural teacher."

Celia nodded, smiled and said nothing as Langer proceeded with the lesson.

"You must control your breathing," she heard Langer tell Nancy. "Controlling the breathing helps steady you for the shot."

Celia watched the way he had his arms around her, steadying her stance and showing her how to sight and ease off the shot by relaxing her fingers in the leather shooting glove. They looked like a happy couple enjoying each other and what they were doing.

Langer was not much taller than her daughter, who was above average height for a woman. He had square firm shoulders under the tennis sweater and muscular wrists showing below the cuffs.

He looks athletic for a sedentary businessman, Celia thought. Or was he a businessman? She had assumed that, but realized that she did not know what he did and promised herself to learn more about him. She also intended to be the concerned mother and to press him on his interest in her daughter, and his intentions.

The lesson likely would continue for another half hour and Celia already had seen enough. She left unnoticed and resumed the stroll she had started after finishing breakfast.

She enjoyed walking after breakfast and did so almost every morning back home. The ship's decks did not offer near the distance and exercise of her morning walks back home, but circling a deck then climbing the stairs to another deck made for a reasonable outing.

Some Saturdays she went with a bush-walking group for daylong rambles at Katoomba on the edge of the Blue Mountains. Bertie had no interest in walking without golf clubs so never joined her. Her walks kept Celia's body fit.

More importantly, walking kept her mind fit. She was a solitary woman, not exactly a loner but one of those individuals unable to completely merge her life into the rest world. Not by choice, but by circumstance.

As an only child she was a piece of her parents' work and her parents' life. Life was the mission and church activities. There was scant time for anything else. Little time and few opportunities to develop her own interests, an exclusive character or a distinct space of her own.

Her sudden meeting and marriage to Bertie redirected her from being a piece of her parents' life into being another piece of her husband's life. Her focus then went to child bearing, household duties and caring for her parents, until they passed. There was little time to determine who she was, who she wanted to be, who she should be or what she wanted from life.

Solitary persons crave thinking time and Celia did much thinking on her walks. She thought often lately on how circumstances and events change lives dramatically; sometimes forcing people to follow a direction they otherwise might not choose. Her thoughts were divided on whether she would allow circumstances to define what remained of her life.

Certainly, this coming-out journey with Nancy was an event that could change their lives. She worried that it would not end with the desired effect: the child advancing into full adulthood prepared to accept the responsibilities needed for a normal, productive life. The mother, her protective rearing complete, becomes a valued, trusted friend.

That's the way the script was written but Celia could not see Nancy following it because she was so focused on herself.

Celia saw her daughter as a person who saw herself as the star of a long-running film in which her charm and brilliance would bring her fame, fortune and everything else she desired, and deserved. Her self-absorption was evident in early childhood when her favourite toy was a mirror. The girl in the mirror had grown into the type of adult narcissistic personality capable of bringing sorrow to others, and eventually to herself.

The arrival of this man Langer was both curious and perplexing to Celia. It was an unwanted element complicating the situation with her daughter. Nancy would use the man's attentions to create a drama in which she filled the spotlight. It was her way of drawing attention and reaction from others. Reaction would be guaranteed to what others would see as a scandalous difference in age.

Celia became aware of the potential complications soon after Langer appeared at their dinner table. She decided that she would be careful not to overreact in any way that would encourage Nancy to overplay the drama.

No mother would be unstirred by a daughter seeing a man more than twice her age. If she displayed much opposition, however, Nancy would use it as more evidence that she was overbearing, and unwilling to allow her daughter to make adult choices. That would show her as the lesser person.

Celia had no doubt that Nancy would pursue the man. She had seen it before. Two years earlier, Nancy began seeing a fellow in his early thirties. They met at the beach and Nancy did nothing to keep their dating secret. In fact, she showed him off. Even Bertie was disturbed but refused to admit it openly and instead passed it off as normal part of growing into adulthood. They had row about that, Celia accusing him of not wanting to recognize the signs that Nancy was going off track. Bertie retorted that Celia was being prudish.

Celia had discerned no hints of Langer's intentions. He seemed drawn to Nancy yet showed no signs that his intentions were anything but honourable. None of the signs one might expect from a type inclined to the perversion of pursuing much younger women.

What type is that, she asked herself? How does that type behave? Appearing educated and refined did not guarantee good character. However, it was early days yet. The trip had just begun and perhaps she was overthinking.

Yet she could not let go of the unsettling thoughts about his appearance into their lives. Showing up for a dinner seat originally assigned to someone else. That happens and is explainable, Celia decided. But bumping into Nancy on the street in Sydney. Again, coincidence? Then his comment that he had seen Celia in the churchyard at Waitara. All possible coincidences, yet unusual.

That pompous other table guest, Carlisle, certainly did not like Langer. He had found Langer's views on the Germans outrageously sympathetic. Celia had overheard him telling his wife that someone should inform the authorities that he might be a Nazi spy. She tossed that off as a ridiculous overreaction.

As she finished her walk – five deck rounds plus the steps between decks – she decided she wanted to learn more about the mysterious Mr. Langer, and would watch for signs that the relationship between he and her daughter was becoming inappropriate.

They would be seeing much more of him whether she liked it or not, Celia thought. The Strathaird had a week of scheduled stops along the Australian coast. Then at least five thousand nautical miles of ocean between Australia and Ceylon, the first foreign stop after the long crossing. It would be more than two weeks before the Ceylon stop and Langer would be a presence at most meals, plus Nancy seemed determined to take up more of his time.

The archery session ended just as she returned from her walk. Nancy bubbled with enthusiastic chatter as Langer put his hand on her back and guided her out of the roped off area.

"That was wonderful, Niles. You are such a great teacher."

Niles smiled as they approached Celia.

• • •

They did see much more of Langer, even more than Celia expected and more than just at meals. The archery lesson extended into more lessons and other meetings. Langer and Nancy often had tea on deck, followed by swimming in the salt water pool, or chatting while sunbathing. There were deck games such as shuffleboard and tennis during the day. In the evenings dinners with their regular table companions, followed by ballroom dancing.

They spent much time together, but never alone. Langer always was careful to have someone accompany them. Usually he urged Celia to join them, and if she was not available, he would ask Vera who Nancy had insisted he meet soon after the voyage began.

Celia enjoyed being involved in these activities, and found she enjoyed being around Langer. He was an impressive organizer of activities. Anything he suggested turned out to be fun. He was fun to be with - pleasant, witty, interesting and highly intelligent but well grounded.

It was, however, awkward being witness to the unnatural relationship developing between her adolescent daughter and an older man. Also, Langer was a contradiction. Celia could not gain an understanding of the core of the man. His views on religion, which he freely expressed as he did with his views on some other matters, were radical to a committed churchgoer, yet seemed grounded in common sense.

She was more concerned about Nancy's gushing infatuation with the man. Nancy dropped many hints, spoken and in body language, that this was becoming a romantic relationship. These were easily noticed by Celia and anyone else in their company. Why Langer did not dissuade them was another puzzle.

"I think it's disgusting," Tom Carlisle said to his wife one morning as they sat in their deck chairs. Nancy and Langer had just strolled by, talking and laughing.

"He's more than twice her age. I think someone should talk to the captain."

"It's not our business, Tom. Her mother is keeping a sharp eye on them, I notice. Although I'm not sure why she hasn't done something yet to stop it."

CHAPTER 7

Heat

THE WEATHER WAS cool and the sea choppy after the Strathaird left the Australian coast, steaming through the South Pacific enroute to the Indian Ocean and Ceylon at the southern tip of India. It didn't slow of the pace of shipboard activities, however. Archery lessons, tennis, shuffleboard, card games continued through the sea's most lumpy stretches.

As the ship approached the equator, however, the sea flattened and the sun became a fixture in the bright sky. The air thickened, becoming warm and sticky at first, then hot and moist to the point of being wet. Temperatures rose into the high thirties on the Celsius scale, ending most of the physical recreation. Passengers took deck chairs to any shaded areas they could find, sipping cold tea while praying for a weather pattern that could bring relief.

Not long into the equatorial heat, illness broke out. It started with a young crew member who developed fever and distressed breathing. Then some passengers fell ill with similar symptoms.

"I wish I could feel more confident in this ship's medical staff," Carlisle said one evening at dinner. "They say it's a virus that comes with the change of weather, but the damn Spanish Flu was a virus wasn't it?"

Conversation stopped like a truck hitting a wall when Carlisle spoke the words Spanish Flu. Everyone at the table except Nancy had memories of the Great Pandemic twenty years earlier. She had been told that her grandfather died in a plague but did not know, and had no interest in, the details.

That flu killed an estimated thirty to forty million around the world. Australia was mildly infected compared with other counties. Fewer than thirteen thousand Australians died, perhaps because the strain that struck Australia came later and was milder than the one that sickened and killed tens of thousands in Europe and the Americas.

The numbers might have been lower than elsewhere but the memories of the Spanish Flu terror remained fresh among family and friends who lost people they loved. Neither Celia nor her mother were infected, which was unusual considering young adults were prime targets of the deadly plague. Two nuns not much older than Celia were stricken and died quickly at the Wahroonga convent. Others were sick but survived. Celia never understood why the flu passed her by.

"Let's hope it's nothing that serious," said Langer. "Probably just something brought on by the temperature change."

Nancy, who had been unusually quiet during dinner, coughed.

"I hope you are not coming down with something, my dear," said Beatrice Crawford. "Your eyes are a bit glassy."

Mrs. Crawford, unable to suppress her motherly instincts, reached out her hand and touched Nancy's cheek.

"You are a bit warm."

"I'm sure she's fine," said Celia. "Just too much tennis."

• • •

Nancy wasn't fine. She coughed throughout the night and did not feel like getting out of bed in the morning. Celia brought in the ship's surgeon who suggested that Nancy be moved to the infirmary.

The ship's surgeon was concerned because Nancy's symptoms were similar to those of the young seaman, whose condition was worsening. Some other passengers were sick but mainly down with heat exhaustion and heat edema. A few, obviously not good sea travellers, suffered the lingering effects of sea sickness.

The following morning Langer knocked on the Coulson stateroom door to inquire about Nancy's condition. Celia stepped into the corridor and closed the door behind her.

"She's about the same," she said. "I'm worried about influenza and pneumonia."

Later in the day, Langer knocked again at the stateroom door. Celia stepped out and was startled by the grave look on his face.

"There's some bad news, I'm afraid. I heard that the young seaman has passed away."

"Nancy," Celia burst out as she set off down the passageway.

"I'll come with you," Langer said.

"Not necessary, I prefer to be alone with her," Celia said as she pushed through the door to the stairs leading to the lower deck infirmary.

A nurse assured Celia that Nancy was stable, and improving. At the moment she was sleeping after a fitful night.

"What happened with the young crew member?" Celia asked. "Was he contagious?"

"We're not sure of his cause of death yet. But he was not contagious, otherwise the surgeon and captain would have ordered a quarantine."

There was a cough and stirring behind one of the privacy curtains in a corner of the infirmary.

"I think your daughter is awake. You can speak to her if you wish."

The nurse pulled back the curtain. Nancy struggled to sit up. She looked pale but the opacity was gone from her eyes.

"Where is Niles?" she asked.

"I don't know, I haven't seen him," Celia replied.

"There was a man here inquiring about her," said the nurse. "I thought perhaps he was a relative."

"We don't have any relatives travelling with us," Celia said. "It's best not to allow any visitors. She needs her rest."

"I expected you to say that," Nancy glared up from her pillow. "You want to keep us apart."

The nurse saw Nancy's anger and sensed the tension between the two women. She wanted no part in this conflict and backed away.

"That's not true. I just want you to rest and get well."

"You want to keep us apart. You refuse to accept what's happening between Niles and I."

"I don't know what you think is happening between you and Niles. All I know is that I am responsible for you on this trip. If anything untoward occurs, your father will blame me."

Nancy glowered and was about to respond when Celia turned quickly to leave, saying over her shoulder that she would be back later to see how she was doing.

CHAPTER 8

Verandah Cafe

WET HEAT SLAPPED Celia's face as she pulled open the thick wooden door leading onto the promenade deck. It was like being whacked by a steamed barber's towel.

The Strathaird was well into the Indian Ocean, moving into the equatorial zone. The sun pounded mercilessly from directly overhead and if the ship had been relying on sails, it would be motionless on the water; becalmed as if a breeze had never blown here. The air was so thick and hot that she had to stop to let her breathing catch up after running up the inside steps from the infirmary.

Few people were on deck. It was too stifling to be outside and the ship offered several public rooms, such as the first-class dining room, that had air cooling, a recent feature offered by only a few ships. The infirmary was air conditioned but Celia did not want to be there while Nancy was awake. She knew her daughter would not let up on badgering her about Langer. What she needed to do was to walk and think, ignoring the heat. Her clearest thinking always occurred when her legs were moving.

She was not much concerned about Nancy's illness. It appeared to be a mild flu, complicated by the heat. Certainly it was nothing serious like the Spanish Flu. The medical staff believed the seaman had something different, or perhaps the mild flu complicated by a separate, chronic condition.

Nancy's mental health is more of a concern, Celia said to herself, then quickly corrected the thought. It was silly. Her daughter was not sick mentally.

"It's just that she's so self-focussed and it is perplexing how she got that way," she said half aloud.

Surely it was not inherited, and certainly not from Celia's side. There were no more giving people than her parents. They lived lives of serving others, not seeking anything for themselves.

Nancy had changed - their family had changed – without Neil's presence. She often wondered what life would be like today if her son was still here. How old would he be now? Twenty-two last August 22nd. Would their family be less anxious and troubled? Perhaps all four of them would be together on this ship, laughing excitedly about the Great European Adventure on which they were embarked.

Laughter, that's what she missed most. His infectious laughter. He would be the centre of attention in the first-class dining room, smiling, laughing, making others smile and laugh. He was the perfect blend of Bertie and herself. Funny and seeing the lighter side of life, much like Bertie. But responsible, thoughtful and giving, like herself.

She had read studies showing that siblings, and families in general, do change following the loss of a child. Yet, Nancy had not been the perfect child before that.

With all her thinking Celia had not realized how quickly she was walking around the promenade deck. Much too quickly in the oppressive heat.

She stopped to rest against the deck rail and patted the sweat from her forehead.

Despite the cloudless sky she felt as damp as she had standing against the ship's rail on departure day. She felt the urge for a drink. Not tea or water. A good, strong alcoholic drink.

She was not much of a drinker. She always said the family could not support two drinkers. There were times, however, when she found a drink relaxing and comforting.

She was thinking about that drink when she noticed Langer approaching. He stopped and leaned against the rail beside her.

"How did you find Nancy? I hope her condition is improving."

"Cranky. The good news is that she appears to have only a mild flu and a bit of dehydration from the heat. Thank you for your concern. The nurse said you had passed by to ask about Nancy two or three times."

"I was concerned, considering how ill the young seaman was."

"You seem to have much concern about Nancy. And much interest."

"She is a very engaging young woman. Fun to be with and quite advanced for her age."

"Yes. That's one of my concerns."

"How do you mean?"

"Well, surely it is obvious. You are at least twice her age and are spending much time with her. People might get to wrong idea."

"People often get wrong ideas," Langer replied softly and seriously before brightening and suggesting they move out of the heat. "I'll stand you a drink in the Verandah Café."

The offer caught her off guard. She had been thinking about a drink and with Nancy not around having one with him alone would be an opportunity to peel away some layers of mystery surrounding him.

The Verandah Café was a lounge and bar where you could get a light lunch and a drink. It had tables and chairs in the Strathaird's art deco style, a couple of couches for relaxing and reading. Its walnut wood bar was centred on the front wall with doorways on each side leading into the corridor which connected the port and starboard sides of the promenade deck.

There were a few people in the lounge, which was not air conditioned, but Langer guided Celia to a secluded corner, steering her gently with his right hand on the small of her back. His hand was warm and easily felt through the light cotton shift she wore to stay cool. It was a guiding touch, not at all provocative, but it was sensual and sent an arousal tingle down her hips and legs.

She wondered how he managed to stay so cool looking in a long-sleeve shirt and slacks. Most of the men aboard opted for shorts, tennis shoes without socks and cotton undershirts. He was dressed for fashion, not for the heat, Celia thought. His shirt was a sporty yellow, red and black Madras pattern. His slacks were cream colour shantung silk.

The table offered privacy, tucked off to one side of the bar, and beside one of the arched windows looking out to the ocean. Celia took a seat on the settee backing against the window and Langer a chair on the other side of the low coffee table. A waiter helped them settle in and took their orders: Celia a gin and tonic, Langer a beer.

"The service is excellent on this ship," Langer as the waiter went off to get their drinks. "It was the same coming out."

"You came out on this ship?" Celia asked, uncomfortable about how to get back into the conversation about Nancy.

"Not the Strathaird but her twin sister, the Strathmore. Same line. P and O has reputation for great service. It was a seven-week voyage, about the same as this one. That's almost two and one-half months at sea, going and coming. Quite a long run when you put the coming and going together, but I have the time."

"You don't mind being away from your job or business interests for so long?"

"I have many interests to keep me busy but it was important to see my sister. I haven't seen her in quite some time."

"One of your interests concerns me," Celia said staring directly at him. "My daughter. She is much taken with you, Mr. Langer, which concerns me greatly."

Her directness took Langer aback. He had viewed Celia as demure and complying. She had appeared so docile when he had watched her at the ship's rail. So sad, almost broken. Her directness now displayed a different personality. The lady obviously could be tough.

"Please, call me Niles," he said with a comforting smile that widened, the skin cracking into crevices at the corners of his eyes. "Perhaps you are concerned because I am a stranger. Knowing something about me might ease your concern, although there isn't a lot to know."

He looked directly into her eyes, and in that quiet but convincing voice, delivered a compact resume that created images as good as any photo album.

"I am what is known in England as a country gentleman. One of the landed gentry with no certified aristocratic ties, just an inherited and failing estate of which my father is the principal. And which unlike many others, continues to produce at least a bit of revenue. My father is alive, active, and still enjoying running things. Which leaves me little to do. Except to ponder and perhaps write what I ponder."

So, Celia said to herself, a loafer. No doubt a playboy loafer.

"As a young fellow I loved writing and dabbled. The war interrupted that but I got back into it when I returned from Europe. I wrote a family history and a couple of mildly successful novels which you likely have not heard of."

He gave the titles, and he was correct, she had not heard of them.

"So that's a about it. I enjoy pondering and writing, but it seems something is always interrupting my writing life."

"Are you married?" Celia, emboldened by the alcohol, asked sharply.

The smile crinkles beside his eyes vanished and he took his eyes off hers.

"I was," he said almost in a whisper.

The conversation stopped there for what seemed an eternity to Celia. Then he continued. He had been married to a woman who filled every part of his life and gave relentless support to his writing efforts. They were childless and she had taken ill three years ago. They had consulted the best doctors in England, then specialists in Switzerland. She died in a clinic there last year. Since then he had been at loose ends, trying but unable to refocus his life.

It was basically the same story he had told Nancy, but with less detail.

"There you have it. Of course, I ended up in your part of the world visiting my sister who went out to Australia with her husband many years ago."

"Those must have been three very painful years for you," Celia offered. "I'm sorry."

Her remarks were sincere; her eyes broadcast compassion. Her thin lips and jaw, however, were firm.

"I am concerned, however, about Nancy. She is wilful and I do not want to see her fall into something that she will regret for the rest of her life."

"She is a spirited young woman seeking attention, which sometimes indicates a calling out for guidance. As for my interest I think you are misinterpreting the situation. . . ."

The conversation was interrupted by the waiter arriving with a second round of drinks. Celia had not noticed Langer signal the bar for another round while he was telling his abbreviated life story.

"Oh, I do not need that," Celia protested. "I really shouldn't have it. I have to get back to check again on Nancy."

"She is good hands. The medical staff on board is excellent. Besides I wanted to ask you more about Waitara. Interesting place with a fascinating history."

"Yes, I believe you mentioned being at Our Lady of the Rosary Church," Celia responded dully, annoyed that he had turned the discussion away from Nancy. She promised herself to return to pursue that topic before their meeting ended.

"Nancy mentioned that you have a strong connection to the church and the fondling home."

Celia sighed inwardly. That's the difference between us, she thought. Nancy is so much like her father, forward and gregarious; always up to telling her whole life story to strangers. Celia did not consider herself obsessively private but took comfort into knowing that people did not know everything about her.

"Yes, my parents were connected to the foundling home in small ways."

Langer urged her to tell their story and listened intently.

Three Catholic nuns, members of the Sisters of Mercy, opened a mission for the poor and disadvantaged on Sydney's North Shore in 1873. They moved across the water from Sydney to minister to the physical and spiritual needs of settlers flowing into the area for work in the timber industry and the developing orchards and gardens.

Jane Sifton, Celia's mother, was seventeen when she was attracted to the sisters' work and entered their convent as a novitiate in 1892. She was on a course for a life as a religious until she met John Dalby, a young fellow her age who worked as a handyman at the mission. They fell in love and she left the convent to marry him. The parting with the Sisters of Mercy was an agreeable one and she decided to work with the sisters as a lay person.

The sisters moved their work to Waitara in 1897 and the Dalbys joined them as they established their new colony of mercy that included the foundling home. The foundling home was the first of its kind in Australia, giving shelter to twenty women and up to one hundred children. Her mother helped the sisters with administrative chores and care of the children while her father continued as a handyman and took on occasional local jobs as a freelance carpenter.

A cottage next to the home became available and John renovated it to become a small but comfortable home. They needed nothing larger because Celia was their only child, an unexpected gift because Jane was considered barren. They named her Celia because the nuns told them it was a name the ancient Romans used for things considered heavenly.

"Impressive charitable work," Langer said when Celia had finished. "I see where you get your religious connections."

"Yes, not everything you say about organized religion is true. It provides many good works."

"No denying that. My only point is that the rituals and dogmas sometimes get in way of the performance of charitable works, and the ability to think for one's self. Organized religion is so much about rules, rules designed to control people, and especially women."

"Perhaps, but organized religion is a comfort to many," Celia said firmly.

Langer decided it was best to drop that debate.

"Nancy told me that her father was too busy with his businesses to come on this trip so if I can help with anything, I'm more than willing. There is a supply layover in Ceylon. I know the governor. Sir David Duncan," he said. "We went to school together. He can arrange some excellent tours for us."

"I'm not sure if Nancy will be up to it," Celia said. "But thank you for the offer."

The alcohol had made her feel unsteady and unprotected. She felt that Langer was pushing her for information.

"I really should go now," she said, standing and shaking his hand. It was an abrupt end to the conversation but she felt the need to be alone.

Langer held her hand for a few seconds as she tried to move away.

"I'm sorry you must leave immediately," he said. "I do hope you realize that things are not always as they seem."

She left quickly and more confused than when she arrived. She had learned a bit more about the man, but not as much as he had learned about her. She was upset with herself for telling him her personal history while not confronting him fully and telling him that she wanted him to stop seeing her daughter.

Yet it was difficult not to feel compassion for the man. There was hurt inside him: his wife's death, and the lack of children, which obviously had created immense loneliness. Or was all that a façade put up to help him get what he wanted, whatever that was. She recalled that first evening dinner and the talk about Nazis and spies and wondered if it was possible that what Langer really wanted was information about Bertie's businesses.

She walked the deck, occasionally stopping to lean against the rail and stare out over the sultry ocean. The heat made it difficult to focus and she needed to focus on her problems with Nancy.

She stopped and asked herself why. Why should she be worried about Nancy and this Langer? She was not concerned about sexual involvement. She had known for some time that her daughter had an appetite for men. Nancy's sex life, however, should no longer be her concern.

The crux of her worry, she concluded, was Bertie. What if Nancy ran off with Langer? Bertie would see it as a catastrophe and would lay the blame directly onto Celia. It would be her fault, just as Neil's loss had been her fault. She solely was responsible for Nancy on this trip. Bertie would see it as another case of not being able to handle responsibility and would hold it, and the accompanying lack respect, against her forever.

Nancy running off was a possibility. She might see this developing relationship as a game that could be played until she was ready to drop it and move on to something else. Langer would not see it that way. Whatever he was after, he was serious and cunning enough to get. Her daughter, so naive beneath her mature and worldly veneer, was no match for this man. He was someone who got whatever he was after.

He seems so genuine, Celia thought. Was it possible he was being deliberately devious? What did he mean by things not always being what they seemed? The more she thought, the more confused she became.

As she walked back to her stateroom, another thought tried to push its way into the front of her mind. It was a thought connected to the feel of Langer's hand on the small of her back. A disturbing thought and she had no intention of letting it advance any farther. The only thought that was completely clear now was that this was going to be an uncertain passage.

CHAPTER 9

The Letter

THE HEAT THICKENED more and lay heavy on the listless sea as the Strathaird continued to nose toward Ceylon, still one day steaming away. The Strathaird's passengers wondered how much more intense the humidity could become before being totally unbearable.

Many lolled in deck chairs, saving whatever energy they possessed for moving bamboo fans across faces dripping with sweat that dried quickly and left them feeling uncomfortably gummy. Others hung limply over the deck railings hoping to catch a freshened breeze. There was none. Even the air stirred up by movement of the ship was warm and wet.

"I swear the humidity is forming mould on the rail as I stand here," said one man as Nancy and Langer strolled past on their way to the lounge to join Celia and the Fenwicks for tea.

Nancy's recovery was complete, despite the increasing heat. She credited Langer for this because he had looked in on her frequently to cheer her up and had suggested drinking huge amounts of water.

Being bedridden increased her interest in him. When she was up and about their swimming and deck strolls resumed with Nancy taking to crooking her arm into his as they strolled and talked eagerly about sights to see and things to do in Colombo.

The developing relationship was obvious to other passengers, notably those who saw them at dining times and at recreation.

"That man is not only sinister, he's perverted," Carlisle told his wife as the pair entered the tea lounge to join Celia and the Fenwicks. "Why doesn't the mother just do something to stop it?"

"I think she is doing something," said his wife. "I saw her posting mail at the Melbourne stop and in Perth she actually left the ship and used the telephone in one of the dock offices. I imagine she has been keeping her husband in Sydney well informed, although I don't what he can do from there."

"He could alert the authorities," said Carlisle. "Langer obviously is a Nazi. Her father certainly knows the right people to talk with."

"What do you mean?"

"The father is a prominent businessman. Well connected. Went to school with people now in the Australian government."

"How do you know all that?"

"The girl told me. At breakfast before anyone else had showed up yet. She's not shy about talking about herself and her family. It seems her parents don't do much together. That's why the father is not on this trip."

Had Celia heard that conversation she would have steamed. To her, Nancy's fondness for telling people details of her life was like undressing in public. She tried over the years to have her daughter understand that, but it was advice spoken to the wind.

Mrs. Carlisle indeed had seen Celia on the telephone and posting mail at the Perth dock area. The Strathaird had a full week's sailing around the Australian coast before heading into the Indian Ocean and setting course for Ceylon. It had scheduled stops at Melbourne, Adelaide and Perth, where Celia telephoned Bertie. It was a brief conversation made annoying and difficult by the interruptions of a noisy line.

"I'll explain it all in a letter," Celia had shouted into the telephone after trying to give Bertie a summary of the events involving Langer.

She went immediately after hanging up to a small café where she ordered tea and sat to draft the letter. It said they had settled into the voyage and that Nancy was being kept well entertained by an English fellow, much older than herself. It explained that Nancy had met the man on the street in Sydney the week before they sailed. It raised the presumed coincidences: Langer's claim to have seen Celia in Waitara, his meeting Nancy by accident, and his showing up at the ship's dining room at a seat reserved for another man. She passed along Carlisle's view that the man had Nazi connections.

Celia crafted the letter carefully. She not want to alarm Bertie, or have him think she was overreacting. He criticized her often for taking some matters too seriously, particularly those involving Nancy.

• • •

When Bertie received the letter he chewed on the contents. His wife could be annoyingly priggish but her judgment was usually sound and reasoned. No leaping to conclusions without collection and consideration of facts.

Their husband-wife bond had begun unravelling long ago, but he still respected her ability to stand unflinching against a torrent of hyperbole designed to make her change her mind. Celia was almost scientific in her observations and her approach to problems. Her favourite saying during their heated arguments, of which there were many, was: "Adjectives and adverbs are not facts, Bertie. Stick to the unvarnished facts," a sharp reminder of Bertie's habit of attempting to win his way through bluster and bullying.

Mention of Langer's possible Nazi sympathies disturbed Bertie more than a man's interest in Nancy. He suspected that she was no saint when it came to men. However, the rise of Fascism was a world concern and like any diligent and sharp businessman, Bertie paid close attention to how it might impact his business interests.

He knew of concerns in Australia and America about pro-Hitler elements in the British aristocracy. The Duke of Windsor, who abdicated as King Edward VIII three years earlier and his wife Wallace Simpson were admirers of Hitler, as were some other prominent British peers. Their support for Hitler was nourished by fear of Communism, and paranoia about a possible union of Communism and Jewish people in a worldwide conspiracy against capitalism.

War talk had been buzzing for months. Australia as a Commonwealth country would be pulled into it, if it ever started. That would create an economic bonanza for he and his business associates. His connections in government circles would give his businesses more opportunities to supply the government with the equipment, clothing and other supplies needed for its troops. A German sympathizer, or spy, leveraging his clandestine work through Nancy was not something to be ignored.

Celia's letter was enough to spur Bertie to learn more about this mysterious Englishman. He telephoned a friend who owned an industrial investigation firm.

"Gerry," he barked into the mouthpiece. "I need to know everything about this bloke. From how he fared in grade school to what type of underwear he wears. And I need it yesterday. OK?"

Before day's end, he had on his desk a slim but informative file. Its contents revealed that the Langer family had German ancestry with aristocratic connections. His father owned a decaying estate in Sussex and an older first cousin was an earl who travelled to Germany earlier that year for Hitler's 50th birthday celebrations. Langer himself had spent considerable time in Switzerland near the German border.

Bertie didn't need more. He was not one to ponder his decisions, nor one for sober second thought. He closed the file, knocked back the remainder of four fingers of whiskey he had been drinking while reading, picked up the telephone and booked passage on the next ship to Europe. He would be only a few days behind them because he had a direct sailing with no stops along the Australian coast. he would telegraph Celia aboard the Strathaird and tell her to wait for him in Colombo.

He would deal with whatever he had to there and hopefully turn around and get back home. He would tell Nancy that she was being manipulated by a man who wanted only to get information about Coulson Industries. She would understand. If necessary he would get the Ceylonese authorities involved, with the help of his friends in the Australian government.

CHAPTER 10

Colombo

COLOMBO HARBOUR APPEARED a cauldron of activity after so many passive days on an empty ocean. Catamarans, flatboats, banana boats, large freighters, even some canoes, floated seemingly directionless, much like sea birds trying to find the best place to fish. The harbour wharves, seen through the heat haze from a distance, seemed to be mounds crawling with insects, which in fact were rickshaws and pony carriages and people on foot.

"Look at the activity," Vera said excitedly from the starboard rail where she watched with Nancy the Strathaird's approach to the Ceylonese capital city. "It's incredible after all those boring days of seeing nothing at sea."

"You can smell the stink from here," said Nancy, putting her hand over her nose.

"That's the smell of spices, Nancy. Cinnamon, cloves and flowers. It's wonderful. When we go ashore, I hope to see one of those men charming a snake out of a basket."

"You truly are demented Vera," Nancy scoffed.

Colombo's docks could not accommodate a ship of its size so the Strathaird anchored in the harbour. A small ferry, shedding decade-old rusty flakes of white paint, took passengers ashore.

Langer and the little touring party he had assembled were going ashore in a private launch sent out by the governor.

"This is stunningly adventurous," Nancy gushed as the launch approached, its deck crew ramrod stiff in crisp white uniforms.

Langer had repeated his offer of a sightseeing tour after he first suggested it to Celia at the end of their meeting in the Verandah Lounge. He had told Nancy of the offer, who in turn pestered her mother about it. Celia finally agreed and Langer invited Cora and Vera to join them. They would see the island's highlights, and have dinner with Sir David. The Strathaird, taking on supplies for the leg to Europe, was to depart the following day.

Sir David, dressed in a white business suit and pith helmet, met the launch at the dock. He was a scarecrow-like fellow with a bushy blond moustache bleached almost white by the sun, which also had turned his sunken cheeks apple red. After being introduced to the ladies, he begged off for an appointment, promising to see them at dinner that evening.

"Sorry about that, Niles," he said. "Something has popped up. All this war talk."

"These fellows will look after you," he said, pointing to two locals dressed in loose shirts, baggy pants and turbans. "Show you the highlights of the city, and outskirts if you wish. They'll get you to King's House in the afternoon for drinks and dinner. It will be good to get caught up with each other."

They set off in rubber-tire rickshaws pulled by reedy men who showed more bone than muscle as their legs pumped and arms pulled their burdens through the morning crowds. Celia and Cora shared one rickshaw, which had a comfortably cushioned double seat. Langer squeezed in between Nancy and Vera while the guides followed behind in another.

"How do such little men pull such loads," Vera remarked as their rickshaw threaded through the conglomerate of pedestrians, carts, motor cars and other rickshaws. The morning heat had begun, intensifying the fragrances drifting from shops lining the street.

"Everyone has to work to live," said Nancy.

'Yes, but this is brutal work best suited for animals."

"These men are from the lower classes," said Langer. "They can get no other jobs. They pull the rickshaws every day just to get food. Many sleep in the streets at night."

"Perhaps we should have taken a motor," Vera said.

"Then this man might not have had a fare and no food for today," Langer replied. "The governor's staff will pay him generously, probably enough for food for several days."

"But it seems so unfair. Every person should have the same chances as everyone else."

"Really, Vera," Nancy laughed. "Sometimes I wonder if you are becoming a Bolshevik!"

The city was an eclectic mix of buildings created by different colonial periods and different cultures and religions. The architecture ranged from the fortress-like Edwardian general post office with its columns of heavy building stones to the Italian Baroque style Christian churches to the exotic Buddhist and Hindu temples. Then there were the stone mansions of the elite contrasting with the stick and mud, or corrugated metal shacks with thatched roofs housing the poor.

The rickshaws rolled east of the old Fort into the Pettah neighbourhood with its series of open air markets and bazaars. They came to a stop outside an odd shaped white church with red roofs.

"This is special," said Langer as he helped the young women from the rickshaw. "This is the famous Wolvendaal Church. Dutch and very unusual."

"What a strange name," said Vera.

"The Europeans saw jackals here and thought they were wolves. So they named the spot Wolvendaal, or Wolf's Dale, or place of the wolves."

Langer explained that Dutch colonists built the church in the shape of a Greek cross with walls one and a half metres thick. Gables had been built on the thick walls to soften the church's stern look. A brick dome roof once struck by lightning had been replaced with iron sheets. Its Mediterranean appearance made it look out of place, but inside the wood furnishings drew awed looks from the ladies. The Dutch furniture was elegant with carved ebony chairs and a raised sculpted wood pulpit with hard-carved ribbon and tassel decorative wood.

Wherever they went they saw a city with one foot in the past, the other in the present. Men waved large fans to separate rice from its chaff. Women worked alongside men scraping and shovelling dirt to make a new road. Oxen attached to wooden draw bars pulled large wooden-spoke carts loaded with goods.

In the crowded market place, Nancy had Vera take a picture of her lighting a cigarette on an ingenious cigar-cigarette lighter; a hanging piece of rope with a smoldering tip. Passers-by needing a light simply grabbed the end, blew on the smoldering tip and placed it to their cigar or cigarette.

"No one ever has to ask for a match here," Nancy laughed.

After lunch at the Galle Face Hotel Langer suggested they should see the Dehiwala Zoo and Kelaniya, the famous Buddhist temple. They could top the day off by watching the elephants take their afternoon break from working in the fields.

"Every afternoon at the same time they stop working and trudge down the path to the river where they roll and spray each other with water before returning to work," Langer explained. "It's like our afternoon tea break. It's amazing to watch."

"I think I'll pass," said Celia, who gave no reason but seemed unusually preoccupied.

"I think I will too,' said Cora. "Perhaps the two of us could spend a bit of time at the market. I hear there is some lovely lace there that I would like to look at."

Celia accepted the idea quickly. The shopping outing would give them an opportunity to talk.

"We'll leave you ladies to the shopping then," Langer said as he and the young women set off for the zoo.

Celia and Cora finished their tea then braved the pounding heat and bustle on the streets to stroll to the market.

"Mr. Langer is so knowledgeable and it's good of him to spend time with us," said Cora. She had watched Celia's preoccupation and raised Langer as an opening for her to talk.

Celia welcomed it and appreciated the chance to feel out Cora's views on the man. They had known each other for years and Cora was the closest to anybody she could call a friend.

"Yes, I sometimes wonder why he has so much time when there are so many men's activities. I gather there are card games every day on board and that some of the men have organized adventurous explorations here on Ceylon."

"Has he not been married?" Cora asked.

"Yes, he said his wife died. He has been visiting his sister somewhere out by Waitara. She is his only family, I gather, except for his father in England."

"No children?"

"I gather not."

"Well, if he is mourning it is good to be around other people," Cora offered while avoiding giving her opinion on what she had been seeing. "Especially younger people. He does seem to have taken to Nancy."

"Or perhaps it's more that Nancy has taken to him." Celia replied. "You know how she is."

Cora did know. Her daughter Vera and Nancy had been friends since starting school together in Wahroonga. Although she was a couple months older, Vera played the little sister role in Nancy's world. Nancy, even as a child, was a commanding – and often demanding – presence and Vera followed behind her like an obedient puppy.

Cora held firm opinions about Nancy but believed that some opinions are best left unsaid, especially when expressing them would create conflict without changing anything. Nancy was Nancy. Cora accepted that while guiding her daughter to be her own person, maintaining Nancy's friendship without allowing it to influence her character.

"Nancy loves to be the centre of attention," Cora said. "Providing it perhaps gives Mr. Langer an outlet for his grief."

"Perhaps, Cora. Bertie will be wild if this develops into anything."

"Are you concerned about Langer's intentions? He seems honourable and I haven't noticed anything untoward. He always makes sure someone is around when they are together."

Celia dropped her eyes to her fingers that were caressing the Ceylonese lace two women were selling from hand-woven baskets at the roadside.

"I'm not so concerned about his intentions. I'm worried about hers. She is so impetuous. Also, I keep thinking about the argument with Mr. Carlisle, who believes Langer is a Nazi. Perhaps a spy."

"That seems a bit farfetched," said Cora. "However, perhaps you should let Bertie know. You should be able to telephone from here."

"Yes," Celia replied. "You know this lace work is remarkable. We should get some for the girls' hope chests."

The group reunited later in the afternoon at the hotel patio where they had drinks before changing for dinner with the governor.

The governor's house, called the King's House, was a white masonry mansion with grand portico arches. Sir David met them out front and after drinks they were shown into a dining room that was less remarkable than expected but graced by exotic hand-carved mahogany table and chairs. The conversation centred on the many amazing sights they had seen.

"Isn't it remarkable the way those elephants stop work for a swim each afternoon," said Nancy.

"Ceylon is a remarkable place," said Sir David. "There is so much more to see throughout the island. The architecture and customs created through the different colonial periods, and of course the Buddhist and Hindu mix make it a remarkably diverse place."

Nancy and Vera told of seeing men fishing on stilts as the tide rolled in, bringing with it sardines and other fish. They learned that the men could perch for hours on stilts pulling up fish and depositing them into their shoulder bags.

"And I loved that church of the wolves," blurted Vera. "The woodworking is spectacular."

"The raised pulpit is a work of art," said Langer. "It is a classic example of the materialization of an organized religion."

"How do you mean?" asked Sir David.

"Well structured religion, it seems to me, always has been a way of exhibiting power, exerting control. The pulpit, magnificent and high above the heads of the congregation is an example of that."

"Your argument seems a bit steep, Niles," said the governor.

"Well look at your own island, David. Centuries of racial hatred and wars mostly created by religious differences. Surely organized religion has been the main cause of the world's most savage conflicts."

This was mainly a man's debate, but Celia's religious interests went far beyond those of a mere practitioner and it was too interesting a topic to leave to them.

"Well, look at all the people that religion has brought together to build new and better societies," she said. "America for instance. It was founded by organized religious groups."

"The point I am making," replied Langer, "is that organized religion is for people who want or need structure and formality and rituals. These things often lead to divisions and disagreements and often violence."

"It is a compass and a comfort for many, however," said Celia. "I mean what is there to replace it?"

"Spirituality," said Langer. "Religion does not probe, nor question. It follows dogmas. It is hypocritical in so many ways. Churches have power and riches while poor people scrabble to stay alive. Religions don't question that enough. Spirituality questions everything. Organized religion is about moulding people. Spirituality creates individuals with freedom to question and think and become better people for it."

What had been a group conversation about sights had become a debate solely between Langer and Celia. Nancy noted her mother's voice raising and that she was becoming jittery.

"So, you are saying that I am not my best self because I follow an organized religion. I think a lot of people would find that a fallacious argument."

"Perhaps Mrs. Coulson," Langer shot back. "My belief is that spirituality is more important than religion because it helps a person question who they really are and helps them to truly be that person. Too many people are not what they should be but what others want them to be."

The debate ended there with Langer and Celia staring at each other. The remainder of the evening was one of light, pleasant talk and good companionship, Sir David arranged transport back to the Strathaird, which would sail shortly after dawn. While preparing for bed Celia thought back on the dinner table conversation and concluded that the debate provoked by Langer had been deliberate and deliberately for her, although she was not sure why.

CHAPTER 11

Tango

THE EXOTIC SCENTS and sounds of Asia faded as the Strathaird steamed west from Ceylon. Talk turned to Europe, England in particular, home or once home to many on board. Many passengers had British connections. They were civil servants returning home from postings, Australians travelling to visit relatives in the old country, business people and recreational travellers.

War talk permeated conversations as the ship's wireless took in more and more dark news about Germany's aggression. The latest was the that Germans, after annexing Austria and taking over the Czech region of Sudetenland, had signed a non-aggression treaty with the Soviet Union.

War was a recurring topic during meals at the Coulson table. Carlisle seldom missed an opportunity to raise it in hopes of getting Langer to rise from the depths of his mysteriousness and reveal his true self.

"That fellow Chamberlink or Chamberpot of whatever his name is keeps giving in to that Nazi Hitler," Carlisle began one evening. "Of course, the Frenchies are no different. They never saw a fight they didn't want someone else to fight for them."

"Your intelligence on world affairs overwhelms me Mr. Carlisle," Niles replied calmly. "The British prime minister, whose name is Chamberlain, is trying to follow the wishes of the British people. We all left sons and brothers buried in Europe just over twenty years ago and have no taste for a return to that kind of war."

"Appeasing that maniac is a mistake. You should be burying the man and his Nazi ideas."

"Hitler is flexing muscles. The Germans are still stinging from their losses in the last war. They want reunification of former lands. What they call lebensraum. Some living space."

"Living space indeed," harrumphed Carlisle. "So, you even speak German."

Langer smiled but said nothing.

Celia wondered if he was being deliberately provocative. She saw the smile as more mischievous than generous. She could not believe that Langer, obviously intelligent and well informed, would attribute the growing German aggression to wanting more living space. Unless Carlisle was right and Langer was a Nazi.

"All this Germany talk is upsetting and is spoiling this trip, Tom," Doreen Carlisle interrupted. "When we get to Marseille, I think we should book for home."

"Oh, don't let all this nonsense spoil your trip, Mrs. Carlisle," said Nancy. "It's all just men showing their muscles are bigger and stronger than others. We'll forget about it all at the dance tonight."

Evening dances were a regular feature of the Strathaird's long voyage from Australia to Europe. They often were pickup affairs in which crew members with musical training and interest got together to provide some entertainment. Or, on many nights recorded music was provided.

This evening's dance, however, was special. A popular British dance band had been touring British government postings in India and had played Ceylon two days before the Strathaird arrived in Colombo. The band had agreed to do one special onboard gig.

Back in England the band entertained Sundays at the popular Palm Court in London's Waldorf Hotel on The Strand. The Strathaird staff decided to decorate the dance hall, located off the first-class lounge corridor, to look like the Palm Court. They added some trellis work and fake coach lanterns on paper tube posts to add some authenticity but could not replicate the Palm Court's famous glass ceiling or its spectacular marble floor. They had brought aboard some small potted palms at Colombo.

The Palm Court evening had been arranged well in advance and was much anticipated. Langer had agreed at dinner one night to arrange for the seating. Tables were for six and the Fenwicks had been invited to sit with them.

Nancy, accompanied by Vera and Cora arrived as the band moved smoothly into its first tune, *The Way You Look Tonight*. The dance floor undulated with swaying bodies as they picked their way through the tables. They found Langer at a table at the dance floor's edge. He was dressed in a white jacket and tie, as were most of the men. The women wore evening dresses, almost all sleeveless because of the warm evening air. Nancy and Vera wore light evening frocks, and Cora had chosen something a bit frillier and more formal.

"Ladies, you all look lovely tonight," Langer smiled. "Where are you hiding your mother, Nancy?"

"When I last saw her she was still fighting with what to wear. She can be so indecisive at times."

They were seated and ordered drinks when Celia appeared. The band had finished its first number and the dancers paused, waiting for the next tune. Many eyes turned to Celia as she walked briskly across the dance floor.

Nancy was chatting with Langer when her mother approached their table. She was dumbfounded. Never had she seen her mother look so . . . so. Her mind was blank on how to describe what her eyes were transmitting to it.

Celia was sleek, an American movie star figure, in a silk-like slacks suit. The slacks were tailored to accentuate the narrow waist and tight buttocks, open to view under the short hem of a matching bolero jacket. She was hatless with her hair brushed to one side and falling provocatively over one eye.

Slack suits, or pant or trouser suits, had become somewhat popular among working women in America, probably because of movie idols like Dietrich, Hepburn and Joan Crawford. In the British world, they were still looked upon as daring, and a bit outrageous.

Celia smiled at the shock broadcast by her daughter's face.

"Well," she said to the group. "You did say it was a Tango Tea evening. I thought it best to dress for the theme."

"Toro. Toro," laughed Langer. "You look spectacular. It's perfect for the evening."

"They've been talking about this tango tea dancing for days," said Vera. "I still don't know what it is exactly. We don't have it back home."

"Of course we do, Vera," Nancy said excitedly. "Where have you been hiding? Under a rock? The tango is everywhere."

"It's very popular back in London," Langer explained. "At the Waldorf it's a Sunday afternoon tea where a popular dance band, often this one, plays and the people request a lot of tango tunes. It's a wonderful afternoon.

They serve twelve different teas, finger sandwiches, scones with clotted cream, and strawberry jam plus an assortment of cakes. My wife . . . ."

He paused and gazed out onto the dance floor as if distracted by something from the past appearing there. Then just as quickly he snapped his attention back to their table.

"At any rate, great fun. Here we go. They are starting a great tango tune."

He reached out, grabbed Nancy by the hand and pulled her up onto the dance floor.

The tune was *Jalousie* and its staccato beat thumped the room as the dancers swayed with vigorous, expressive movements. Nancy bent back into the crook of Langer's arm and made dramatic head snaps while holding her right hand on his lower hip. She flushed with excitement.

The tango was a sensual dance, a sexual pantomime, but the Strathaird dancers, exercising traditional British reserve, toned it down. Nancy was intent on casting off all reserve, however, exaggerating some of the sultry movements, accompanied by surly but sexy snarl of the lips. Langer declined to fully play his part.

When the song ended, they returned to the table, breathing quickly, perspiration beading their foreheads. Langer offered his handkerchief to Nancy, then his hand to Celia.

"Your turn madam."

"Oh no. I'm not a dancer."

Langer pulled her hand gently and guided her out to the floor as the next number was beginning, then turned his face back to the table.

"Then it's your turn, Cora."

As he guided her onto the dance floor a young singer with slicked back hair, cheek hollows and hooded eyes began the next song in a soft, sleepy voice.

When they begin the Beguine
It brings back the sound of music so tender
It brings back a night of tropical splendour . . .

It was a rumba-like piece with slow and deliberate steps that allowed the dancers to roll their hips in a sensual display. Celia caught on to it quickly. She and Langer moved smoothly with the music, looking as if they had invented the dance.

Nancy had not seen her mother dance in years. Out on the floor was a woman very different from the one she knew as her mother. The eyes of all the men still seated were on her, watching her lithe and lively movements. The auburn hair flew side to side catching the light reflected from the mirrored alcoves. When she snapped her head back, she smiled broadly revealing a set of perfect teeth and a personality never seen before by her daughter, who felt a touch of envy flutter inside her.

Langer was sweating profusely, but Celia looked exhilarated but cool when they returned to the table.

"I'm no match for you Australians," Langer huffed as he sat to catch his breath. "Where do you people get all that energy?"

"You didn't do badly yourself," said Celia. "It must have been the tonic of the Australian air at your sister's farm."

"You dance expertly," said Langer. "It must come from a lot of practice."

"She never dances," Nancy interjected sulkily. "In fact, she never goes out. Except to go to church."

"I don't imagine you learn tango and rumba steps in church," Langer laughed.

"Almost," said Celia. "The nuns at the foundling home taught me to dance. They had music and dancing sometimes in the evenings. The younger ones, especially the novitiates, loved dancing."

"It was the same where I grew up," Cora said. "The nuns at our girls' school organized dance lessons."

"How ridiculous," said Nancy. "They can't drink, they can't smoke, they can't date or get married. But they learn to dance."

"Just because they can't date or get married doesn't mean they can't have fun," Cora said.

Langer offered her his hand. "Let's see what they taught you."

Nancy had started to rise from her seat, expecting that Langer was asking her to dance. She pouted as she watched them take the floor. What a waste, she thought. Mrs. Fenwick's steps were sluggish and clunky. What could you expect from someone taught to dance by nuns. She danced worse than her mother.

Nancy promised herself she would never become like them. Dreary housewives. Cleaning the house and minding the dog. Evenings knitting and listening to the radio. They all followed the same pattern: an unexciting courtship, marriage, raising the brats.

Langer and Cora returned to the table before the song ended.

"My that's much too fast for me," said Cora.

Langer, slightly exhausted by trying to guide Cora through her missteps, offered his hand to Vera. She accepted happily and they danced off into the centre of the floor as Nancy stood and huffed off to the washroom.

Vera and Langer were an interesting couple to watch. They both danced in fluid, relaxed movements, which was surprising because off the dance floor Vera appeared gangly and awkward. She wasn't exactly a homely girl, but she wasn't pretty either. She was just plain looking with straight, dull blonde hair but she had a contented smile on a comfortable face that broadcast friendliness.

• • •

Nancy's little snit over not dancing every dance with Langer passed and the dance party became an enjoyable affair. The table conversation, loosened by drinks, was gay and friendly. There were laughs as Langer told stories and jokes about the British monarchy, still suffering the effects of King Edward's abdication to marry twice-divorced American socialite Wallis Simpson.

"Imagine giving up your throne for a woman, and such a social climber," said Vera.

"Such is love," Langer said mockingly. "The truth is he probably didn't want to be king. Too much public exposure and too much responsibility for a playboy."

"I think he made the right choice," said Nancy. "Royalty is so boring. Tied to all those rusty traditions. Cut loose. Have fun. That's what I say."

"Now who is talking like a Bolshevik," Vera answered.

"The newspapers say they are Nazi sympathizers," Cora offered. "But you don't know what to believe anymore."

"They took their honeymoon in Germany," said Celia. "There was a story in the Sydney Morning Herald that said they met with Hitler. In fact, the King . . . or the Duke now . . . called him a great man."

Langer thought about that for a few seconds.

"He is an appealing figure. Look at him and you see someone who is bearing intolerable wrongs. His face broadcasts the hurt. That smudge moustache and the locks of hair falling across the forehead. He is the

---

face of Germany. The hurt party reunifying the country and the German people."

There was a silence as the women were uncertain what to take from that remark. Celia looked across the room to the table where Carlisle and his wife sat. She saw Carlisle glaring at them.

Later, the ladies all agreed the dance evening had been a fun time with a sense of growing companionship. The apparent developing relationship between Langer and Nancy had moved off into the background, replaced by a group of people just enjoying each other's company in a festive setting.

For Langer it had been one of the most pleasant evenings in years, free of tensions. Unleashed from memories of the past and the possibilities of the future. He thoroughly enjoyed the music and the dancing. The tango, which evolved from music African slaves brought to South America, was dramatic, but nostalgic. It reflected a profound sense of loss and longing for people and places left behind.

He stood in a dark corner of the promenade deck smoking and staring out onto the placid sea while thinking about that. Was it possible for someone to leave a former life completely behind and escape into another? To leave behind all of life's deeply rooted attachments. It was comparable to tearing a tree from the soil, then replanting it in a new and strange environment with vastly different circumstances. The tree could survive but would it be the same? What would be the effects on the other trees which had grown beside it and were part of each other's existence? Would they be able to carry on?

On another section of the promenade deck Celia sat on a bench reflecting on the sense of freedom the evening had given her. For once she was just herself, free briefly of the life complications and complexities following her across thousands of miles of ocean. Best of all, Nancy was not the sole centre of attention, if only for a brief time.

CHAPTER 12

Life's Dream

NANCY MADE HER decision at the horse races. She had bet on Life's Dream to win and he had, if only by a nose. She saw that as a good omen, one signalling that she was ready to bolt from the family barn and run her own race.

The horse races were a popular entertainment aboard the Strathaird. There were card parties, a variety of sports activities and games, and of course, the evening dances. The horse races always drew the most participants. They featured six wooden horse heads painted with bright colours; dappled greys, chestnuts, palominos and black beauties. They were caricatures with painted large grinning teeth and rope manes.

The horse heads sat on poles attached to small wheels. Six lanes were created on the dance floor with masking tape. Each horse had a lane on which it rolled up toward a finish line at the end of the room. How far each moved was determined by a ship's staff member rolling a pair of large wooden dice. If the dice produced snake eyes, the horse for which the dice were rolled moved a measly two taped blocks. If the dice produced a pair of sixes, that horse jumped ahead twelve blocks.

Passengers picked horses and bet on them. The betting was pari-mutuel, a betting pool in which people bet on horses to finish first, second or third.

At dinner, Langer invited everyone at the table to the races that would begin after the evening sitting. He was in an expansive mood and offered that he would treat each person to a bet on the first race. Carlisle looked at him curiously, and said he and his wife had something else planned. Celia and Cora were bridge partners for an evening competition, but the two young women and Beatrice Cross accepted.

Life's Dream was a long shot in the first race, but surged well ahead of the others and paid five to one.

"I've won. I've won," Nancy shouted, jumping up and down, then throwing her arms around Langer's neck.

Vera had bet the favorite, Abbey Road, who finished last. Aces High ran a good race for Mrs. Cross but finished just out of the money.

"Niles, you bring me such luck," Nancy gushed, waving the pound note winner's share enthusiastically.

"Luck is fleeting, my dear," said Mrs. Cross. "It's always best to rely on sound thinking. Sound reasoning. That's what my husband used to say."

Nancy glowered and did not reply. Sound reasoning was not for her. She relied on what felt good, not what felt right. To her, Langer felt good. Certainly, he was older than her, perhaps by twenty-five years. He had been married before but had no children. Nancy saw that as one reason he was falling in love with her. She was young and beautiful and one day off in the future when she had enjoyed a large slice of life, she would bear him the child for which he no doubt yearned.

Unsophisticated people would see their relationship as morally unconventional, if not scandalous. Let them think what they will, she thought. What others think matters little. It was like standing in the spotlight with everyone looking at you. You smile back at them and they begin to understand you had the courage to do what they only dreamed of doing.

Life's Dream was a talisman. Its surge ahead of the others clinched her decision. She would have Niles. They would marry and travel Europe. Her mother would pitch a fit so it was critical that she win her father over. He would accept the situation when he saw the happiness Niles brought to his daughter. Her mother would wail but do nothing because she was indecisive. She was bound by character traits frozen in the past. She could never sway off the marked path because she lived a life directed by old fashioned ideas.

The dreaming and scheming in Nancy's mind left no room for absorbing what was going on outside her bubble of self-absorption. The ship's conversations drooped with war talk based on increasingly worrisome news arriving through the wireless. The Nazis had occupied Slovakia, the British navy reservists had been called up to active service. The latest news was a major British conscription push that called for enlistment of all men ages twenty to twenty-one.

"That might lessen the field for when we get there," Vera said as they lounged at the pool.

"I've got my man," Nancy replied.

"You're not serious," Vera said with some genuine surprise. "I thought all this Mr. Langer business was just another Nancy lark. You do push the limits sometimes, you know."

"There are no limits," Nancy smiled, rising from her lounge chair to run and greet Langer who had appeared at the far end of the pool deck.

Langer was pensive, his high brow puckered in concern, when he joined them.

"British citizens have been warned to get out of Germany," he said.

"Well, there are many other places to visit in Europe other than Germany," Nancy said with a laugh that rang with less than her usual enthusiasm.

"Worse news still," Langer continued. "There are rumours that the British admiralty is going to close the Mediterranean to all British flagged ships."

"Surely they can't stop us," Nancy said looking at Vera.

"They certainly can. Closing the Mediterranean means closing the Suez Canal, exactly where we are headed."

That evening at dinner there were rumors that the Strathaird's planned Red Sea port stops and land excursions might be abbreviated, or even cancelled. The ship might steam directly to Suez and get through the Mediterranean to Marseille before any closures.

"That's ridiculous," Nancy told the table indignantly. "We plan to visit the pyramids and ride the camels."

"More likely you'll be preparing battlefield dressings in London, my dear," said Carlisle. He turned and glared at Langer.

"And now sir, how do you feel about the chances of war? And, on which side will you be betting?"

The Strathaird received more frequent news about deteriorating relations between Germany and its neighbours as it steamed into the Gulf of Aden and up the Red Sea toward Suez. The speculation about the Egyptian stops was ended when the captain decided to proceed immediately to Suez and directly on to Marseille.

The cancellation of the Egypt day tours created unhappiness among some passengers, notably Nancy. She was among a minority who could not accept or comprehend the seriousness of the fact-moving events in Europe.

"How patently ridiculous," Nancy had scolded a ship's junior officer who announced the news casually while passing through the sun deck. "You've ruined the best part of our trip."

"I'm sorry, miss," said the officer, who seemed surprised by her reaction. He immediately regretted having said anything. "I didn't mean to upset you. I just heard it from one of the other officers, I'm sure the captain will make a formal announcement."

"Well, the captain certainly will hear from the passengers."

She turned to Niles, who had turned to his book to avoid being involved in the scene.

"You will talk with him won't you Niles? This is outrageous. We all were counting on such fun. Riding a camel, seeing the desert, and the pyramids."

"Again, I'm sorry, miss," the officer said turning quickly on his heel. "This is nothing else I can say."

"The ship is run by fools," Nancy snorted, encouraging other sun takers to share her indignation.

Celia had sat silent in her chair, also deep into a book. She said nothing, hoping that Nancy's rant would reveal her immaturity to the others, notably Langer.

The captain's decision was the right one. The Strathaird was one of the last ships through Suez and made Marseille just as the canal and the Mediterranean closed to British Commonwealth shipping.

CHAPTER 13

Marseille

A WIND GUST, AN omen of a world being blown into madness, snatched the slip of paper from Celia's willowy fingers, and lifted it above the heads of passers-by. None noticed the paper rise and dive across the busy avenue where it vanished among an even thicker crowd of Marseillaise out walking with the worries of the day.

You could not blame them for not noticing one slip of paper cavorting in the wind. The city brimmed with preoccupation over the German invasion of Poland. Headlines screamed from the front pages fluttering in the breeze at sidewalk kiosks.

Celia, who had a bit of French from school, had scanned the headlines posted outside the telegraph office. The German Luftwaffe had attacked unexpectedly and destroyed much of the Polish town of Wielun, killing twelve hundred people while German infantry and Panzer divisions razed the towns of Krzepice and Starokrzepice, expelling their citizens.

Britain and France reacted by giving Germany a deadline to withdraw from Poland. If the deadline was not met, both countries would be at war with Germany.

Many French out on the sidewalks in the late summer sun walked with heads down, contemplating the events in Poland and wondering whether their country might be invaded next.

Many believed the Germans would not withdraw and would march across western Europe.

Celia lunged for the slip of paper as it took flight from her hand but the breeze was playful. It lifted it higher just as her fingers almost snatched it back. The lunge unbalanced her and she was pushed aside by the jostling pedestrians outside the telegraph office. It floated farther away and out of sight far down La Canebière, the broad boulevard flowing downhill toward the Old Port.

She panicked. The paper was a telegram from Bertie. If she needed to reply she had no return address. Then she calmed herself, realizing that the telegraph office would have a copy and she had already read the message:

SUEZ CLOSED. STRANDED CEYLON. SEEKING ALTERNATE TRAVEL. BERTIE

"What a mess," she muttered as the river of pedestrians carried her downstream like a broken branch. She needed to think, calmly and rationally and out of this flood of pushy people.

She spotted an unoccupied chair at a crowded sidewalk café and lurched sideways out of the flow and into the chair as someone else reached for it. She sat, feeling like a piece of flotsam come to rest on a river bank, but anyone watching her would not have thought that. Her makeup remained perfectly in place.

She removed sunglasses and pushed a few wisps of displaced auburn hair off her forehead, which although heavily tanned, was smooth and fresh looking for a woman of middle age. She ordered coffee with hot milk, which she did not want because it would aggravate her overloaded nervous system, but she needed something to do with her hands.

Outside the flow of pedestrians, she relaxed and her thoughts found some order. The telegram now drifting aimlessly somewhere in the city streets was the second message from Bertie. The first was a shipboard wireless, which arrived as the Strathaird approached Colombo, and said he was sailing to meet them and they should wait for him.

That cable surprised her and she worried that the letter she posted to him from Perth had contained too much information. She had tried to be careful not to alarm him, yet wanted him to understand her predicament with Nancy. Either way she could not be right. Bertie always either blamed her for overreacting to their daughter or for not doing enough to ensure that Nancy behaved herself.

That news of Bertie's coming had troubled Celia throughout the day in Colombo, distracting her from the sightseeing and shopping. She had not expected him to react so quickly and decisively, but Bertie never did anything in half measures. His impulsive departure left her muddled.

She needed to talk with someone but certainly could not tell Nancy that her father was enroute. How could she explain that? Perhaps Bertie suddenly accepted that he should take a vacation and decided to join them? Nancy would not buy that. She would have accused Celia of concocting an elaborate Langer story that upset her father and brought him running.

Celia had wanted to tell Cora everything during their shopping outing in Colombo, but could not. There was nothing Cora could do to help. Bertie had sailed. God only knew about Langer. Would his pursuit of Nancy continue? If it did, what would happen when Bertie arrived?

Now sitting and sipping her coffee Celia felt relief overtaking her anxiety. She no longer had to worry about a showdown when Bertie met them here in Marseille. At least not in the immediate future.

It could be weeks before Bertie reached Marseille. Certainly many days. She assumed that he could take a boat across the channel to India, then a tortuous rail adventure through the Indian sub-continent, across the Middle East and into Europe. That seemed impractical and would be too much for Bertie's fragile patience.

She recalled that Langer and the governor had talked about the new scheduled air mail service that had started in Ceylon a couple of months back. The mail carriers sometimes took a passenger but that service, if it could be called that, was not reliable.

Most likely any Europe-bound ships would divert around the southern horn of Africa then steam toward Britain or the west side of Europe. Whatever. Bertie would connect with them one way or another. He was the man of action on matters important to him, and Nancy and business were important matters. He would be a charging bull in his efforts to get here.

She had thought about chucking the whole trip when they reached Ceylon. First, Nancy's infatuation with this man easily old enough to be her father. Then Nancy's illness. Her instinct urged her to turn around when reaching Colombo and go home. These problems did not exist in her gardens.

Returning home after reaching Ceylon had not been an option, however. Nancy would have gone off like a frog in a sock. Perhaps even run off with Langer. Then of course Bertie would blame her.

During one of their arguments over Langer, Nancy had she hinted at running off. However, she was underage and until she turned twenty-one she would not have her own passport. She could have problems crossing international borders without her mother on whose passport she was listed.

Celia could feel the eyes of people standing at the café's edge staring at her and her empty coffee cup. Bugger them, she thought as she signalled the waiter, ordered another coffee and returned to her thoughts.

Returning home now, she reasoned, was not just an option. With a war started it was a necessity. She would have to find passage from Marseille out of the Mediterranean, down around the tip of Africa and on to Ceylon. She could cable Bertie there now and tell him to wait for them. If he was still there when the cable arrived. She could tell Nancy that her father gone to Ceylon on business or that he had come looking for them when the war started.

Did any of that make any sense? Sound reasonable? Celia's head spun and her mind, super-charged by caffeine, raced and swerved through a jumble of thoughts. One thought, which had been hiding among the others came clearly into view: life back home, outside of her gardening, was a life she no longer wanted.

Not that her life in Wahroonga was miserable, by any means. She was Bertie Coulson's wife and as such received a life of privileged comfort and safety, seldom questioning whether it could be better or worse. After more than twenty years of marriage, she knew he was not her best choice as a husband.

Life with Bertie was not easy. He was intelligent and quick, never slow to see and admit his weaknesses, but never able to carry through with needed corrections. If he genuinely tried she could accept and find it easier to excuse the indiscretions that widened the chasm in their marriage.

Bertie saw their daughter's flaws, but procrastinated in doing what was needed to correct them. Perhaps he recognized the same flaws in himself, flaws that he was in no rush to correct. Correcting his flaws would mean depriving himself of some necessary pleasures.

Over time, Celia accepted his faults and their consequences on her. She was not, however, willing to accept Nancy's faults, which now created a new and untenable situation that Celia must deal with alone and thousands of miles from home.

This trip to Europe was to have been a break from life in Wahroonga. It had been talked about as Nancy grew into womanhood. The Grand Tour of Europe was a tradition among well off Australians. After a good wool years, Australian mothers took their daughters abroad to Europe and to England where many still had relatives. These were usually lengthy coming-out voyages for the young women and offered opportunities for meeting well-reared and well-placed young Englishmen who might be interested in marriage.

The trip would give Nancy opportunities to grow into the woman Celia expected her to be. Someone mature, settled, respected; someone who accepted the life carved out for them and who didn't waste time and energy questioning why it could not be different.

Celia believed that Nancy had difficulty accepting anything about their lives, especially the things that were decent and honourable. She was developing a reckless disrespect for life's accepted conventions. She showed no interest in settling into a marriage with any of many suitors. She was becoming, in her mother's eyes, a reckless girl capable of pulling down the stable lives of those around her.

Celia wanted this trip to help her daughter grow up, deepen her understanding of the world and help her find a respectable place in it. Seeing Europe's architecture, sculpture, paintings and other works of art tended to humble the viewer. Anyone with an unusually high opinion of herself had to feel smaller when standing below the works of da Vinci, Michelangelo and van Gogh.

For Celia, this trip was jumping off the conveyor belt life that moved relentlessly through the same cycle year after year. An escape from a life and people that she wanted to question openly, but could not without turning that life upside down.

She sipped her café au lait and gazed beyond the flowing sidewalks and into the Marseille skyline, painted golden by the retreating afternoon sun. The beauty of the place was more than she had expected. Ancient buildings bathed in soft sunlight mixed with blue reflections from the sea. Every square foot of the place soaked in centuries of history incomprehensible to anyone from new worlds such as Australia or North America. She had not been to Europe before and was looking forward to travelling place to place, tasting and feeling the freedoms of escape from a life where everything was the same from day to day to day.

None of that matters now, she told herself. It was foolish to think about proceeding with their set plans. Not just foolish, but dangerous. Probably the best idea was to get to Britain where it would be relatively safe for now and plan from there. Perhaps get across the Atlantic to the safety of Canada, then find a way home from there.

Langer certainly could be helpful in getting them get to England. He was a widely experienced traveller who knew Europe inside out. She had got to know him better after the Strathaird left Colombo. He had taken to having breakfast some mornings and often joined Celia, who was an early riser. Nancy slept late as did the other members of their table.

She had been uncomfortable at first during those breakfast times alone with Langer. His showing up to eat with her seemed planned. Perhaps, she thought, he hoped to gain her approval of a relationship with Nancy. Uncomfortable as she was, Celia did not pursue the conversation that he had deflected during their lunch at the Verandah Café. Nancy and his interest in her, unnatural as that might be, was something to be settled later.

With that issue pushed off to the side, she found him pleasant company. He conversed easily about topics that interested her – gardening, interesting books and things to see in Europe. As a listener he came across as genuinely interested. He made her feel that her and her interests truly mattered. In all, Celia found that she liked being around him.

She especially enjoyed the dinner conversations in which Langer baited Carlisle, who reminded her of the rainbow lorikeets that frequented her gardens in Wahroonga. They were colourful parrots, often puffed up and noisy, too often showing they thought too much of themselves. Langer led Carlisle into conversations that appeared deliberately designed to confirm Carlisle's belief that he was a Nazi.

He was charming and funny and could be helpful in getting them to Britain but Celia dismissed that thought. It would create even more complications. Better to get Nancy away from him now.

The waiter, impatient with her day-dreaming over the coffee, broke into her thoughts.

"Qui soit tous, Madame?"

Celia did not understand but his voice and manner indicated he wanted her to order something more, or give up her place to others waiting for a table.

"Oui," she replied obediently and fetched coins from her purse. As she did, a couple approached to take over her table.

"Well, look here, Doreen. It's Mrs. Coulson."

Celia looked up into the grinning face of Tom Carlisle. She had no choice but to invite them to join her, despite getting ready to pay her bill and leave.

"We were seeing the sights," Carlisle said excitedly. "Out finding our land legs again. Good to feel solid ground again."

Celia could tell from the higher pitch of his voice and the exhilaration sparkling in his eyes that he had seen more than the usual sights and he had stumbled on the one person he wanted to tell.

"We were over at the grand staircase. We saw your daughter's friend Langer."

He paused to let the suspense build. Celia thought perhaps he had seen Langer and Nancy doing something risqué in public, like embracing, or kissing. She glanced at her watch.

"Yes, Mr. Langer was talking to a very furtive fellow. Trench coat and fedora in this warmth. Little fellow with a moustache. I believe they were speaking in German."

"Tom, you can't be sure of that," said Doreen. "They might have been speaking French."

"I could tell by their faces and their gestures," Carlisle insisted. "It had to be German. Whatever, it was certainly sinister."

He paused again to let that sink in. Then he leaned forward, lowering his voice.

"I'm telling you Mrs. Coulson, the man is up to no good. I'm certain he is working for the Germans. A lot of those Englishmen are. I don't know what he wants with your daughter but I suggest you get her as far away from him as you can."

Celia did not know what to say. The Carlisles were busybodies and gossips, but they were not deliberately vicious. They likely believed everything they heard or saw, never questioning the accuracy of it.

"Well, thank you," said Celia. "I must be off to find Nancy. We are cancelling all our plans and will try to get home through England. Thank you again and I hope you also get home safely."

She forced her way into the people stream on the sidewalk and went with the flow, heading nowhere in particular, but knowing she needed to end up at the rail station. She had decided not to wait in Marseille for Bertie. She would get to England and figure out how to get home. What she needed to decide was how to convince Nancy that returning home was best for them now.

Nancy would fight her decision, but would have little choice. With the war, security would be heightened by the day. Travel for anyone without their own documents would be difficult. She would explain that she had legal responsibilities as a parent at least until Nancy achieved legal age. Then she would have her own passport and could return to Europe if she wished or do whatever she wanted. Until then, it was Celia's duty to protect her.

She turned onto Boulevard d'Athenes and found herself approaching the grand staircase leading up to Gare Saint Charles, Marseille's main rail terminus. The grandness of the wide staircase made her pause before starting to climb the one hundred and four steps. It was a true marvel, connecting the city with the rail station that had been built on a hill not easily accessible to the streets below. Its steps were broad enough to carry tall lamp posts in their middle and its sides were decorated with marble statues glorifying France's colonial past in Africa and Asia.

She was breathing hard when she reached the top and turned to take in a sweeping view of the city. Off her right shoulder was Basilique Notre Dame de la Garde, Marseille's signature landmark. It sat on the city's highest point, its soaring bell tower topped by a spectacular golden statue of the Virgin Mary, the guardian of the city whose citizens called her 'la bonne mere,' the good mother.

The terrace outside the station held puddles of people, mostly tourists come to see the grand staircase and the views from the little summit on which the station sat. Inside the entrances of the station people streamed, flowing in all directions amid the clatter of baggage carts, the hums of idle locomotives and the scratchy announcements from the intercom speakers. The morning train from Paris had just arrived and Celia had to push through hurrying knots of people to get to a ticket window.

"Un horaires de trains, s'il vous plait," she said in mangled French made worse by the sharp Australian accent.

The clerk looked at her as if he were deaf. She repeated then he reluctantly reached behind him and plucked a sheet of paper from a rack and tossed it across the counter. Celia took the timetable and made her way through the crowd to outside where she found a bench on which to sit and study the timetable.

"What are you doing here?" said the voice off to the side of her.

It was Nancy with Langer close behind her.

"Did you see all the wonderful statuary?"

They had come up the magnificent staircase to the cobbled terrace leading into the station.

"I saw them only briefly. I came to check train schedules. How was your morning?"

"Glorious! What a wonderful city. Niles knows all the highlights. Why do you need a train schedule? It's wonderful here. The weather's perfect and it will take a few days to a week to see everything."

"I'm afraid all our plans have changed. We need to find the safest way home. We've sailed into a war. It's only going to get worse."

"Oh nonsense. Just because the Germans have invaded Poland doesn't mean we are in danger. It's not anywhere near here."

"Your father has cabled and wants us home," Celia replied, her voice rising slightly as she got up from the bench. She could sense a shouting match coming.

"What did he say? Let me look at it."

Celia hesitated. "I can't. Walking up here the wind blew it from my hand."

Nancy rolled her eyes. It was as she thought. Her mother had not heard from her father at all. She was making this up in hopes of getting her away from Niles.

"I'm sorry but your father is worried about our safety. Shipping is closed the way we came so we have to find another way home."

"I don't want to go home," Nancy persisted. "You can go home. I want to stay. The war means nothing to me."

"I've already told you that your father is worried about the war and wants us home. You can't stay in Europe on your own."

"Niles will watch over me, won't you Niles?"

Langer had detached himself from the conversation, but listened and watched the tension thickening between the two women. They were bonded by birth but it had been evident to Langer early that there was no usual mother-daughter bond now. Their personalities were galaxies apart.

Nancy was an easy study, one to take action without thinking, seeking instant results and gratification. Celia was reflective, though there was a flintiness about her that he suspected could spark and ignite dramatic change once she thought it through.

"I won't argue it anymore," said Celia. "We must leave."

She offered her hand to Langer.

"Thank you, Mr. Langer. You have been kind and much too generous with your time."

"My pleasure," said Langer, taking Celia's hand and shaking it.

"If you do need any help I plan to stay at the hotel until tomorrow then catch the early train to Paris and Calais. I have decided to go back to England. Your mother is right, Nancy. Now that it's started I'm afraid all Europe will become battleground."

Tears welled in Nancy's eyes.

"I can't believe this is happening. Everything is being ruined!"

"I tell you what," Langer said, looking at Celia. "Let me buy you all a farewell dinner tonight. I'll leave a note at the hotel for the Fenwicks to join us. It will be a bon voyage party and we can reminisce about the trip. There's no use letting it end on a sour note."

The suggestion brightened Nancy and for Celia it at least delayed the screaming match. They parted, agreeing to meet for dinner at six o'clock.

CHAPTER 14

Le Poisson d'Or

L ANGER CHOSE LE Poisson d'Or, a small restaurant next to their hotel, for the goodbye dinner. It was quaint, very old and with an earned reputation for outstanding seafood dishes. The place had a Mediterranean flavour with white plaster arches opening onto a terrace that overlooked the lower part of the city and the sea. The walls held paintings of coastal scenes radiating the blues of the sky and sea and the golds of the warm days. Only the oak table and chairs, darkened by decades of age, didn't fit the theme.

Langer had arranged a bouillabaisse, the famous regional fish stew. That took some arranging because the restaurant usually declined to make a bouillabaisse for fewer than twelve guests.

"What makes the Marseille bouillabaisse different from other fish soups is the selection of Provençal herbs and spices in the broth," Langer told the four women.

The meal, in the opinion of everyone at the table, was superb. The conversation was light and loose, aided by some dry white Rhone wine, plus a local light red.

"This is certainly a wonderful way to end the grand tour," Cora said, lifting her wine glass for a toast. "Thank you, Niles, and may we all get safely to our destinations, whatever they might be now."

Cora and Vera were leaving for London the next day to seek out relatives and to watch how the war developed before deciding when and how to return to Australia.

"We might see each other on the same train," Langer said. He turned to Celia and Nancy: "We could perhaps travel as a group to London if you wish."

"That would be wonderful," said Nancy but her mother broke in quickly.

"We will stay in Marseille a day or two," said Celia. "I want to contact my husband and get his advice on what we should do. I know he's concerned about us being stuck in the middle of this."

Nancy said nothing else. The dinner party broke up soon after with everyone promising to look each other up at some stage down the road.

Nancy was strangely calm during the parting. She kissed Langer on the cheek and said she hoped to see him in England.

Celia shook his hand and simply said: "Goodbye."

• • •

Celia slept soundly through the night, which was unusual for her recently. It likely was the couple of glasses of wine with the dinner. She awoke as dawn spread light through the hotel room shutters, looked over to Nancy's bed and saw it was empty. The bathroom door was ajar and unlighted.

She climbed out of bed and called "Nancy."

There was no answer. She shouldn't have expected one because the room was small and anyone in it would be easily visible. She noticed the wardrobe's doors were open and saw that some of Nancy's clothes and a small valise were missing.

She should have been shocked, but wasn't. Nancy's calm at the parting the previous night was unexpected. She should have suspected that she was planning something. Apparently that something was to run off to Langer. Had she done it on her own, or had he compelled her?

Celia dressed quickly and went to the hotel concierge. She learned that the young lady had left carrying a valise and had ordered a taxi and was overheard to tell the driver to take her to Gare Saint Charles.

CHAPTER 15

Departure

THE TRAIN WHISTLE signalling departure pierced the cavernous space of Gare Saint Charles as Nancy half ran, half stumbled along the platform. The train jerked into forward motion as she reached the second from last Pullman car, grabbed the handrail and pulled her and her valise onto the step. A trainman grabbed her hand and said something in French that she did not understand.

Once she caught her breath, she walked through the cars her head swivelling right and left as she looked for Langer. She found him in the dining car, reading a paper while he drank his tea with a croissant. The croissant crumbled between his fingers as he saw her. She was dishevelled, her hair shot out at several different angles under her hat, her face red from exertion.

"Nancy! Did your mother change her mind about staying in Marseille? Sit down, you look like you have just finished a foot race."

"I have," she laughed. "The train was trying to leave without me."

"I'm glad it didn't. Where is Celia?"

Nancy fussed with her hat and her hair then grabbed the arm of a passing waiter who she asked to bring her a coffee and some rolls.

"I was so rushed I didn't have time to get my morning coffee," she said, still not answering the question that Langer had asked twice.

"Will your mother be joining us?" Langer asked.

"Celia decided to take the southern route. She'll meet up with us sometime later. You know how she wanted to visit Lourdes. Apparently it's on the way to Bordeaux and she'll figure it out from there."

Langer, who had brightened at seeing her again, became uneasy. She obviously had left her mother, presumably after a disagreement.

"You have plans to join up somewhere?"

"We left it open. I thought you probably would have some ideas on where I might go and what I might see."

"It's not the best time for sightseeing in Europe. I'm heading to London, then out to Sussex and away from all this war news."

"I'd love to spend some time in the English countryside."

Langer sipped his coffee thoughtfully. "Your mother will join us before crossing the channel then?"

"I'm not sure. You know how she is. Stubborn. And moody. She likes to spend time alone."

"You can't very well get into England without her. You are on her passport."

"Oh, that's just a formality. I have a birth certificate. I'm sure you'll help me convince them."

That might take some convincing, Langer thought. Bringing a young, attractive and underage woman into the country without a passport. Some immigration officers might simply wink and let them pass. However, some might not. What if Celia has gone to the authorities in Marseille to report that her daughter had taken off, or been abducted?

His thoughts were broken by an excited voice.

"My goodness. We can't seem to get rid of each other. Nancy. What a surprise." It was Cora and Vera who had just entered the dining car. Langer invited them to sit with them as he ordered more tea and croissants and jam.

"I'm happy that Celia changed her mind and decided to leave Marseille," said Cora. "Is she coming to get a bite of breakfast?"

Langer looked to Nancy who buttered a roll and appeared not to have heard the question. There was uncomfortable silence that Langer felt obliged to break.

"Nancy tells me she decided to go on to Lourdes, and join her later."

"Oh," Cora muttered, looking confused. Another uncomfortable silence followed, one that Nancy ignored. She busied herself with the roll while Cora summoned a waiter and Vera stared out the window at the passing scenery.

Langer's mind rolled into crisis mode. It was like watching the German soldiers of more than twenty years before spill out of their trenches and advance toward him. He needed to do something quickly. Mrs. Fenwick and her daughter no doubt were getting wrong images of what was happening here. He turned to Nancy, who remained focused on her coffee and rolls.

"I'm concerned that your mother might not know exactly where we should meet. Maybe it's best to go on from Paris to Calais and give her a meeting point there. I can send a telegram to her hotel. If she has already left they can forward it to Lourdes. They likely arranged Lourdes accommodation for her so they will know where to send it."

Langer was up from the table and on his way to the train's wireless counter three cars back before Nancy could say anything. He took a pencil and paper and scratched out a staccato message telling Celia that Nancy joined his train unexpectedly. She was with him, plus the Fenwicks, and they would wait for her at the Calais boat-train dock hotel.

He gave the paper to the operator and said he would return later for a copy and a receipt. He wanted evidence that he had tried to contact Celia to tell her that Nancy had joined him unexpectedly and on her own volition.

Thank God, he thought, that the Fenwick women had shown up on the same train. Their presence could be more evidence that he had not run off with the Coulson girl.

CHAPTER 16

Pursuit

Celia scolded herself for not suspecting something from the evening before. Nancy was unusually unruffled when they said goodbye to Langer after dinner. No protests, no histrionics. She already had planned to sneak off, possibly with his encouragement and his assistance.

The obvious action now is to go to the police, Celia thought. That would end all this drama that had accompanied them since leaving Sydney. The police would pick them up in Paris, if not before at some station stop enroute. They would arrest Langer and return Nancy.

Celia walked to the hotel entrance and stood there considering what to do. A gendarme stood on the corner a few dozen yards down the avenue. She took a step in his direction, then hesitated. The police would go hard on Langer. Possibly charge him with abduction, even if Nancy did a drama queen performance explaining how she loved him and had followed him. Or, if she was worried about what her father might think about the whole mess, she might just toss Langer to the jailers by saying he had lured her away. She was not above doing that.

Celia did not believe her daughter had any true feeling for Langer. He was simply her prop in a drama starring her. A way to gain attention, and of course to irritate her mother. Langer was using Nancy for a reason, some reason which she had yet to figure out. Perhaps Carlisle was correct in saying he was a Nazi. Maybe the true purpose of Langer's attention was to gain passage into Bertie's business affairs, now closely tied to the war effort.

Best not to approach the policeman, she thought. Instead, she turned right and walked three doors down to the telegraph office. She needed to tell Bertie that Nancy had run off. He had just arrived in Colombo, according to the telegram she received earlier, and no doubt was still there waiting for the steamship company to sort out what to do now that its ships could not enter the Mediterranean.

Inside the office she wrote out a seven-word message telling of Nancy's running off and addressed it to Bertie care of P&O Colombo. The clerk handed it to a telegrapher while Celia dug into her purse for the money to pay for it.

"Oh, Madame Coulson?" the clerk asked after reading the name and address she had printed on her message. "There is as message come for you," he said, fetching a newly-arrived cable.

Celia read it, smiled, then shouted to the clerk not to send the telegram addressed to Bertie.

"Please, it's a mistake. It should not be sent."

The telegrapher shrugged and said something in French.

"It is already gone, madam," said the clerk.

Celia sighed. The inbound message was from Langer. Nancy was on the train with him. The Fenwicks were with them. They would wait for her at the Calais train terminal where passengers caught the boat-train to England.

There was no sense in sending Bertie a second telegram saying Nancy was found. She would do that when she caught up to her in Calais and tell Bertie to meet them in London after he sorted out a travel plan.

She returned to the hotel, packed a travel bag and arranged to ship the heavier luggage to The Waldorf Hotel on The Strand in London. She left quickly for Gare Saint Charles where she learned that the Golden Arrow express train was leaving for Paris in thirty minutes. She would not be far behind Langer and her daughter.

Aboard the train there was little to do but sit, read, stare out the window and think. Celia's mind was too crowded to read and the scenery was pleasant but not spectacular. It would not be until later when the train passed into the Rhone Valley region where the villages nestled under the regal mountains.

She had much to think about. She had known for some time an unalterable and disheartening fact: she and Nancy never could be friends. Most girls went through that teenage period when their mothers were the enemy because they stood between them and the things they thought they should be allowed to do. Some girls also developed rivalries with their mothers. It was all part of the transformation from child to adult and was a phase that passed, sooner for some, later for others. When it did pass. the relationship between daughter and mother often grew into friendship.

Mothers and daughters who became friends treated each other as equals. They laughed together, shared the joys of life and genuinely enjoyed each other's company.

That will never happen to us, Celia thought as she stared out at the groomed French vineyards flashing by. She did not know why. She understood that difficult mother-daughter relationships were common, but their relationship was too constantly difficult to explain as hormonal, or as simply expected individual disagreements. Throughout her childhood Nancy had been egocentric and emotionally manipulative, and had adopted that strategy as her main means of communicating with her mother.

Certainly, Neil's death had changed Nancy, as it had changed them all. Celia had suggested they see a psychiatrist to help them deal with the tragedy and its effects on them. Bertie had refused. Only weak people needed psychiatrists, he said, and when psychiatrists got hold of them the usual treatment was electroconvulsive shock treatment.

"Most psychiatrists are half nuts themselves," he said.

Celia went to one on her own. His views were helpful, at least in helping her understand how the death of a child changed a family. She learned that surviving brothers or sisters often were left with enduring symptoms, sometimes distorted personalities. Most were tormented by guilt. Rivalry exists between siblings and creates petty hostilities. It was part of life. But when one sibling died, the living ones could experience an unnatural guilt stemming from things they might have said, thought or done to the dead brother or sister.

A surviving child might develop an unhealthy fear of death. If a brother or sister could die, so could he or she. This often led to an unnatural craving for attention. Perhaps, Celia told the psychiatrist, but long before Neil's death Nancy was different; demanding, difficult to reason with and much focused on herself.

She did accept the theory that fathers who lost a son tended to have a daughter take his place. They put the daughter on a pedestal, ignoring and not correcting developing faults. Nancy already had completed the journey from rebelliousness to friendship in terms of her relationship with her father. They were good friends, possibly because they were so much alike.

When all was considered, said the psychiatrist, families warped by tragedy seldom recovered fully, especially when they had troubles to begin with.

Perhaps now, Celia pondered, Bertie will see clearly the dangerous and destructive side of his daughter's personality. Direct her to change, with counselling if necessary.

First he had to find his way out of Ceylon.

CHAPTER 17

Bertie

BERTIE COULSON LEANED into the wind created by the motor launch as it pushed across the calm but cluttered waters of Colombo harbour. His jaw was set tight with tension, his angry eyes scanned the crowded pier ahead for a glimpse of Nancy or Celia.

It was ridiculous to expect to find them in that mass of people. They no doubt were at one of the two main hotels and likely had left a message for him at the P and O passenger desk. He had no idea what to expect when he found them, but he was prepared for anything.

"Hopefully, this guy has bored and simply buggered off," he mumbled to himself.

From a distance the pier was an anthill onto which someone had sprinkled Demerara sugar. It pulsated with bodies in frenzied motion, producing a din that became audible as shouting voices as the launch came close. The bodies and the din swallowed the passengers disembarking from the launches.

Bertie found himself surrounded by yelling, gesticulating hawkers as his first foot landed on the pier. They waved and pushed pieces of silk, necklaces, booze, and other items for sale into his face as he elbowed them away and headed up the pier to the building marked by a massive P and O Lines rooftop sign.

Inside the stone building it was cooler despite being wall to wall with passengers seeking information on alternate travel now that the Mediterranean was closed to British civilian shipping. The closure was announced aboard his ship as it approached the Ceylon coast, setting off various levels of concern and talk about alternative travel. Some people raised the possibility of travelling overland through India. One man even suggested that anyone in a real hurry might consider tagging along with one of the airmail pilots now flying in and out of Colombo.

It didn't really matter to him. He would settle Nancy's latest infatuation and they could all return to Australia together. There didn't make sense for them to carry on the grand tour. Britain's closure of Mediterranean shipping indicated that war was much closer than anyone had anticipated.

When he bulled his way through other passengers and got to the P and O passenger counter, Bertie was told the ship's captain was meeting with P and O officials.

"There should be announcement by this evening," said the P and O agent.

"I'm not concerned about that," Bertie said. "Are there any messages for me from my daughter and my wife?"

"Ah, yes. Havard Coulson. There is a letter left for you." The agent disappeared briefly then returned to the counter with an ivory-coloured envelope bearing his name. He recognized the handwriting right off. It was Celia's.

He read the note, flushed with anger, then slammed his fist on the counter.

"Goddamn her! This is ridiculous."

He looked at the letter again.

Bertie:

I decided it was prudent to continue on to Marseille. The situation between Nancy and this man Langer has not improved. I feared a confrontation by telling Nancy we must remain in Ceylon. She is much enamoured with this man, although I'm not convinced it is not put on just to draw attention and upset me. Perhaps the situation will resolve itself by the time we reach Europe. If not, we will be in Marseille and you can handle it upon your arrival. It will be much easier for me to make excuses for delay in Marseille rather than here in Colombo.

Celia

He crumpled it with both hands and tossed it to the floor.

"What the hell is she thinking?" he said aloud.

"Pardon me?" said a tall, thin man standing beside him. Bertie recognized him as one of the ship's passengers who he had identified as a busybody.

Bertie knocked the man aside with a pulverizing look. "Never mind. It's my business," he snapped as he pushed off through the crowd.

Now what to do? She ignored his order to stay put and wait and now was God-knows where. All this mess might be resolved now if she had done what she was told. Instead, he was stranded in this hot dusty hell hole not knowing anything more than when he left Sydney. Was this man Langer still hounding Nancy? What had Celia learned about him? Had he been asking questions about his business or his contacts?

He must carry on to Marseille, but now this Suez closure had made that impossible. P and O had arranged rooms for its first-class passengers at the Grand Oriental Hotel, a four-storey whitewashed edifice within shouting distance of its waterfront offices. Bertie told the agent he was continuing on to wherever P and O decided, was assigned a hotel room, then went there to contemplate the situation and to await word on what the steamship line planned next.

Bertie believed the best course was to take the ship and make for England around the horn of Africa. The old, reliable route, and the only sea route between Europe and Asia before the Suez Canal was built. It was much longer but the ship would reach England in perhaps ten days, depending on weather and the need to resupply along the way. At least once there he could carry on to find Celia and Nancy.

He was standing on the room's balcony, admiring the view of the magnificent clock tower and the governor's residence, when there was a knock on the door. He opened it to find a small brown lad with an oversized turban holding two pieces of paper. One was a telegram that he assumed would be from Celia, whom he expected had reached Marseille. He ripped it open and the large capitalized teleprinter letters jumped off the page.

NANCY GONE WITH HIM. PURSUING TO PARIS

Bertie felt the bravado leave his body. It was like someone had turned on spigots in his ankles allowing the energy and confidence to drain onto the marble floor. He felt cold despite the tropical heat and oppressive humidity.

He glanced at the second piece of paper the bellboy had placed in his hand. It was a note from the hotel saying P and O had decided to sail for London in the morning. It would take the Horn of Africa route.

He pulled himself back together and decided there were two things to get done before the morning sailing. He had to telephone Sydney and tell his security people to double vigilance on all operations, particularly any files relating to government contracts. That done he would go to the downstairs bar and get the two things that always saw him through a crisis: good whiskey and a woman.

CHAPTER 18

Calais

"S HE'S A BIG girl and capable of looking after herself," Nancy said as the train chuffed to a halt at the Calais terminus. "Besides she's the one who wanted to go to Lourdes for her religious vacation."

The debate over whether to wait at Calais for Celia or proceed directly to England started long before the train pulled into the coastal town where train service connected with the water ferry between France and England.

Langer reasoned that they should wait in Calais for Celia. He was uncomfortable leaving one of the group to find her way to England alone. It might be acceptable under normal circumstances, but a war was on, even if only in its earliest days.

Also, he questioned in his own mind Nancy's story about her mother telling her to go ahead while she took a side trip to Lourdes. Celia had said at the dinner that she planned to stay a couple days in Marseille to contact her husband, then decide what to do. She gave the distinct impression that the war outbreak meant the Lourdes trip was out.

If Nancy was lying about Celia going to Lourdes, she had run off without telling her. That set up all sorts of possible repercussions, which he did not want to contemplate right now. He had to get Celia back with the group and have her understand he had not encouraged Nancy to run off. He hoped she had remained in Marseille, received his telegram and was on her way to reunite with them.

"And, there is the issue of you not having your passport, Nancy," he said. "Everyone trying to enter Britain now will be checked closely. We don't want them to think we are sneaking you in illegally, do we?"

Nancy was not impressed with that argument.

"I am a Commonwealth citizen with an Australian birth certificate. I can't see how they could refuse me entry."

Langer turned to the Fenwick women for support, but was not confident he would receive it. Vera was nervous and given the option of being magically whisked back home to Australia, she would have jumped at it. Cora worried about the war affecting border crossings.

"The borders could be closed at any time," said Cora. "Who knows what the Germans are planning, or even where they are. They could be marching on Paris."

She is right, Langer thought. They should leave France immediately, but his life experiences had given him the strong belief that no one ever should be left behind. Also, leaving now would strengthen the impression that he had enticed the girl to leave her mother and come away with him.

"Shouldn't we at least wait for the next train to see if she's on it," Langer asked.

"But we don't even know if she received your cable, Niles," said Nancy. "She might be saying her rosary in Lourdes and not planning to travel to England for a couple of days. That was her plan."

The train doors opened and people were stepping on to the platform. Langer, unsure of what he would do next, helped the women down with their hand luggage. He was about to suggest they find a café for lunch and discuss further what they should do when he saw people beginning to queue under a hand printed sign directing British citizens to a doorway. He edged toward the queue to see what was happening.

"Major Langer. Hello!" a male voice sang out as its owner approached, his hand out in greeting.

"Timothy, how good to see you again." Langer took the man's hand and placed his other hand on his shoulder. Obviously they were friends from somewhere. "What are you doing here?"

"The foreign service sent me over to help the Consulate here. We have instructions to get all our nationals safely back home. France could be a war zone any day now."

Cora, Vera and Nancy watched from a distance as the two men conversed. Langer explained that he was helping two Australian women and their daughters get to England. Through some confusion one woman had been left behind in Marseille and Langer did not want to leave her behind.

"Don't fret, sir. It is best is you go ahead with the ladies. We'll look after the other woman. Give me her name and I'll check the boarding lists from Marseille. The French are providing us with the names of all passengers with tickets to Calais and the other embarkation points along the coast. Give me a moment and I'll ring the Consulate office here."

He strode off and the three women stepped up anxiously to ask what was happening.

"Major Langer! How impressive," said Nancy. "You never told me."

"It was a long time ago. Timothy and I did some time in the Army together. It's ancient history. He's gone off to get some information for us."

Timothy returned twenty minutes later. "Got lucky. Couldn't find a thing, but a new cabled list came in as I was ringing off. A Mrs. Coulson is on the late train from Marseille."

"Excellent," said Langer. "We should wait then."

"It won't arrive until early evening. It's best you get these ladies across the channel. Don't worry about the other. I will watch for her and look after her. I'm returning to London later tonight and will escort her."

"We'll need a meeting point in London," said Langer.

"You still have the place in Sussex, I assume? Why not go there. London is a mess. The place is on war footing, expecting German aerial attacks at any time. You'll be safer out in Sussex."

"He is right Niles," Nancy broke in. "Let's go to your home. I don't want to be in London if there is an attack."

It was settled that Langer and the three women would board the ferry and go to Sussex. Timothy would intercept Celia, take her to London and she could arrange transport to Sussex in the morning.

CHAPTER 19

Langer Manor

THE FIRST VIEW of Langer Manor did not disappoint, but neither did it stir much excitement. It was a grand place, in its day, but passing time and changing style and fashion left it sagging, wrinkled and sad. Climbing vines, planted decades ago to provide life and colour contrast to the masonry exterior, were untrimmed and each year crept across increasingly larger pieces of the mansion's brown brick and sandstone face.

It was a wide, squat two-storey place with oversize windows, each of which contained eight rectangular glass panels separated by strips of grey lead. The Mansard roof was shingled with heavy grey-black slate and made interesting by a row of small semi-circular dormer windows drawing in shafts of light into a low-ceiled attic. A viewer looking up from below could have expected to see the contorted face of some confined mad woman staring from one of the windows.

The house dominated the setting, which consisted of a series of knob hills overlooking a pastured valley in which the closest village rested quietly. The house sat on one of the lower knobs and behind it rose another knob, much steeper and from its top offered a splendid view of the countryside surrounding it.

Concealed by the manor house were several other buildings clustered like a mushroom patch out back and to one side. Some of the buildings presumably were stables because the breeze from that direction carried the tang of horse manure and old wood. Steam rose from all the buildings, the product of a warm autumn sun rolling over a morning of cold showers.

Celia arrived at the village on the late morning train, and as suggested by Langer when she talked to him by telephone from London, she found the village taxi nearby. It was a short taxi ride, perhaps not a kilometre, along the narrow, paved road leading past the dirt drive up through a hedgerow of shrubs dwarfed by aged oak and ash trees.

The taxi man deposited her and two bags at the front entrance portico, whose sullied white columns added to the wan look of the place. There was no greeting party, and it appeared no one had used that entrance in a long time. Obviously another entrance was used regularly, perhaps on the other side of the house because no one had heard the taxi's approach. It was near luncheon and Celia assumed everyone was gathered in whatever corner of the building that dining took place.

She had been uncertain about coming here and had considered insisting that Nancy come back to London, but felt unprepared to face the argument that would create. Also, it was hard to argue against the relative safety of Sussex considering the threat of air attacks in London where war tensions weighed on the city like a heavy fog.

She had arrived in London at midnight on the last evening boat-train from Calais, escorted by Timothy Ryan of the British consular staff. She was alarmed initially when he approached her as she stepped from the Marseille-Paris train in Calais. He introduced himself and explained that Miss Coulson and the Fenwick ladies had gone on to England with Major

Langer, who had offered them accommodation at his place in Sussex, well outside the London turmoil.

"London is a mess," Ryan said. "People have realized we are in to a real war and don't know how long it will last."

"Major Langer?" Cecil asked.

"Well, Niles. Mr. Langer now, but I don't really know him as anything else. We served together back in '18. He was a young major and I was his attaché."

He explained that he was in Calais to help any Britons needing to get off the continent. He had met the major unexpectedly after not seeing him for many years. One of his party had got separated, he told Ryan, who suggested going on to London and he would look out for Mrs. Coulson and explain to her what was happening.

"I'm returning to London on the last boat train tonight and would be happy to accompany you and see that you get settled. It will be too late to go on to Sussex but I'm sure he can contact your daughter and the major in the morning."

Ryan guided her to the boat-train waiting area, then went to find other British passengers to assist. He said he would check with her on the train when the boat reached England. They met again later on the train as it began the trip from the English coast down to London.

"Good to be back on home soil, isn't it," said Ryan as he took a seat beside her. She had not expected to share a seat with him but was glad to have the company. He was a chatty type and seemed happy to have someone to listen to him.

Celia pegged him as a drinker, although there were no indications that he had been drinking in Calais, or now. His face was red and prematurely wrinkled, much like an overripe tomato.

"I never imagined we would go through this after the last one," he said. "Wretched times. I thought everyone had learned from the hard lessons of war."

"You and Niles were in Europe for the last war?" Celia asked.

"Yes. It was a bad time. His older brother was killed in France, then he was wounded and sent home. That was more than twenty years ago. I haven't seen him much since. A couple of regimental reunions. That sort of thing. I heard he had gone abroad was living in Switzerland or Germany. There was some tragedy there involving his wife. I never heard what it was about or what he has been doing since."

"I don't really know," Celia said. Ryan was an opportunity to learn more about Langer, but Celia, for some reason, did not wish to learn more.

"He's been quite kind and helpful. All this is a shock. We left Australia planning on months of seeing the sights of Europe, and of course England. Now we must get home the best we can. Perhaps through Canada or the U.S."

"You'll want to arrange that quickly. German submarines are out on the Atlantic. It soon will become one of the most active war zones."

Their train pulled into Waterloo Station just past midnight, but chaos had replaced the late night calm expected in normal times. People jammed the platforms and connecting corridors, many disembarked from the European-connection trains. Others, in various stages of nodding off, slouched on overcrowded waiting room benches. They were among the many waiting out the night for the early morning trains that would take them away from London.

The city held its collective breath, listening for the drone of Hitler's Heinkel bombers expected to appear any night now, pushing through the air space along the Thames. Anxiety heightened when the Fuhrer broadcast a speech from Danzig boasting that Germany had a secret weapon that would win the war. Londoners understood the threat of bombs and gas attacks but feared a new secret weapon. Many suspected it involved missiles that could be launched at them from afar, therefore saving Luftwaffe bombing fleets for other nasty work.

Outside Waterloo Station there was only blackness. A total blackout was in effect, so strict that anyone caught lighting a cigarette on the street could be arrested.

"London has not been so dark since the Middle Ages," said Ryan as he helped Celia with her bags. "Thank God it's not far to the hotel. I don't know how they drive without headlights. There's the taxi rank over there," he added throwing up his hand and hoping one of the waiting drivers had good night vision. He did and gunned the black cab forward in the pitch black night.

The taxi crept through the dark streets, pausing frequently when the driver made out another car or someone foolishly trying to cross the street.

"Bloody awful," shouted the driver as he drove the taxi down the white centre lines. Others were doing the same so it was a constant game of what oncoming car would move off the line first.

"There's talk the government is at least going to allow us to hood the headlights. Too many accidents already and the war is barely started."

On the train Celia had read a newspaper report of lampposts, post boxes and pedestrians being knocked down by vehicles struggling through the darkness.

"The Luftwaffe already has killed dozens of people without dropping a bomb," said Ryan.

The taxi pulled into the kerb in front of the Waldorf without incident. The hotel staff had done a fine job of covering all windows with special blackout covers put up every evening and taken down every morning.

Ryan brought her bags through the doorway and into the lighted lobby.

"There you go. All safe and sound. This is a fine hotel. I hope you will be comfortable here. Take breakfast at the Palm Court. It's an institution. Famous for its Tea Dances. I came here some years back, with Major Langer as a matter of fact. He came here often with his wife. She loved to dance and especially that Latin music. A lovely, beautiful lady."

"You've been very helpful and very kind," Celia said, offering him her extended hand.

"My duty, and my pleasure. Enjoy Sussex and best of luck getting back home, And, say hello to the major. Tell him it was good see him again even under these unpleasant circumstances."

Celia rose early, after a fitful night, and took Ryan's advice to breakfast in the Palm Court. It was everything she had imagined that night of the tea dance aboard the Strathaird. The ship's staff had done a fine job of recreating the setting for that event, but could never come close to the real thing.

The room was created for elegant dances. Light danced across acres of mirror and glass, the marble flooring, the high arched walls and the ceiling with its panels of what appeared to be cut glass crystal. She closed her eyes and heard the music and could feel the breeze made by the swish of evening dresses.

The hotel was nearby the Australian consulate. After breakfast she walked there hoping to get information on how they might get back home and anything on Bertie's whereabouts. She could leave a message there for him and try to reach Nancy by telephone.

People on the sidewalks along The Strand scurried with purpose, faces tense, but focused and determined. Most wore a shoulder strap holding a small cardboard box that held their government-issued gas mask.

Workers on the other side of the street were placing posters designed to boost morale.

**"Your Courage, Your Cheerfulness,
Your Resolution Will Bring Us Victory"**

"Freedom is in Peril"

Lorries rumbled past, heavily weighted with dirt to fill sandbags, sturdy rows of which were starting to appear around petrol pumps and important buildings. The sky above the buildings reflected silver flashes from the sun hitting barrage balloons floated to complicate the work of German fighters and low-level bombers. German planes had not appeared yet in the London skies, but they were expected. People seemed prepared, possibly because they already had experience with exploding bombs planted by the Irish Republican Army. England had suffered a dozen such bombings that year, including explosions at nearby Kings Cross station and Victoria station only a few months before.

The consulate people were kind and helpful. They believed that Bertie's ship had left Ceylon enroute to London via the horn of Africa route. If so, it could arrive in London in a few days. They also allowed her to telephone out to Sussex and she spoke to Langer who gave her instructions on what train to take and from what station. Nancy and the Fenwicks were still sleeping, he said. It had been a long and tense journey for them from France.

A train that would take her to Sussex was leaving Waterloo Station later in the morning. She packed a small bag, arranged for the rest of the luggage to be stored at the hotel, and caught a cab.

It was hard to imagine that a cab had navigated basically the same route in the pitch black the night before. The streets were now filled with motor cars and people, many of them part of the massive evacuation of London. Hundreds of thousands of children were being removed to the countryside in a government organized operation named Operation Pied Piper.

Sidewalks around the station overflowed with lines of children queued for trains. Each child had a label pinned to his or her jacket and each carried an individual gas mask and carrier bag containing pyjamas, underclothes and a sandwich or two.

Celia had to manoeuvre between frothing pools of noisy, fidgeting schoolchildren just to get inside where more queues formed for trains being stuffed with children and accompanying women. The train trip was miserable for any form of life aside from sardines. The children's' cardboard mask boxes pushed against the shoulders and faces of the seated passengers. Mercifully, the trip to West Sussex from London was short; one hour and a half.

Now, feeling some relief at being out the crowds, Celia fingered a rust-encrusted knocker on Langer Manor's heavy oak door. It was stiff with lack of use but she freed it enough to allow three solid raps that echoed within a large space inside. She was about to rap again when the door creaked open revealing a superannuated butler. He seemed astonished to find someone at that door, although he had been told to expect another visitor.

"Good morning madam. We don't normally use this entrance." The voice gurgled, a bit like water percolating through gravel. "Mr. Langer senior prefers using the side entrance. I'll take you through to the others."

Inside the front door, the house retained some elegance. The entrance hall was massive with an ornate vaulted ceiling busy with sculpted stucco floral patterns and carved oak trim. The walls were the original wainscoting form, floor to ceiling, with oak cut into square panels. A curving staircase, with hard-carved decoration, flowed up to the second storey.

Langer, Nancy and the Fenwicks were having tea in a well-lighted room at the rear of the house. Aside from tall windows allowing light in from ceiling to floor, the main feature of the room was a large stone fireplace flickering brightly as it consumed three fat logs.

"Excellent! You have arrived safely," said Langer standing and inviting her to take a seat. "I hope the train journey was not too dreadful. We really could have picked you up."

"Ours was a nightmare," Nancy interjected before Celia could answer. "Screaming and squirming brats everywhere. At that time of night they should have all been in bed."

Celia and Nancy stared at each other. They did not go to each other and embrace. Nor did they specifically greet each other. Their reunion was as if Celia had just popped out to the corner store and returned minutes later. Neither said anything about the events of the past couple of days. It was apparent that neither intended to. The subject was a woolly mammoth standing in the middle of the room and everyone was talking around it.

The relationship between mother and daughter is becoming even more unnatural, Cora thought as she raised her teacup in hopes of preventing anyone from reading her face.

Neither Cora, nor anyone else, had time to dwell on the reunion because of the appearance in the room of Conrad Langer, Niles' father. Nancy and the Fenwicks had met him earlier, but all conversation stopped to allow Niles to introduce him to Celia.

The senior Langer was a beanpole of a man, frail looking and obviously not in top health. He had been wounded in the Second Anglo-Boer War and never recovered fully. Niles was an infant when his father left for Africa so did not know him as anything but an invalid who needed a cane to stand and walk.

The sub-surface flesh of his face appeared to have melted, leaving a thin and sallow membrane stretched across protruding bone. Only the blue eyes, dancing in their watery film, declared the face still alive. His hands trembled when making gestures, which he did a lot, and his voice, although strong, quavered.

None of these signs of age and illness prevented him from being an informed and fascinating conversationalist. His knowledge of current affairs was up to date and so was his vocabulary, which Celia thought unusual for an older person who existed beyond active society. She liked him immediately.

They chatted easily about her overnight stay in London and rail trip into the country. For Celia, it was a relief to chat. The group fell into conversation as if this had been their normal life for many years. Then Langer suggested a tour of the house and the grounds. His father begged off saying he would save his energy for his daily stroll up the hill behind the manor.

"It's not the most interesting house around," Niles said as he directed them out to the main hallway, then outside. "But I think you'll agree it is placed in a magnificent setting."

Langer Mansion's hilltop perch offered a panorama of cultivated fields, a forested hillside and the green valley cradling the village. There were stables for a few horses, a tack room, horse walk and three separate cottages for staff and overflow visitors. Only one of the staff cottages was occupied. Staff had been reduced to the butler, a cook-housekeeper and a couple of part-time men who maintained the stables and general outside work and they came out from the village daily.

The gardens were large and well laid but wilted and rusted like a flowering potted plant left unattended outside. At the back of the garden was a swimming pond fed by a hidden spring, and beyond that a wheat field, now ripe brown and undulating in the afternoon breeze, which carried the scent of roasted bran. There was no glint or sparkle in the scene, presumably because pruning and painting the property to make it postcard pretty required more staff.

"And it has no mysterious or exciting history, but it has had some interesting neighbours," Langer told the four women as they strolled the property.

Langer Manor, he said, dated to 1799 and had been in his family since the beginning, but it was becoming more difficult to maintain enough revenue from farming its fifty acres to pay all the expenses. The acreage had been triple at one time but pieces were sold for cash invested to produce regular revenue. Agriculture activities such as the wheat field and vegetable garden produced revenue, but much of that went to the tenants who worked the land.

"At any rate, it's father's place, his heritage and he intends to hold on to it until the end. What I'll do with it after, I'm not sure. I've never been the country squire type. But the history around here is fascinating."

The ladies were anxious to hear about the fascinating history of the neighbours. They were captivated when Langer told them that a nearby estate had been owned by Sir Harry Fetherstonaugh, a carousing playboy whose party life was deliciously scandalous and stoked the gossip mills from Sussex to London.

"He had a teenage mistress named Emma Hart who later became Lord Nelson's lover. He threw elaborate and wild parties but then settled down to a quiet, reclusive country life. After he turned seventy, he married his dairy maid, who was twenty-one."

The silence of stones dropped over the group. Everyone had the same thought: was the story true and told for a purpose? Langer lowered his head sheepishly and stared at the ground. He was uncharacteristically embarrassed, realizing that all four women connected the Fetherstonaugh situation of two hundred years previous with his attention to Nancy.

"Well," he hurried on, "that's not the most interesting part of the story. H. G. Wells lived at the Fetherstonhaugh estate at one time. His mother was the housekeeper there and his father was the gardener. So here you are in a historic part of the country. Lots of fun stories."

Small talk about Langer Mansion's surroundings and neighbours continued through lunch. Each of them avoided the important topics occupying their minds, and the decisions that must be made soon.

"I think we should go into the village, Nancy," Vera said. "They must have some interesting shops."

"Excellent idea," said Nancy. "You will drive us down won't you Niles?"

"Certainly, but I can't stay. You'll have to walk back. It's a pleasant walk. I promised father I would go over a few things with him this afternoon."

Cora said she would tag along, but Celia said she would pass. Langer brought a car around to the rear entrance as the women organized themselves for the trip into town.

"Are you sure you won't come along?" Langer asked Celia. "It's not cosmopolitan but it does have some interesting shops."

"Thanks, but I think I'll just rest here," She still felt uneasy being in close quarters with Nancy.

She stood in the drive and waved and when she turned to go in bumped into the elder Langer leaving on his daily walk.

"I'm off on my afternoon hike," he said. "Will you join me?"

"That would be lovely," Celia said, happy to have something to take her mind away from the troubling thoughts that had been building.

The manor sat on a broad shelf nature had cut into the hill overlooking the valley in which the village rested. It was not on the top of the hill but about two-thirds of the way up. The other one-third rose steeply, concluding with a wooded knoll not spacious enough on which to build a house. One side of the knoll was cleared enough to accommodate a small flower garden and a rock slab bench that sat two. It provided a restful spot to sit, read or meditate while gazing into the valley below.

Conrad Langer made the climb every day, staying perhaps an hour to read a book, which he carried tucked between his arm and body during the climb.

"I'm glad Niles brought you out," Conrad said between languid steps. "It's good to have some female company about. Good for Niles. He's been lost since Margaret died."

"Were they married long?" asked Celia.

"Eighteen years. Never had children. So, my only grandchildren are in Australia, which as you know is planets away."

"How true. So far that after just a matter of weeks it is hard to imagine that it even exists."

"Your husband is there, I assume?"

"Yes," she answered quietly. "The war is making for busy times for his businesses."

"Yes, the war," he said, turning his head and looking away into the distance. There was a catch in his voice and Celia thought she had seen a tear. He turned back to face her, pausing to wipe the backside of his trembling right hand across his cheek.

"Niles probably told you we lost Mark during the last war."

"He hasn't mentioned anything about the last war."

"Not surprising, I suppose. Mark was his older brother. He died fighting in France. Niles also served in France but thank God made it back."

"I'm so sorry. It is so difficult to lose a child," she said with authentic sadness. "It must have been hard on both you and Niles."

"Niles was an officer in the Royal Sussex. Saw horrid times in France. It was a miracle he came back. He never talks about it. He's a solitary one, my son. Always been like that. A bit of a clam that snaps shut its lid when it senses trouble. He's social enough and a good talker but a lot of things he keeps to himself and his writing. Genuine history buff. I worry sometimes he prefers past times to the present."

"He is a bit mysterious, or some of the passengers on the ship thought so."

Conrad laughed.

"Mysterious! Perhaps that's from being cooped up here with me. He never had many mates out here in the country. His favourite people he found in books. You learn a lot in books and for some people what you learn and think you don't want to share with others."

Celia pondered that, trying to analyse what he meant by it.

"He has done some writing of his own, I understand," Celia said.

"Yes, he works at it. Hasn't found the groove yet. He did a history of West Sussex and a history of families that went to settle America. He's had some short stories published and I suspect he would like to be a novelist. Perhaps he will be later. He could sell off this place, live comfortably in London and devote all his time to writing."

Celia shivered despite the sun's warmth. It was an odd conversation. Standing in soft, warm sunshine discussing personal matters with a failing man who only a couple of hours ago had been a stranger. Now he seemed part of her life, someone she had known forever and now was sharing his end-of-life reflections. He spoke as if double checking a checklist prepared to ensure that the end of his life and his legacy would be natural and without chaos.

Their conversation also created for Celia a different image of the son, the man who had occupied much of her thoughts since leaving Sydney. The mysterious and calculating man who often turned up unexpectedly seemed less of a dark shadow, more of fallen leaf pushed by the wind and unable to find a place to land and anchor to get its bearings.

"It would be a shame to see this wonderful place gone from your family after so many years. So much family history is here."

"Nothing is permanent, my dear. It's a problem for us humans. Too many of us don't recognize the inevitability of change, or cannot accept it if we do. People would be much more content in life if they would accept that change will come and do their best to manage it instead of fighting it. Older folks like me should not tie the newer generations to the past."

"Surely the newer generations have a responsibility to ensure the past is not lost and to look after the older people who were a part of it."

"New generations should be free to build their own lives. I don't want my son lingering here looking after this place and me when he should be living his own life. Old people should not block the path. I've read that in Canada elderly Eskimos sometimes walk out into a blizzard and disappear so not to be a burden on the younger ones."

"Someone must look after those who have difficulty looking after themselves, the elderly or others. Surely that is the responsibility of families."

"Perhaps, but times change. Look at the talk now of the 'new philanthropy' in which there is growing co-operation between state and voluntary groups. We are developing a full-fledged welfare state in which agencies, not family, look after the old and the infirm. I expect that sometime in

139

the future we might see a plethora of homes for the aged and few elderly living with their families."

"Out of sight out of mind. Then you are alone."

Conrad shrugged and gazed over the valley.

"True, but that is the reality of the future. The world now is moving faster and will move much faster in future. Life is for those who can keep the pace."

Maybe Conrad Langer is right, she thought. Maybe he is a visionary. She felt however that his son, despite his strangeness at times, was not the type to put his father in a home and forget him. What about her own daughter? What would she do years from now?

They talked a bit longer before Conrad Langer made his way slowly down the hill. Celia remained for quite a while, brooding and trying to sort out what to do now. Bertie would arrive in a few days, perhaps even a day or two for all she knew. They should go back to London to wait for him. How to explain that to Nancy? She could say they were going to do London things, then Bertie would appear by surprise.

Nancy would want to stay here at Langer Manor. That would be disastrous when Bertie arrived in London. She would have to tell them where they were and she could not have him coming here for a confrontation.

The whole thing was a mess. She had to find an escape route.

CHAPTER 20

Dawn

CELIA AWOKE AS the first faint light of pre-dawn diluted the darkness of the room. She was uncertain where she was until the dregs of sleep cleared and she sat up. She was in a large bedroom on the second floor of Langer Manor. She and Cora had their own bedrooms while Nancy and Vera shared a room on the same floor.

She got up quickly, splashed water on her face, straightened her hair and tossed on sweater and slacks for a walk before the house woke and began its daily routine. She needed to walk and think.

She was in England to escape war in Europe. She was here in West Sussex to be distant from the bombing threat in London. Her husband was enroute to help rescue his daughter from a possible affair with a man more than twice her age. They were guests in the house of this man, whose purpose in having them as guests perhaps was not entirely altruistic. Celia needed to think all this through and figure out what she should do.

It was cold outside but the sweater would provide enough warmth as she hiked up the hill to watch the sun come up. She would be sweating by the time she reached the top and the sun would warm the air soon after.

Grey light pushed away dark shadows as she reached the top of the hill. The brightening created a halo effect around the bench area where a solitary figure sat staring down into the dimness of the valley. It was Niles Langer. His presence surprised her and she was uncertain what to do or say.

"Oh, I'm sorry to intrude," she blurted nervously knitting and unknitting her fingers. "I didn't realize anyone would be here at such an early hour. I thought I was the only insomniac."

Langer stood and turned slowly to face her. He looked smaller and less powerful in the weak light of dawn.

"I often come here to watch the sun rise. Father likes the sunsets. I like to see the sun rise. It is positive. Gives hope, much like religion."

Celia cocked her head quizzically and took a step toward him.

"I got the impression that you disliked anything to do with religion. That's what you said one night at dinner on the ship and several times since."

"That's what you might have understood, but it's not what I meant," Langer replied. "I believe I have said that organized religion is sustained by fear and is the cause of some of the world's greatest ills, such as war."

"And, as I've said before it is also the cause of many of the world's good works. The homes for unwed mothers and orphans, for instance."

"I agree. But it does tend sometimes to hold people back from following their own natural instincts, or their hearts."

"You mean their urges," Celia replied quickly.

"A person's urges and what they feel in their heart are two different things," Langer shot back.

"Is your interest in Nancy an urge or a feeling of the heart?"

The question brought a pained expression to Langer's face.

Celia continued.

"What do you want from us, or more specifically my daughter?"

Langer looked at the ground and did not answer. This was a new, combative Celia Coulson he was meeting. Much different from the one he seen throughout the voyage from Australia.

"I don't know the reason, but you have been pursuing us. I thought I made it clear at our shipboard lunch that I find that unusual . . . in fact it's offensive and I'm bothered. Nancy is half your age at least. It's not right. It's . . . it's . . . it's lavicious behaviour."

Langer was shocked. He turned away and stared down the hill where light mist was forming, only to be consumed by the rising sun.

"That's insulting. I told you before that things often are different from what they seem. Obviously, you have an overheated imagination, or Nancy is telling you something that is not true."

"She has said that the only thing preventing her from leaving and travelling with you as your mistress is her age and not having her own passport. That is not the work of an overheated imagination!"

"And you think that idea came from me?"

"You've stuck to her like glue. Where else would she get the idea?

"Perhaps she made it up to get at you."

Celia turned, lowered her head and stared into her hands. Maybe he was right. Nancy loved to walk the cliff's edge with a spotlight shining on her. She delighted at times in shocking to entertain.

"And what about the roses? Is she making those up too?"

Langer turned back to face her. A morning breeze had risen and was roistering his sandy grey-flecked hair. A slight smile wrinkled his cheeks flushed from the morning coolness, or perhaps from a controlled anger. The smile reached up to crinkle the corners of his cool grey eyes, which showed more sorrow than amusement. He shrugged his shoulders while opening the palms of his hands.

"Things sometimes are not what they appear to be."

Celia sighed audibly, a sigh of frustration. She turned quickly and headed back down the path. Two-thirds of the way down she met Nancy coming up. It was a single footpath so they could not avoid each other, even though both wished to.

"You're up early," Celia said.

"It's a glorious morning," Nancy answered. "I thought I'd get some exercise and some air."

Celia tilted her head toward the upper part of the trail. "Our host is up there watching the sunrise. When you come down we need to talk."

Nancy said nothing as her mother stepped off the path to let her pass.

At the bottom of the path Celia heard a whinnying from the stable. She walked over and inside in the first stall she found a chestnut mare nickering and looking hopefully over the stall gate. The stable hand had not yet arrived to take her for her morning walk.

Celia patted the mare's muzzle and rubbed behind her ears.

"It's alright. Someone will be here soon. I know what it's like to be alone."

She felt dizzy, perhaps from walking the hill on an empty stomach. Her head spun and she felt suspended above the ground. Spinning, then falling. Like Alice falling down the rabbit hole. Twisting and turning. Her whole life a twirl. The Strathaird flew by. Then Ceylon. Then Marseille and London, finally landing in this place. What was she doing at the bottom of this rabbit hole? With a confused and hostile daughter in the home of a man whose actions were incongruous and his intentions a mystery.

She laid her face against the mare's muzzle, and began to cry.

CHAPTER 21

A Distant View

NANCY ARRIVED ON the hilltop lookout just as Langer was about the leave.

"Good morning. This is a busy place this morning. Your mother was just here."

"Yes, I met her on the path," Nancy said, catching her breath. Langer smiled at that.

"I thought you Aussies were rough and tough outdoor types."

"Rough and tough yes, but not mountain goats," Nancy said, sagging to feign exhaustion.

"Here, sit and rest a moment," he said, touching her elbow and guiding her to the rock bench. They both sat and fell silent, taking in the view and considering where the conversation should go next.

Their relationship had intensified, at least in the eyes of anyone observing it over the past month or more. To some it was downright scandalous with many whispered conversations about why the mother, or least someone, would not do something to stop it.

Despite the whispering there was no evidence of anything truly improper.

Among the whisperers only Carlisle had believed that Langer was after more than a sexual relationship. He was convinced that Langer was a Nazi working a larger plan through the girl. He theorized that the Coulson girl's father likely was privy to Australian war effort information that would be valuable to the enemy. The girl could be a key to getting to that information.

Nancy was aware of the whispering and enjoyed feeding it. It satisfied her appetite for attention as well as a perverse urge to upset her mother. Why she wished to hurt her mother she did not know. It was something inexplicable inside her. Perhaps it was because her mother was a safe target. Mothers do not usually strike back.

Whatever, neither daughter nor mother felt comfortable with each other and if ever asked would not be able to explain why.

Having Niles gave Nancy a sense of power and control. Niles understood and appreciated her. He accepts, she told herself, that I am different, a person who must be allowed wider boundaries. Her mother could never see that and often harped about not always being the centre of attention and developing some appreciation for the feelings of others.

Her mother was in for a terrible shock when she learned that Niles wanted Nancy to stay at Langer Manor. He had not asked her yet, but he would. He loved her and she loved him and there was nothing her mother could do to stop that. Celia would never understand it all, but her father would, once he understood what Niles meant to her.

She turned her gaze away from the countryside stretched out before them and looked directly into his eyes.

"You mentioned earlier that you are not sure what you will do with this wonderful place after your father is gone," she said. "With some attentive management it could be polished back to its former glory."

"Yes but finding the attentive management is the rub. It's not in me, or at least I couldn't give it the time and effort that it needs and still do some of the things I wish to do. Write more. Travel."

"What about finding a partner? My father says partnerships are the thing of future for business."

"Bringing a partner into this situation would mean paying him or sharing profits. There is not enough revenue in this place to be sharing with a partner who expects a good financial return."

"What if the partner did not expect a financial return?"

"What kind of partner would provide the work required here for no financial return?"

"A wife."

Langer flushed, suddenly feeling unsure of himself, and feeling unsure led to hesitation and hesitation led to poor decisions. And, Niles Langer did not make poor decisions.

"This is a wonderful place, Niles. It just needs some focused direction. It's the kind of place I believe could be turned into a profitable business. Perhaps a combination working farm and tourist attraction. Drag it out of its stuffy past and into the new century."

"I love your enthusiasm. It's the enthusiasm of youth. Obstacles simply do not exist."

"Of course they exist, but you simply run over them with a solid new business plan and a good business manager. My father taught me that."

"What if the obstacles are people? Do they get run over in the drive to progress?"

"People have two choices: join the flow to a better life, or get out of the way. There have always been many people too stupid or weak to get out of the way."

Langer thought on that for a few moments. The comment did not shock him. No one expected compassionate attitude from this younger generation. The first war, the Spanish flu pandemic, then the Depression had toughened people and made them more cynical about life. The horrors of those events had changed society, producing phenomena such as the flappers, the 1920s breed of young women who rebelled, in dress and attitude, against the precepts of their elders. They were outspoken to the point of being foolish.

"This estate has been here for a couple hundred years and presumably will be here for a while yet. It is a discussion for another day. Decisions are like that field off in the distance. They need to cook in the sun. You can't make a decision on harvesting it until the sun has baked it ripe."

Nancy's smile contorted into a pout and her face darkened. She had not expected him to be so unforthcoming. She did anticipate having her plan diverted, however, and was about to lay out her thoughts more forcefully when Langer pointed down into the valley.

"We have visitors."

A dark coloured sedan had turned off the village road and was heading up the long drive to the manor.

"We had best go down to see who it is. We don't get many visitors here."

He offered her his hand, helped her off her rock seat and they headed down to the steep path that led into the manor yard.

CHAPTER 22

Tweed Suits

LANGER KNEW WHO the visitors were when he reached the lower end of the hill path and saw them emerge from the car. The tweed suits, double breasted overcoats and fedoras were the first clues.

Their stealthy movements and furtive looks at the manor and its surroundings confirmed they were MI5 men. He had learned about MI5 people during his army service. Before going to France in charge of a combat unit he had spent some months in military intelligence, which worked closely with the secret service.

The two men saw him coming off the bottom of the trail and paused to wait for him.

"Good morning, sir," said one, a tall, thin fellow with a sallow look that matched the yellow nicotine stains on the two first fingers of his right hand. Too much time sitting in rooms and cars waiting, watching smoking, Langer thought.

"Good morning," he replied. "Are you looking for directions?"

"No, we are looking for Niles Langer," the MI5 man said peering behind Langer at Nancy.

"I'm Niles Langer. What can I do for you?"

"We would like to talk with you. Inside if we might."

Langer took the two men into the library and shut the door. The second man, short and lumpy but fastidious in his dress, said nothing. He stood in a corner absorbing the room's details into large dark eyes. The tall man, evidently in charge, produced identification and introduced himself as Charles Banning.

"We have been asked to interview you about your sympathies toward Germany."

"Pardon me? What business is it of MI5 how I feel or don't feel about Germany."

"That should be obvious to you, Mr. Langer, now that we are at war with the Germans. Specifically, we have some reports that during your recent voyage from Australia you, on several occasions, expressed sympathies for the German cause. Obviously His Majesty's government needs to know whether its subjects are for it or against it."

That fool Carlisle, thought Langer. He actually filed an information with the police when he reached England. Carlisle, the ultimate busybody, did not conceal his objection to the amount of time Langer and Nancy spent together, and had worked himself up into a frenzy of fantasy. During his visit to the police he no doubt had passed along comments that Langer had made about Germany during dinners and other social occasions.

"That's gossip," snapped Langer. "Totally unworthy of MI5's interest and time. Surely there are more critical matters on which His Majesty's secret service should be directing its efforts."

Agent Banning consulted a fat black notebook. "Several passengers heard you express the belief that Germany has legitimate grievances and good reasons for going to war."

"So what? Many Englishmen no doubt feel that if the surrender terms after 1918 had been less severe, less damaging to German pride, they would not be trying to regain their former position in the world now through another war."

"Well," said Banning. "That can be construed as a strong sympathy."

"My brother lies in a military grave in France," Langer said angrily. "I held a King's officer commission as a major. I fought the Germans in France, killed a few myself and have piece of German shrapnel in my thigh to prove it. That is all that needs to be said and I suggest that you leave my house, sir."

Banning smirked and threw a glance at his partner across the room.

"I first need to talk to the ladies who accompanied you on the journey and who you have brought here."

"Do what you need to do and then leave," Langer said as he stormed from the room.

Cora and Vera were interviewed first. Banning took them into the library off the entrance hall and closed the door. They had little to say except that Langer had been a gracious host, on the journey and here at his home. He had helped them reach England without incident. They knew nothing about his politics. They understood that he became friends of the Coulsons after meeting Nancy in Sydney. They had relatives in Weymouth and we leaving today to visit them. Both were confused about why these men were here and were happy to be leaving to visit relatives.

They left the room and Celia and Nancy were summoned. The questions were quick and not particularly probing. Was Langer a family friend? How had they met?

Celia, having advised Nancy to stay quiet, did the answering. They had met Langer on board the Strathaird. He had been an impeccable travelling companion, looking after all four of them, showing them some sights, then ensuring they got to England safely. He had invited them to the Manor to be out of the chaos of London and the possibility of bombings.

"Do you have any concerns about his political sympathies?" Banning asked.

"None whatsoever," Celia replied.

"And, any concerns about any unusual interest he might have in the young ladies? Some of the passengers said he spent much time with your daughter."

"What business . . .," Nancy burst out before being cut off by her mother.

"Mr. Langer has been a perfect gentleman and a friend," Celia said sternly. "The 'some' passengers no doubt are the Carlisles, busybodies with large imaginations. Now, I presume that is all. We need to pack."

Nancy, surprised by her mother's defence of Langer, was shocked by her statement about packing.

"You are leaving here?" asked Banning.

"Yes," Celia replied. "I have booked us passage on the Empress of Britain, leaving the day after tomorrow for Canada, where we will find our way back to Australia."

"A wise choice," said Banning. "England will be under attack any time now. It's best to get across the Atlantic before commercial shipping is closed down completely. Thank you for your assistance, and have a safe journey."

As Banning and his partner stepped toward the library door, Nancy turned on her mother.

"What do you mean we are going home? I have no such intention."

"I received a cable from your father. He wants us home. He is concerned about the war and our safety. He had hoped to come and fetch us but the shipping closures at Suez made that difficult."

"I'm not going home," Nancy protested. "Niles has said we will be safe here."

"It's for the best, miss," said Banning. "And, you might not be aware of the recent changes in Australian passport regulations. Single women are not allowed to go abroad against the wishes of their parents. So, in fact, I could force you to return home, although I hope that will not be necessary. Good day."

Banning was correct but not totally accurate. Australia had changed its passport regulations and could refuse travel papers to single women wanting to accompany a man abroad, or a single girl wanting to travel abroad to marry against her parents' wishes.

Celia gave off a conciliatory sigh as the agents left.

"I know how you feel. There's no use arguing about it now. Let's seek Mr. Langer's advice. He has to take his father somewhere but we can discuss this later. Now let's help Cora and Vera get ready and see them off."

They found the Fenwicks closing their suitcases and preparing to lug them downstairs. The old butler was there offering to haul them to the entrance where the taxi would arrive, but they waved him off politely. Celia and Nancy helped them and stood with them waiting for the car to arrive.

Cora took Celia aside, just out of earshot of the girls who were recalling some of their best times aboard the Strathaird.

"I feel awkward leaving, Celia," Cora said quietly. "Will everything be all right?"

"I've booked passage to Canada for us. We'll find our way home from there. Once we get to Canada we'll be well out of the war."

"Everything is all right with Nancy?"

"Yes, we 're working it out. She'll insist on staying but I think I can enlist Mr. Langer to help her understand the realities."

"I hope so. Good luck to you both."

"And to you too. Hopefully we'll all meet back home soon enough."

Celia and Nancy stood and waved until the taxi was out of sight. No sooner had it disappeared than the Langer car rolled up the driveway.

Langer helped his father out of the car and into the house.

"Father is not feeling the best. I'll take him to his room and stay with him for a while. We have some business to discuss as well. You'll have to dine alone tonight, I'm afraid. But we'll catch up on everything in the morning."

Nancy was stunned. She had not seen him like this before.

"Is his father that out of sorts?" she said as they watched him guide the old man up the stairs to him room. "I thought we were going to talk with him about returning home. It's a ridiculous idea."

"Tonight's not the time. We can do that in the morning. Let's get something light from the kitchen, then turn in early. Tomorrow is a big day."

CHAPTER 23

Homebound

NANCY CAME DOWNSTAIRS early next morning and saw the door to the library open a few inches. Through the open space she could see her mother and Langer talking. They appeared to be in serious, but friendly, conversation. Nancy wondered if Langer was convincing her to allow her daughter to stay in England. She imagined so.

Her mother seemed to becoming more relaxed around Langer. She was less hostile to him and the idea that he and her daughter could have a relationship despite their age differences. Nancy found the changing attitude settling and hoped this meant the way was being smoothed for her future plans.

Nancy's head swam with plans. She was certain that Niles would ask her to stay in Sussex. There was no question in her mind that they would marry. The differences in age would be accepted eventually. However, a dilemma existed: England versus Australia.

Her father had plans for her in the business. Life in England as restorer and mistress of Langer Manor would be interesting for a while, but it was best that Niles sell this place. His father, if he lived much longer, would be better off in an old age home than out here. Much to plan and decide, she mused.

Celia and Langer were startled when Nancy entered the library. Her appearance so early was unexpected. For her to be up early two mornings in a row was unheard of.

"Good morning," Langer said cheerfully. "We were just talking about you. You slept well I hope."

"No. Not at all."

"I know you are upset about returning home," said Celia. "However, Niles . . . Mr. Langer agrees it would be best for us to return home through Canada. It's a long trip but safer and less complicated."

"You mean when our holiday ends as scheduled," said Nancy.

"No, I mean now," Celia answered. "There is no guarantee of safe sailing to Canada over the next few months. In fact, there is no guarantee as of now."

Nancy became agitated.

"What is the point of leaving. There is no threat to us. We should just carry on as planned for the next couple of months."

"The timing is not for anyone's choosing," said Langer. "There is only one passenger sailing to Canada scheduled now. The Empress of Britain tomorrow morning. After that there is no telling whether any passenger sailings will be available."

"Canada!" Nancy appeared incredulous. "Last week the Germans sunk a passenger ship bound for Canada. It's much more dangerous out there than here."

"No," Niles said firmly. "It's safer. The Athenia sinking was a mistake. The Germans have said they will not attack passenger ships. They will, however, begin bombing us. Even out here away from London."

"Your father will be wild with worry," Celia added. "At least once we reach Canada he knows we will be safe."

"But this is so fast, and so unfair," said Nancy, voice rising, dark eyes burning. She turned and stared directly at Langer. "What about the future? What about our plans?"

Celia looked to Niles.

"All of us need to focus on now," Langer answered, more sternly than Nancy had ever heard him speak. "England is becoming less safe by the day. We need to do whatever is necessary to ensure everyone is safe. It will all work out eventually."

Niles was rushed and seemed to want the conversation cut short. His attention span seemed to be increasingly short when it came to her.

"My father has a doctor's appointment in the village. I'll take him and drop you at the train at the same time."

Before anyone could say anything else, he was out the library door calling for the aging butler to help his father get ready for the trip to the doctor.

"We must finish packing," said Celia, leaving Nancy standing in the empty room with no one to hear her continuing protest.

By early afternoon Celia and Nancy were on the London train waving goodbye to Langer through the window. On the platform he had hugged Nancy and shook Celia's hand, saying he would come to see them at the hotel tonight, or at the ship's departure lounge in the morning.

Seats on the London-bound train were plentiful. Few people were travelling into the city and there was none of the chaotic congestion Celia had experienced coming out to Sussex.

Nancy took a seat by herself, so mother and daughter did not speak during the trip. Celia wondered what thoughts were percolating in her daughter's mind. Langer's plan to come to their hotel in London or to the ship's dock for departure had calmed Nancy for the moment. However, how would she handle a final goodbye, or in fact would she?

The MI5 man had made clear he could force her to leave Britain but Celia was not certain that had any effect on Nancy.

They took a taxi from the station to the Waldorf, where Celia dropped Nancy while she walked over to the Australian High Commission to pick up any word from Bertie. There was an envelope for her, a cable from Bertie saying he expected to reach London in two days. Celia folded the cable, then deposited it in a waste basket and walked back to Waldorf.

She opened the hotel room door and found Nancy on tiptoes with ecstasy.

"Niles telephoned," she blurted, half laughing, half crying. "He's coming back to Australia!"

"Really," Celia said nonchalantly.

"I don't know any of the details. He couldn't talk long. He said he would be in touch. It's glorious news!"

This explained why he had been so short with her. He was planning to leave for Canada with them but was preoccupied with how he was going to tell his father. He said it would all work out, and it had.

CHAPTER 24

Molly

BERTIE LEANED ON the ship's rail and flipped his cigarette butt into the breeze. He watched it float on the air currents, then drop into the froth created by the ship's hull. He stared out over the flat sea and let his random thoughts float like the cigarette stub.

In two or three days the ship would dock at London and he would learn what was happening and do whatever had to be done. He had been to London once before and found it noisy and dirty compared to Sydney. He disliked Londoners, who he called Pommies, finding them dull and daggy. He wouldn't be in that city long, but should not have had to go there at all. If Celia had stayed put in Colombo like she was told to do, they could be on their way back to Australia by now.

It was another example of her not being able to handle their daughter. Nancy could be difficult for sure. Headstrong and pushed the limits too far sometimes, but you just had to know when and how to rein her in. Celia, instead of trying to guide Nancy, always was trying correct her and make her change.

Celia's note left for him in Colombo said they were continuing on to Europe because she feared Nancy would refuse to stay in Ceylon. She was obsessed with this older man, so much that Celia feared Nancy would run off with him. Obviously, she was not thinking clearly, Bertie thought.

She never did when it came to Nancy. Why had she not just arranged a telephone call to him? He would have talked to his daughter and diffused the situation, if there really was a situation. Or, if there was a real and serious situation he could have said he had decided to take a vacation and join them on the grand tour, and they should wait for him in Colombo.

His wife's overreaction to everything their daughter did was perplexing. He could not understand and sometimes thought that perhaps it was overreaction caused by fear. Fear of losing another child. Neil's death had shattered her and Bertie wondered if she ever would be her normal self again.

He considered himself responsible for some of the guilt she carried over Neil's death. He had blamed her, openly at first, then subtly. It was she who encouraged the boy to be an outdoor fanatic. Hiking, exploring, camping out. Find your true inner self and build self-determination by running free in the great outdoors.

"The bush is for aborigines and other wild things," he once told her. "Not for human beings who have spent centuries learning how to build cities that advance their lifestyles. If the outdoors were so great, the aborigines would have made something of themselves long ago."

Bertie believed that the cities were where a person learned how to live, and how to develop the smarts to become prosperous and powerful.

"Starlit nights and quiet campfires are for people without the granite knackers needed to ram their way into the prosperity of this changing world."

He carried little guilt of his own over Neil's death. If he had had his way, Neil would never have been on that trip; never been encouraged to pursue the outdoors.

He was not a man without guilt, however. His guilt was that of an unfaithful husband and occasionally it caused him some mild anguish. He accepted that his unfaithfulness was unfair.

Despite everything that had developed between them, he still loved Celia. She was a loving person who would sacrifice anything of herself to help others. She was intelligent and funny, especially before their lives began to change. She was a good person who tried to make him a better person in spite of himself.

There had been a couple of brief affairs before Neil's death. They meant nothing and he was regretful. The affairs increased after the accident, then became regular. Perhaps deep down they were a way of punishing Celia for the loss of their son.

As time passed they settled into separate lives. His life was mainly downtown, hers almost a return to her convent-like upbringing. He regretted their distance from each other, and their arguments, which usually began over Nancy.

Life now should be good, he thought as he gazed over the ocean. He was reasonably wealthy and had some influence, but missing was the open happiness they knew in earlier times. He wished for a return of those times, but accepted that there is no going back. Hurt reshapes people.

Lost in his thoughts, he felt the light, sensual touch on his shoulder, then the warmth of a body against his back.

"You are not planning to jump over are you," she said with a soft English accent. "Was I that much of a disappointment?"

He turned and pulled her hips into him.

"You never disappoint, my dear."

They had met in the bar at the Grand Oriental while the steamship company was figuring an alternate route to London because of the Suez closure. She was sitting alone at a table with a postcard view of Colombo harbour. She was a redhead, with shoulder length tresses, and full ruby red lips. Roughly his age, pushing fifty. Tall, even seen in a sitting position, and slightly chunky but not enough to spoil a shapely figure.

She had smiled provocatively as he entered the room and the smile, combined with the table with a terrific view, convinced him to walk over and introduce himself. After a few drinks and some enjoyable conversation, they had gone to her room and spent the night together, then much of their time aboard ship after leaving Ceylon.

Her name was Molly Wilson and she was the wife of a bureaucrat for some British tea company with a large plantation in the distant green hills outside Colombo. Molly was taking home leave while the husband remained at the plantation.

She was good company. Comfortable within herself, no inhibitions and a captivating conversationalist. She was obviously well read and could talk on most subjects, but with a light sense of humour and a beguiling laugh.

There was no question of an attachment that would be difficult to untangle. She had made that clear that first night: she and her husband were good partners with no plans to go their separate ways. That did not mean, however, that she could not enjoy life while they were apart.

Her presence certainly made this passage much more enjoyable than the one from Australia to Ceylon. Bertie was fortunate to have seen her in the Grand Oriental bar that evening. Of course, he had a knack for finding pleasure within adversity. When they were young Celia used to laugh and say that he could fall into a dunny and still find fun.

Aside from sex, the most enjoyable times with Molly were in the evenings when they played cards and shared light conversation and drinks with a few other couples in one of the ship's lounges.

One evening somewhere off the African coast a week away from England, the conversation turned heavy and dark when a porter, out of breath and pale as the moon over the ocean, entered the lounge.

"It's war," he said excitedly. "We are at war with Germany! Britain and France have declared war."

"My God," exclaimed Bertie. "My daughter is in France."

"You said you were to meet her in London," said Molly.

"Yes, but I don't know if she had left for England yet. The last I heard she was in Marseille. I hope to God her mother had the sense to leave for London."

"I'm sure they are there or will get there and will be safe."

News of the war declaration cooled their relationship as Bertie spent much of his time pacing the ship and thinking. They did have some meals together and spent a couple more nights together but Bertie was like a caged tiger. He felt helpless, unable to communicate with Celia directly; unable to make the ship go any faster.

He could only hope that they had gone to London and were waiting for him there. The ardent admirer pursuing Nancy no longer was the big issue. It faded and was swallowed by worries about the war. Hopefully Nancy was in London but even that was not a safe place to be. The Germans certainly would launch air attacks to terrify the population in preparation for an invasion. There was regular shipboard speculation about bombing. London was not a safe place to be.

If the pursuer was still around he would deal with that quickly while figuring out how to get back to Australia with his daughter. Home was the place to be now and he needed to get back with her quickly.

Australia was thousands of miles away from the war. Secluded and safe but producing war goods that would swell his cash flow.

CHAPTER 25

Blackout

A LATE SUMMER SUN spilled unexpected warmth and brightness over the Tilbury docks on the Thames, just downriver from London's centre. It did little, however, to raise the spirits of passengers boarding the Empress of Britain bound for Canada. They shuffled up the gangways, heads down, chins locked. The usual bon voyage frivolities were missing as passengers and crew focussed on safety preparations necessary for crossing the North Atlantic.

Any North Atlantic crossing now was worrisome. It was a bit early for the vicious autumn storms, but not totally unheard of in September. Storms and icebergs always were a concern for ships making the crossing. A new threat now caused not just concern, but fear.

Even before war was declared, Germany had submarines on the North Atlantic, positioning themselves to pounce on Allied warships and merchant vessels travelling the shipping lanes. U-boats prowled those waters, hungry for any prey that would help Germany intimidate and gain an early advantage in a war at sea.

The German propaganda machine pledged that its submarines would not target passenger vessels. The reassurance didn't help the innocent souls aboard the SS Athenia, enroute to Montreal from Glasgow, when it was torpedoed in the opening days of the war. Most of the fourteen hundred passengers and crew were rescued from the sinking Athenia, but more than one hundred died.

Any remaining Atlantic passenger crossings now were for emergency evacuations with most of the luxurious comforts and service abandoned. Getting from England to Canada was the goal, and passenger comfort was low in the ship's new priorities.

"This is depressing," Nancy complained as she followed her mother up the gangway while glancing down the ship's side where several crew were suspended on rope scaffolds. The men on the scaffolds dipped brushes into paint pots then smeared black paint over the portholes.

"Look, they are painting the portholes over. We won't even be able to see outside."

A ship's officer standing at the top of the gangway overheard her.

"It's to keep light from shining onto the sea at night," he said. "Even a pinprick of light can be seen at a long distance over the sea at night."

Also darkened were the powerful floodlights that illuminated the ship's three distinctive funnels. When lighted, the funnels could be seen by other ships thirty miles distant, and served as a beacon for trans-Atlantic aircraft crossing the Atlantic.

"Also, smoking above decks after dark is forbidden."

"Where are we supposed to smoke then?" Nancy asked, in a tone that challenged rather than sought information.

"In your cabin, miss. Or there are no restrictions during daylight hours."

Celia and Nancy found their cabin to be huge, a full twenty-seven feet long, room enough for two double beds a mirrored dressed, sofa style chairs, an immense wardrobe and sink despite the separate bathroom.

There was no bustle of staff arranging their quarters when they arrived. Their suitcases and their large travelling chest sat on the floor in the middle of the room.

"I suppose we are on own to sort and hang our clothes," said Nancy. "What are these? We didn't get extra luggage did we?"

Celia turned from checking out the large wardrobe and saw two unfamiliar fine leather suitcases among their bags and chest.

"They're not ours. They must have been dropped here by mistake."

As she spoke, the apartment door swung open, revealing a vibrant, well attired young woman about Nancy's age. Her fashionable ankle-length skirt with a natural waistline and short jacket made her look tall and slim but she actually was two or three inches shorter than Nancy. She had short, dark hair, arranged in finger wave style that added to the impression of an animated woman seldom still. Hanging from her hands were an overnight bag and a bulky hatbox.

"Hello! I'm Helene. Helene Paquette. I understand we are sharing the apartment on this voyage."

"We are what?" said Nancy with a look of astonishment. "That's not likely."

Helene, unfazed by the unwelcome reception, stepped into the apartment and closed the door behind her.

"Yes, this is a last ship out because of the war. The place is stuffed to the rafters with people desperate to get to Canada."

She spoke with a very light, almost indistinguishable, French accent.

"There is little room here," snapped Nancy. "You'll have to look elsewhere."

Celia stepped between the two young women. She offered her hand to the newcomer.

"I'm Mrs. Coulson. Call me Celia."

"I'm really sorry for the inconvenience, but the purser gave me this note and directed me to come here. I'm going home to Montreal. I was just starting my final year at school in Paris when this started. My father insisted I leave Europe immediately."

"We'll work it out somehow," Celia said, looking sideways at her daughter. "It's not a holiday cruise, after all."

"Someone said they would deliver a cot and a divider sheet for privacy," said Helene.

"It won't much matter," replied Celia. "We've been advised to sleep in our clothes clutching a life jacket. There are a few tense days ahead."

Nancy gave up protesting the intruder's presence. She was preoccupied. Everything in her illusory world had gone cyclonic. The prospects of settling into more pacific days in West Sussex were torn apart by this mad dash to leave England.

At least Niles would be with her. It would be a great adventure travelling across Canada with him. They would be away from this panic with time together. The cross-Canada train trip would take days. They would be in close quarters and she could see her mother coming to accept Niles and their plans for the future.

She was annoyed that he had not joined her already. In his telephone call he had said he had much to do but would book passage on the Empress and see her on board. She had hoped that they would meet at the dock before boarding. She worried now that perhaps he had not been able to secure passage. What if he missed the ship? How could she contact him? How would he be able to catch up? Could he ever catch up, considering the war?

Celia was making a fuss over settling their new shipmate so Nancy left abruptly, to scour the ship for Niles. People jammed the decks and passageways, many made cranky by the squeeze of overflow passengers, others becoming undone by war anxiety.

The Empress of Britain normally held five passengers short of twelve hundred, four hundred and sixty-five first class, two hundred and sixty tourist class and four hundred and seventy third class. She was carrying an additional one hundred for this evacuation voyage, variously bivouacked in the squash court, around the pool, and in lounges. The crowding, special safety precautions and high tension made provision of normal service impossible despite good efforts by much of the crew. The critical goal now was to get the ship across the Atlantic to Quebec City where it would be converted for troop transport.

In the squash courts people hung sheets around their newly set up cots in an effort to create some privacy. They were too preoccupied to stop and recollect whether they had seen a distinguished looking man with piercing blue eyes and silver sideburns. Each of the lounges she visited were too crowded and fogged with cigarette smoke to distinguish anyone clearly.

Nancy pushed her way through bustling staff and people dragging suitcases to reach the purser's office, which was crammed with passengers upset by a variety of unexpected circumstances ranging from shared accommodations to the hardness of cots set up in temporary sleeping quarters. She waited in line for her turn to be served and listened to the constant refrain from the counter staff:

"Please we must all be patient. These are difficult circumstances and we must be patient!"

When her turn came she was confronted by an overwhelmed agent who said he had no time to spend helping passengers connect with each other.

"But he's my fiancé," Nancy lied convincingly. "He requires medication that I am carrying for him. We became separated in London and I need to make sure he made the ship. His name is Langer. Niles Langer."

Reluctantly the agent thumbed through a sheaf of paper.

"No. No one named Langer," snapped the agent tossing the papers aside and signalling to next person to push forward. "But everything is a balls up right now. We don't have a complete list of names. I'm sure he'll turn up."

Nancy intended to push the matter but a long blast from the ship's whistle made her jump back and before she could recover, the mob lined up at the purser's counter had pushed her aside, eddying her away like a piece of flotsam.

She walked more of the ship, hoping to spot him somewhere. She imagined him doing the same, walking and scanning the decks with those winter blue eyes. She took the stairs to the Lounge Deck and walked the promenade where people lined the rails watching the departure. She elbowed through people to reach the rail and scan the pier below for any sign of him. Nothing.

She continued along the deck. As she passed the Cathay Lounge she spotted her mother sitting at a table beside one of the windows. She went inside.

"There you are Nancy. Helene was looking for you. She wanted to invite you for a departure drink so you could get to know each other."

"I've been looking for Niles. The purser's office doesn't list him as a passenger."

"It's such a panic. They probably don't have a complete list. He's quite organized, so he's no doubt aboard somewhere."

A waiter brought the tea Celia had ordered and promised to return immediately with another place setting for Nancy.

"Well, if he isn't. I'm sure you'll be happy," said Nancy.

"Actually, I could care less. I'm tired of all this intrigue. I'll just be happy to get across the Atlantic."

"Intrigue! That's what you think this is! Obviously you have no intention of seeing our situation seriously."

"I don't know what your situation is," Celia said coolly as she poured hot tea.

"Well, it's obvious that his return to Australia means he plans to marry me."

"I don't see how he intends to do that. You are still under age and cannot marry without your parent's permission."

"I believe that's why Niles is returning to Australia. We can all get to know each other better and plan a wedding for June or July. What we need to discuss is whether we live in Australia or England. There's nothing much to keep him in England."

"I would think his father, the estate, and a couple hundred years of family history in Sussex would be an attraction. His wife is buried there."

The wife reference was an overhand smash intended to score, and it did.

"You may be against this, but it is going to happen." Nancy said defiantly. "There are obstacles like the age difference but we can overcome them."

"You have worked all this out between the two of you then."

"We haven't had much time but we will during the this voyage and the trip across Canada."

"It seems to me you are assuming much based on little mutual discussion."

"Niles loves me and I love him. That's all that matters or counts for anything."

Celia sipped her tea calmly, staring over the teacup rim at her daughter. Her eyes narrowed and clouded quickly like a gathering summer storm as Nancy waited for the expected explosive reaction. It did not happen, and Nancy was perplexed. She felt it was time for her mother to let loose a torrent dammed up for the weeks since they left Australia. Cracks in the dam were evident throughout the trip and it was a good time for it to burst. They stared at each other in silence until a light and happy voice broke the impasse.

"Oh there you are. I've been looking for you. Let's go out. There's too much gloom and doom on this ship."

It was Helene.

"Go out?" said Nancy. "Go out where? We are on a ship."

"There's jazz band in the other lounge," Helene chirped. "Let's go and get some music!"

Nancy hesitated. She needed to find Niles, but she also was overdue for some fun.

"Come and get me if you hear from Niles," Nancy told her mother as she turned to follow Helene, leaving Celia alone with her tea and the unfinished argument.

Celia sat for a few minutes, delaying what she knew she must do. She was leaving England without leaving any message for Bertie. He would arrive in London tomorrow, or the next day for sure, and would be alarmed not to find them or any message from them. She had intended to leave a note for him when she was at the High Commission building. However, her mind was muddled. She was uncertain of exactly what she planned so had put it off, telling herself she would compose something before going to the ship.

Now here she was and the only option was to send a ship-board cable to him in care of the High Commission.

"He'll go off like a frog in a sock when he receives it," she said aloud, but no one was around to hear her.

She would have to decide what to say to explain her actions. That was difficult because she was having trouble explaining them to herself. She decided that she had had enough tea and needed something stronger to help her compose a message. She got up, and walked across the carpet to the bar where a waiter intercepted her.

"I would be happy to bring you something, ma'am," he said apologetically. "I didn't realize you wanted something else."

"I needed to stretch," Celia replied. "I would like a whiskey. What do you recommend?"

"We have some excellent Canadian whiskeys," said the man.

Celia sat down at her table with a pen and paper while the waiter fetched his recommendation. She finished the message and the whiskey about the same time.

"Sailed Canada. London too dangerous. Booking passage home from Vancouver. Waiting there. Hotel Vancouver."

Although this Empress of Britain sailing was the next last scheduled passenger trip between England and Canada, Britain had to continue merchant shipping to North America for oil, food and other supplies needed to survive. The British merchant navy, the largest in the world, carried civilians so Bertie could find passage on one of those ships, now travelling in packs for more security against the German U-boats.

Celia deliberated over the message before taking it down to the cable desk. Bertie, having received all her messages, might conclude that she was trying to run away from him. However, surely he would see that there was uncertainty, and danger, in London. When he arrived there he would see the faces creased with anxiety and taste the sour scent of worry hanging in the air. And, see everyone carrying the gas masks.

Yet, staying and waiting for him in London was clearly a sensible choice. Bertie would have resolved the Langer situation, one way or another. Then all three of them could have tried to get passage to Canada on a merchant ship. Life would get back to what it was a couple of months ago. But what life? Was it the life she really wanted?

She ordered another whiskey and drank it quickly. All it did was make her drowsy and cloud her thinking.

She returned to her cabin and lay down on the bed. Within seconds she was asleep and dreaming. Painters dangling on the side of the ship floated through her dream. Then there was a woman dangling above the churning sea. Nancy and Bertie were down in the water pulling the woman's rope toward them. On deck above, Niles Langer was trying to pull it up.

CHAPTER 26

Tensions

"I'T'S PATENTLY RIDICULOUS," Nancy groused as she picked at the food on her plate. "Chubby over there is having a hard time getting his fork over the front of it," she said, pointing her fork at a large man trying to navigate his fork over his bulky life jacket and into his mouth.

"Maybe it will help him lose weight," Helene said quietly.

Some diners in the Salle Jacques Cartier were wearing the life vests given to them on boarding. The passengers were advised to wear them, or at least keep them at their side, at all times.

It was impractical, and unnecessary, for passengers to wear the life vests at all times. The advisory from the crew, however, was to get people to remember to have them easily reachable in case of a torpedo attack. There always are people who, lacking good common sense, follow the extreme side of any caution.

Celia and Helene draped theirs over the backs of their chairs, but Nancy had refused to carry hers about and had stuffed it in a closet in their room.

They had a table to themselves, tucked off in a far corner of the dining room. The room was only half filled and was missing the elegance that it displayed during cruises in normal times. The serious moods of the diners, and the presence of the life jackets, dulled the usual sparkle of the first-class dining room. People spoke in whispers, heads lowered.

Many passengers had decided to stay in their cabins, or to get something lighter to eat in one of the lounges. It was the second full day at sea and they were traversing the area where German boats might be expected. The entire ship held its breath.

Nancy's nerves were frayed but it had nothing to do with fear of a German attack. She was confused and perplexed over Langer's failure to show at the ship.

"I'm sure Niles wouldn't put up with all this nonsense," she said. "He said all along that this war business was being exaggerated."

"I'm not so sure he felt that way after it actually started," said her mother. "He said the danger was enough that we should get out to Canada."

"That's certainly how my father felt," said Helene. "He feels it will be a long war and that Germany might take over much of Europe."

"I wish we would hear from Niles," said Nancy. "It's not like him. He said he planned to book passage on this ship and that he would let me know."

The uncertainty about his whereabouts gnawed at her, although she tried not to let it show. She fretted inwardly about how he had become so distant. Yet in his telephone call to the hotel he had sounded enthusiastic about sailing for Canada. Had he changed his mind after? Obviously he was not on this ship because they were into the second day of the voyage and he would have appeared by now.

"He could have been delayed for a number of reasons," said Celia. "Perhaps something with his father. At any rate, if he really wants to come to Australia he no doubt will be able to find passage on one of the merchant ships."

"What do you mean if he really wants to come?" Nancy snapped. "He wants to be with me."

"Can I offer tea or coffee?" said a voice behind her. It was a young waiter who had attracted Nancy's attention earlier. They had been playing eyes throughout the dinner.

"I'd love coffee," said Nancy.

"Don't you find it keeps you awake at night?" Helene asked.

"I'm not interested in sleeping tonight. Too tense. I'd like to walk the ship."

"There's much to see on this ship," said the waiter as he poured the tea and coffee. "It has one entire deck devoted to recreation and sports."

"I must see that. Do they have archery?"

"Certainly," said the waiter. "Although activities are limited because of the situation."

The ship's crew carried too many extra duties now and had little time to help with recreational activities. They had to deal with the overflow of passengers, plus take on security roles such as standing watch for ships on the horizon, and ensuring there was no light leakage from the ship after dark.

"I love archery. Perhaps you could show me that area when you are not working."

"I would be happy to. I'm off for the evening soon after the dinner hour ends. My name is Andy and I can meet you on the rec deck later."

Celia made busy fixing her tea, but took in the exchange.

After dinner Nancy said she wanted to walk the deck. When Helene offered to accompany her, she said she needed to be alone to do some thinking. Celia and Helene returned to the suite to read. The walk back to the suite was short, but rocky. The ship had started to heave and roll in increasingly heavier waves.

"I think the ocean has some indigestion," Helene laughed bravely. "I hope it doesn't pass it on to me."

Inside the cabin she looked pale, steadied herself on a chair arm, then made a stumbling dash for the toilet. Having purged her dinner, she crawled into her cot and fell asleep.

The pitching and rolling of the ship intensified and Celia found it difficult to read. She fell into a fitful sleep, moving into semi-consciousness when the ship banged and shuddered when hitting a rogue wave, or when Helene moaned loudly.

At one point she was awakened by the cabin door opening. Nancy struggled through the doorway, closed the door as carefully as she could with the ship rocking and fell into her bed.

Celia opened one eye slightly and saw the bed table clock reading 4:07. The sour smell of gin and cigarette smoke, mixed with the musky scent of sex, drifted lightly across the room.

Celia could not fall back to sleep. She stared into the cabin darkness, wondering what had changed the precocious little girl with the dark hair and dark eyes into the woman that she had become. Nancy had lost every vestige of childhood innocence, and most of the good teachings provided by home and school. Perhaps not lost. Deliberately discarded. Why, Celia found difficult to contemplate let alone understand. It was as if her only daughter, the child she expected to grow up and be like her, had become possessed by an unseen force.

Nancy had become sexually active early. Celia had come to accept that, as mothers must. They might not like what they learn about what their daughters do with their bodies, but there is nothing they can, or should, do about it. She had raised her concerns with Bertie who said sex is part of growing up.

"It happens to all of us," he laughed. "Humans are animals. Animals have sex. The difference is humans are smart enough to protect themselves against the unwanted. Nancy is smart enough to know that."

Sometimes she wondered if her daughter was a nymphomaniac, but she knew that was not so. Her daughter's relationships were not about an urge, or a need, for sex. They were about control. She had a compulsion for control.

Most young women never would want their mothers to know about their sexual activity. Nancy wanted her mother to know. It was another way of shining the spotlight on herself. Part of that hunger for attention and control that grew out of the fear of being left behind and lost like her brother.

CHAPTER 27

Landfall

T HE WATERS CALMED and the tensions over U-boats eased as the Empress steamed into Canadian waters. The first shores that would have been visible were passed in the night, but as dawn spread the ship was deep into the Gulf of St. Lawrence and moving steadily along the St. Lawrence River toward Quebec City.

The Coulson women and Helene missed the first views of the Canadian shores but were up, washed, fed and on deck as Quebec City came into view. The voyage ended there and the three would travel together on the four-hour train trip to Montreal.

"Have you ever seen anything so picturesque," Helene said, pointing at the city occupying the hump of land overlooking the river's northern shore.

"It is spectacular," said Celia. "I didn't think it would have such a European look."

The buildings along the shore and on the hill were a mix of medieval, chateausque and classical elements. The old Citadel and the copper-plate

Chateau Frontenac roof contrasted, yet somehow blended, with the recent Price Building and its art-deco architecture.

"Imagine what it was like for the explorers coming here four hundred years ago. They would have seen that magnificent hill but only a clearing with Indian houses in it."

Helene bubbled enthusiastically at being back in her home province of Quebec. On the cab ride from the docks and on the train she assumed the role of tour guide, pointing out historic points and explaining that Quebec was the oldest city in Canada.

She told them that high above the river were the Plains of Abraham. During the war between the French and British in North America, the British general James Wolfe had his army scale the cliffs at Quebec City to surprise the French soldiers. A fierce battle ensued on the Plains. Both Wolfe and French General Marquis de Montcalm died in the fight. The British won, taking control of Canada.

The train's lurching and rocking was a reminder of the days on the North Atlantic. It had been a horrid crossing. All three women had spent all of Day Three in beds, rising only to go to the washroom. The following days were little better. They moved about shakily, took some soup but did not leave the cabin. The ship's crashing against huge waves and its heavy, sickening rolling eased only when the ship slipped in behind Newfoundland and nosed into the Gulf of St. Lawrence.

All three had been too seasick to talk much or even think much. Nancy was too occupied with her swimming head and rolling stomach to think much about Langer and where he might be. It was possible he was aboard, and as sick as the rest of them. Either that or he had missed the sailing and would be trying to get passage on a merchant ship. She would insist to her mother that when they reached Canada they would wait until they heard from him.

Andy, the young waiter who Nancy had spent the night with, stopped by the cabin once to bring some tea and to inquire how they were, but Nancy was too ill to pay him any attention. She had not seen him again.

Despite the train's swaying and shaking, it was a relief to be warm and safe on firm ground. The angry ocean, the U-boats and the war were behind them. The windows were not painted over, allowing them to see the countryside rolling past them. The sun shining on the passing forest made brilliant the autumn colours of the trees.

Helene told them there were many exciting sights at Montreal. She begged them not to rush their train reservations to Vancouver and to allow time to see some of Montreal.

"You must see Mount Royal, which overlooks the entire city. And, Mrs. Coulson, the oratory is there on the mountain. St. Joseph's. Thousands go there looking to be cured. They say miracles happen there. It is something that you would enjoy."

Nancy rolled her eyes and looked out the train window. Her mother said it sounded like a worthwhile place to visit.

It seemed no time before the train slowed and lurched into Montreal. Helene pressed her face close to the window, looking for her father then waved excitedly to a man standing on the platform.

Helene's father embraced his daughter and spoke happily about how glad he was to see her home safely. Charles Paquette was a handsome man with an effervescent personality. He shook hands enthusiastically during the introductions.

"Thank you so much for looking after Helene during the crossing," he told Celia. "I can't thank you enough. If there is anything I can ever do for you . . . ."

Helene and Nancy had stepped away to talk to a porter who had their bags, so Celia said there might be something he could do.

"Helene said you are a lawyer," she said quietly. "I do have a legal issue that needs to be resolved. Perhaps I could visit your office before we leave for the West."

"I would be delighted to help," Paquette replied handing her a card. "Just telephone or stop by.

I'm only a block or so away from the Windsor Hotel, where I presume you are staying."

"Yes, we are. I will arrange to come by after we settle our plans."

They said goodbyes, with Helene suggesting that they all meet for dinner. Perhaps the next night after everyone had some time to settle after the harrowing crossing.

The Coulsons took a taxi to the nearby Windsor Hotel, which was a short walk along Dominion Square, but not an easy walk with luggage. The Windsor was a nine-storey palatial granite and sandstone building, considered the best hotel in all of Canada. It had six restaurants, two ballrooms and a concert hall. King George and Queen Elizabeth had stayed there on their Canada visit six months before.

A porter appeared with a luggage cart before they were out on the sidewalk.

"You go on up with him," Celia said to her daughter as they entered the hotel's spectacular rotunda lobby with it ceiling paintings and gold embossing. "I have a call to make."

"Call?" asked Nancy. "You don't know anyone here."

"I need to start organizing the rail travel."

"I'm sure the room has a telephone," Nancy said, the sarcasm twisting her mouth. "The place looks expensive enough."

"It's easier from down here in case I need help from the desk."

Fifteen minutes later Celia opened the door to their suite and found her daughter sitting on the edge of one of the beds, holding a crimson rose to her nose.

"I can't believe it," Nancy exclaimed, rising to show her mother the rose. "It's Niles," she said. "He's here! He did make it. I knew he would."

"It might be just from the hotel," said Celia, showing little interest. "Or, if it was from him, he could have wired it from somewhere."

"He's here. I know he's here. He obviously found a ship."

No more was said about the rose. They unpacked and organized their clothes and Celia suggested they have a late dinner in the hotel dining room.

"In the meantime, I thought it would be good to visit that Oratory Helene mentioned. Why not come along, then we'll do dinner." She knew before asking what her daughter's response would be.

"You don't give up, do you mother? I'm done with that. I'm not a child anymore."

"It's apparently one of the most interesting and popular sites in French Canada. And, the faith you were born into doesn't end with childhood."

"It did for me. At any rate I want to stay here and wait for Niles. He sent the rose so he's sure to call."

Celia said no more. She took her purse and gloves and left saying she would be back in time for dinner. She was content to be going alone. The outing would give her a chance to think. And she had much to think about. Much to plan.

The short taxi ride up Mount Royal provided little thinking time. She instructed the driver to drop her partway up the hill on which Oratory sat and she would walk the rest of the way.

The view in all directions was as impressive as Helene had said. The city spread out below; the massive Oratory and its long run of ascending steps looming to her front. She had read that the dome of the basilica had been completed only recently and from somewhere up above was an even more spectacular view of the city and its surroundings on the river.

She strolled until she found a bench in a copse of trees off to side of the Oratory. There were plenty of people coming and going, yet there was serenity there. She felt embraced by a peacefulness not experienced in a long time. It was the perfect place to sit and reflect and she assumed that whoever managed the place had picked this spot for exactly that purpose. She thought back on the last few months, which it seemed had been spent on a storm-rocked sea.

Her life had not begun that way. Life had been so simple for a single child raised by simply-living parents who believed their life's mission was helping others. Then came life with Bertie. It brought unexpected prosperity and it seemed to Celia that increasing affluence made life more complex and brought more problems.

It was the same story of the world, she thought, gazing out over the Oratory grounds to the wide steps leading up to the church entrance. Advancements that she had seen since she was a child – electricity, motor cars, airplanes, radio – more prosperity, yet more difficulties. So many changes, seemingly for the advancement and benefit of society. Yet life was more complicated with more problems. That first war, the flu pandemic, the Depression and now another world war. The world had become a depressing and dangerous place.

Hard times had changed so many lives. Some people coped by turning to religion. Others turned away from it, not being able to comprehend how a supposedly kind and protective God allowed so much suffering and death. Perhaps that was Nancy, blaming God for the loss of her brother and the suffering and changes it caused in her family.

She recalled the dinner table debate with Langer in Colombo. His view that organized religion was stuffed with hypocrisy. Poor people starved while princes of the churches lived in luxury.

Maybe he was right that organized religion caused young people to drift off from the traditions and beliefs that their parents and grandparents had held fast to for decades.

Her thoughts were broken by the, throaty toll of the Basilica's bells. She glanced at her watch and saw it was three o'clock, not time for the bells to be calling people to Mass. Some other service perhaps. She got up and walked over to the stairway leading up to the Basilica entrance. It reminded her of the grand staircase of Marseille, although not anywhere near as grand. It consisted of two sets of concrete stairs divided by a set of wooden stairs on which some people were ascending on their knees as a sign of faith, and penance.

Inside, a prayer service was underway, not the best time for sightseeing. Celia slipped into one of the wooden pews at the rear and scanned the church interior from there. From there the altar looked much smaller than it really was and the priest and attendants but small specks in the vastness of the place.

Murmured prayers drifted upwards into the cavernous space of the dome, which had been completed only recently. She could see the stained glass windows running along the base of the dome but they were too high up to distinguish the actual scenes.

When no service was underway, the church buzzed with the whispers of groups of people walking about, exploring the Basilica. Most of the interest was in the crutches and canes hanging in displays on the walls.

These were left behind by people said to have been cured by praying to St. Joseph, and to Brother Andre, a simple monk and founder of the Basilica.

Celia passed a table piled with pamphlets, picked one up and sat to scan it. It gave the history of the Oratory and summarized the story of Brother André Bessette. She read that Brother André was a saintly figure who died two years before at age 91. One million people filed past his coffin and devotees now petitioned the Vatican to begin the process of his beatification, one the steps toward being declared a saint.

Brother André, the pamphlet said, was sickly from birth and unable to find work suitable for his condition. He became a novitiate in the Congregation of the Holy Cross, which has taken over operating Notre Dame College in Montreal. Brother André became the school's doorman, which included doing some cleaning, handling mail, and nursing sick students.

Some visitors to the school asked him to pray for them and he began visiting ailing people at their homes. He told people to pray to St. Joseph and gave them St. Joseph medals and drops of oil used for votive burning in front of a statue of St. Joseph in the school's chapel. People began reporting cures and partial cures.

He took people to pray before a statue of St. Joseph he had placed in a niche on some school property on Mount Royal. The numbers of people expended as reports of miracles grew by word of mouth. Brother André wanted to build a chapel at the niche and people began raising money for construction. His followers increased by the thousands and the chapel grew bit by bit until it was the magnificent basilica in which Celia now sat.

An interesting story, Celia thought. A sickly orphan becomes a diminutive doorman reputed to be a miracle worker and who builds the largest Basilica in the Americas.

Outside again Celia pulled her coat around her neck to protect it from a chilly autumn wind blowing up the hill. She watched a procession of pilgrims singing as they climbed both sets of the concrete steps, while a few dozen others climbed the centre set on their knees. There were two hundred and eighty-three concrete steps but the centre wooden set was only ninety-nine steps, still more than enough to do on your knees, Celia thought.

She felt a presence beside her and turned to face Niles Langer.

She expressed little surprise, nor for that matter did she feel any. His sudden appearances from nowhere had come to be expected.

Before either could speak, they both saw a young man struggling to climb the centre steps on his knees. He was dragging crutches with one hand, pulling himself up one step at a time with the other. His legs were dead for movement and he reached down behind the knees to pull the legs over each step, one at a time.

His face broadcast the pain of the effort needed to do a single step. His eyes bulged with the intensity of unshakable belief. He was not much older than Nancy. Twenty-one, perhaps twenty-two. Though his face twisted in agony with every painful movement, it shone with determination and the conviction that once he reached the top and got inside of the shrine, he would hang his crutches on the wall and fall to his knees to offer prayers of thanks.

"Hail Holy Queen, Mother of Mercy and Light . . .," his lips muttered. "St. Joseph pray for me," as his right hand pulled his right leg onto another steps. "Brother Andre pray for me . . ."

Celia watched his excruciating struggle and wondered how a person develops such intense faith. Was it because he was crippled and desperately wanted to walk again? Was faith fuelled by the need to believe faith could make you better? She doubted it was just that. There were others at this

189

holy place who exuded powerful faith and belief but appeared untouched by disease or maiming. Or was it something you had to work to build day by day just like the priests always said? More prayer, more penance to build a stronger faith. She didn't know the answer but hoped something or someone would lead that boy to a cure.

"I hope God grants him his miracle," Celia said, turning quickly to walk down to the street below. When her back was turned to Langer she pulled a tissue from her purse and wiped her eyes. She was not a person to allow someone to see her cry.

"He already has," Langer said as he stepped quickly to catch up with her. "Faith like that is a miracle."

On the street below Celia waved toward the line-up of taxies parked farther up the street. Langer had caught up to her and she turned to face him.

"This is a place where one does not expect to see non-believers."

"I'm neither believer, nor non-believer."

"I thought you were an atheist."

"An atheist is someone who lacks belief. That doesn't mean he is not searching for truths that might lead him to form a belief."

Langer paused, looked searchingly into her eyes, then turned his gaze to the Oratory on the hill.

"The problem with searching for truth is that when you find it, it can be unexpected and painful. Truth can set us free, but we must be willing to bear the disruption and pain it might bring."

He opened the taxi door for her and they got in together.

CHAPTER 28

Louis Quinze

CELIA RETURNED TO the Windsor Hotel to find Nancy spinning with excitement. She had heard from Langer.

"I told you he was in Montreal," she said as he mother stepped inside the suite. "I knew it when I saw the rose. He telephoned just now. He is staying at the Ritz-Carlton."

"Yes, I know he is here. I saw him on the street. He was going to his hotel."

"He didn't tell me he saw you. What did he say? Did he say how he came to Montreal?"

"We talked only briefly. He said he would explain all when he saw you."

Nancy was happily excited, but perplexed.

"He said he wants to have dinner, but Helene called just before he did and has arranged a dinner for us with her parents. I'm going to call her back and cancel. I can't have dinner with them both."

"She obviously wants us to have an evening with her parents."

"But what about Niles?"

"Have him join us. I'm sure Helene and her parents won't mind. I'm sure it will all work out. Meanwhile, I need to go downstairs and organize the rest of the trip home and I need to cable your father to let him know."

"I suppose you have informed him about Niles?"

"No, I haven't. I think that's up to you, isn't it?"

"Father will accept Niles. He's always accepted my decisions. I'll send him a cable just before we reach home telling him I have a surprise."

"It will be a surprise indeed. I think you would be best to sit down and compose something thoughtful in a letter. Do it soon and it will arrive before we do."

Celia had no contact with Bertie since sending the cable saying they were leaving for Canada. She hoped he would find passage on a merchant ship, then take the train to Vancouver.

Nancy worked out the dinner dilemma. She rang Langer at the Ritz-Carlton and invited him to join her and the Paquettes at a famous old town restaurant, whose name she could not pronounce. They would meet in the Windsor lobby and take a taxi, or even walk if they had time. She was excited about showing him off to Helene and her parents.

• • •

Langer was waiting for them in the lobby. He looked trim and well rested, greeting them with his wide smile that spread between the smile dimples on his freshly-shaven cheeks. Nancy rushed to him and embraced him.

"Niles," she exclaimed, planting a kiss on the side of the mouth "I'm so relieved to see you. I was worried."

He appeared slightly embarrassed and moved her to one side as he extended a hand to Celia, greeting her as Mrs. Coulson.

"Tell us how you got here," said Nancy. "It must have been an adventure."

"I was delayed by family business and missed your ship. But I got very lucky with a merchant ship. You probably didn't know you travelled across the Atlantic with a pack of ships. Safer that way. I actually got here a bit ahead of you because my merchant ship steamed directly up the St. Lawrence to here without the Quebec stop."

"It's wonderful that everyone made it across safety," Celia said as they all made their way outside to a taxi.

"I really wish we could tell the Paquettes not tonight," said Nancy. "It would be good to dine alone and hear all about your adventure, Niles."

"That would not be right," Celia said. "Helene was helpful on trip. It was good to have her company. And her father seemed a good sort at the station."

They met the Paquettes at Louis Quinze, a small, intimate restaurant in one of Montreal's oldest areas. The Paquettes were a charming, vibrant couple. It was easy to see where Helene sprang from. Monique Paquette was a bit above average height for a woman, slim with murky blonde hair.

Celia introduced Langer, before Nancy could, explaining that he was a friend who they met in Europe as the war started. He had been helpful to them, had taken them to his country place in England and now was enroute to Australia to visit his sister who needed help.

"I hope it's nothing serious," said Monique. "She's not ill is she?"

"Oh, not at all," Langer replied brightly. "She is trying to get our father to emigrate to Australia so she can look after him in his remaining years. It is a bit of a struggle."

"He certainly would be safer in Australia," said Charles Paquette. "This war is worrisome. God knows how it will all end. However, I suppose if he has spent his entire life in England the move would be disturbing."

The dinner conversations were varied and pleasant. An eavesdropper might have assumed that this group was well acquainted, perhaps even long-time friends. The ladies moved along to fashions while Langer and Charles discussed mutual interests in history.

"We don't have the depth of history that England has," Charles said. "But what we do have is very interesting. Mount Royal and the St. Joseph Oratory make for interesting visits."

"So I've heard," said Langer.

"Another is Caughnawaga. It's not far. Just across the river and it provides a looking glass at the early development of North America. It's an Indian reserve and the final home of Kateri Tekakwitha, the Indian woman who many people are promoting for sainthood."

After dinner the Paquettes suggested a calèche ride through Montreal's most interesting areas. The most available calèche would take only four passengers. The open carriage was pulled by a horse, which stood wearily at curb side. It was decorated with ribbons that dangled from its halter and a hat with holes cut to fit over its ears. Paquette offered to take another with Celia. Langer rode with Mrs. Paquette and the two girls.

"Your friend Mr. Langer seems like decent type," Charles told Celia. "He will accompany you and your daughter to Vancouver and on to Australia?"

"Yes, and that is what I need some legal advice on. I can't say much here. I will explain all the details when I come to your office."

It was a brief ride, perhaps thirty minutes. The calèches stopped together at the Windsor Hotel to drop Celia and Nancy. Langer went on to his own hotel but not before suggesting they meet for breakfast.

"We are here for another day because of the intercontinental train schedule, so why don't we plan an outing tomorrow?"

"That sounds excellent Niles," Nancy said. "Where should we go?"

"Charles Paquette suggested this place called Caughnawaga on the other side of the river. Lots of Indian history apparently."

They agreed to talk about it at breakfast.

CHAPTER 29

Avocats

T HE LAW OFFICE was a short walk from the hotel, on Saint Jacques Street above a fur store. Celia had telephoned and a few minutes later found herself climbing a set of stairs leading into an oak-panelled corridor and a set of doors with a brass plate announcing the offices of Messieurs Martin, Paquette, Robertson, avocats. She had skipped breakfast with Nancy and Langer, saying she needed to shop for something.

Charles Paquette confirmed Celia's impression of him from the evening before. He had a wide smile on a trusting face that you would bet had never, ever, scowled. He shook Celia's hand vigorously, like he would on meeting a college roommate who he hadn't seen for years. After exchanging the mandatory niceties and chat about the previous evening, they got down to business.

"The situation is embarrassing and quite difficult, and delicate," said Celia. "It is not a typical legal matter but we are so far from home that I have no one else to turn to for advice."

She told him the entire story, from its beginning in Australia just before setting off on the coming-of-age tour for Nancy. How Nancy had met Langer on a Sydney street. Then how he had appeared at their dinner table on board ship. How some of the passengers believed he was a Nazi spy and his unusual interest in Nancy.

Then how Nancy had taken to him and how he had followed them across Europe, eventually staying at his estate in West Sussex. Then when Celia decided to return home, how he decided suddenly to return to Australia and was here now in Montreal. There was never any suggestion that he had taken advantage of Nancy. Every outing they had had included someone else, usually the Fenwicks, who had remained in England.

"She very taken with him, my daughter. She also can be very difficult and that is why I have tried to play along. I have not put down my foot on the matter because I fear they will run off together."

Paquette had already heard part of the story from his daughter and had observed Langer at dinner. He hadn't formed any negative impression from that meeting.

"Are you certain he is pursuing the girl?" he asked.

"The evidence points to that."

"You said your husband is a business owner back home. Does he have any connection to war supply production?"

"Yes," said Celia watching the lawyer make detailed notes. "They are supplying many materials to the government for the war effort. Also, he has college mates who now are in the government."

Paquette nodded and continued to listen and take notes.

"Nancy has convinced herself that he intends to ask her to marry him. He's more than twice her age."

Paquette stopped taking notes, leaned back in his chair and offered an opinion.

"The most efficient way to handle this would be to have someone take him into a back alley. Unfortunately, there are laws against such solutions."

"I don't know what his plans are for getting to Vancouver," said Celia. "I'd like to find a way to stop him there so he can't pursue Nancy to Australia."

"We have a Vancouver connection. One of the partners here has a cousin who is a lawyer in Vancouver. I can contact him and explain and he likely can work something with the immigration authorities there. They certainly would be amendable to helping stop this kind of perversion. Meanwhile I'll think about what might be done to hold him up here."

"I expect Nancy's father will catch up to us in Vancouver. It would be wonderful to have all this cleared up when he arrives. Bertie doesn't much concern himself about the letters of the law, so . . . ."

"Well I think we can arrange a plan that will remove your husband from perhaps doing something he might regret."

He gave her the name and contact information of Jonathon Blight, the Vancouver lawyer and said he would begin organizing a plan immediately.

"That's so helpful and I truly appreciate your assistance." She opened her purse, preparing to pay whatever was necessary. Paquette said that when a plan was arranged and executed, the Vancouver firm would tally everything and give her an accounting of expenses and fees.

After she left, Paquette began composing a letter for Vancouver. It was an odd situation. Helene of course had given her impressions of the Coulson women and the Englishman Langer. She had said there was an unnatural tension between the mother and daughter. They didn't seem to like each other.

Perhaps it was one of those mother-daughter competitions, the lawyer mused. The daughter was exceptionally attractive. The mother was no less attractive, he thought. A petite shapely woman with an interesting face featuring prominent cheekbones and full sensuous lips. Langer could be after the daughter, or the mother, or maybe he was interested in neither and really after information about the husband's company. It was certainly confusing. He picked up his pen and began scribbling notes.

CHAPTER 30

Caughnawaga

"WHY WOULD WE want to go to such a place?" asked Nancy. "It's bound to be dreadful. I've heard that the Indians are worse than the Aborigines."

"That's being uncharitable, my dear," chided Celia.

"It will be an interesting outing," Langer offered. "The Mohawk are an interesting people. Very influential in the development of North America. It would be a shame to have been to North America without absorbing some of the history."

"You are so into that stuff, Niles," Nancy laughed. "Me, I'm totally into the present."

They were riding in a taxi over a relatively new bridge connecting the southwest corner of Montreal with the south shore of the St. Lawrence River. The flatlands at the edge of the river held the village named Caughnawaga, which had been established two hundred and fifty years previous by Jesuits wanting to protect Iroquois people who had accepted Christianity.

Nancy had no interest in the visit but agreed to go to please and be with Langer. Celia would have preferred to stay at the hotel and prepare for the rail journey west but Langer had been persistent. She had booked reservations on the trans-continental train leaving Montreal the next afternoon. Langer, she assumed, would do the same when he learned of their plans.

It was a short ride from the hotel to the Mercier Bridge, a single arch steel structure with some similarities to the Sydney Harbour Bridge under which they had sailed months back. In fact, Langer noted, it had been built at roughly the same time as the Sydney Bridge, opening in 1934.

"Many of the workers on the bridge were Indians from the reserve on the other side," said Langer as their car travelled the slight downward slope onto the south shore and into the Mohawk community. Just off the south end of the bridge was a small shack offering native souvenirs and Langer asked the driver to stop.

"Let's see what handicrafts they have," said Langer.

The shop was an open front lean-to that sheltered its occupant and goods for sale from the weather. The occupant was a middle-aged Mohawk woman, startlingly attractive except for her hands, which were thick and tough presumably from years of needlework. She was pleasantly chatty and Langer learned that she was the owner of the shop and the artisan who produced many of the goods.

Business was not like the old days, she told them. Before the bridge she sold her handicrafts from a stall along the road leading into the ferry terminal on the north shore. People waiting for the ferry would browse the roadside stalls to kill time and often returned to their cars having bought at least one item. Now most of the cars coming off the bridge slipped past without stopping.

"These look like your size," said Langer, picking up a pair of floral beaded moccasins and showing them to Nancy. They were soft deerskin with velvet cuffs. The intricate beading on the instep vamps and the cuffs was red, black and green in the shapes of small flowers and leaves.

"They are beautiful," said Nancy who had not been impressed with the shop until she began examining some of the goods.

"We'll take them for the young lady," said Langer pulling out his billfold.

"If she likes them, I will pay for them," Celia interjected.

"It's my treat," said Langer. "Something to remember the trip by."

It was a brief drive along the river road to the St. Francis Xavier Church that Langer had suggested would give some insights into Canadian history. The village was not what any of them had expected, especially Nancy. There were no bark lodges or tipis that they had read were the main forms of North American Indian dwellings. The houses were wood siding or stone, many two-storey structures with French Canadian style gables and porches.

The church was nothing like the grand religious edifices of Europe, or the Oratory that loomed in the distance above the north side of the river. It was a narrow stone building with a steeply pitched gable roof fronted by a square tower running straight up the front of the building. The tower had three simple rectangular windows running up its face to below an octagonal belfry with silver painted spire.

The St. Lawrence River flowed wide and fast not more than a couple hundred yards behind the church. From the yard there was an impressive view of Montreal with Mount Royal and the Oratory dome filling the background. Nancy stayed in the yard chatting and smoking with the taxi driver while Langer and Celia went inside.

The interior was much more impressive than the exterior. It was spacious and airy with white plaster walls rising above wooden wainscoting. The floors were wooden and well used as were the rows of pews.

"This is interesting," said Langer taking Celia by the elbow and guiding her toward a wall holding the Stations of the Cross, sculpted scenes tracing Christ's journey up Calvary. He noted that they had been made by an Italian artist named Guido Nincheri.

"But most interesting, look, the captions are written in Mohawk syllabics, not French or English."

High above them, the barrelled ceiling was brightly painted with different scenes from the New Testament. Langer had read about that, as well. Because of the moisture from the nearby river the usual fresco painting method could not be used.

"So the artist took pieces of canvass, painted the scenes, then glued the canvass to the ceiling."

Celia did not appear impressed with that piece of history, but Langer had something more interesting.

"Beneath us are a lot of buried bodies," he said. "They used to bury the bodies of the most faithful in the basement and the burial spots were marked with wooden crosses bearing the names of the deceased. They don't allow that anymore."

He paused to let that sink in but he still had not captured Celia's interest.

"The most important person buried here is the woman that some people want to be made a saint. Kateri Tekakwitha. I don't know if she is still buried here but she died in 1680 and was buried at the church that this one replaced."

"She was a native, obviously," said Celia. "What made her so saintly?"

"It's a complex story about a woman caught between two cultures. Caught between two lives and how she found a new life."

They sat in a pew at the rear of the church and Langer told her the story of the Indian woman people wanted to be named a saint.

"Tekakwitha," said Langer, "was born in the Mohawk Valley of New York about 1656, to the south of where we are now. Her younger brother and her parents died in a smallpox outbreak. Kateri also caught smallpox but survived and was left with a terribly scarred face. She took to Christianity, which many of the Mohawk people shunned and ridiculed. Religious tensions built until Jesuit missionaries in the Mohawk community left, moving north this spot here. They brought with them some Mohawk Christians, including the girl Kateri who was about 19 and had been baptised.

"Kateri was always in poor health partially because of the smallpox but her health worsened because she fasted and inflicted pain on herself as penance. Her poor health overtook her and she died at age twenty-four. Witnesses said that when she died all the smallpox scarring on her face disappeared and left her unblemished in death."

"Twenty-four!" said Celia. "So young!"

"Not really," said Langer. "Life was different back then. By twenty she had lived through much more than many of us experience by the time we are sixty. I often wonder why so many people have to wait for death to get relief from their suffering. Surely, a truly merciful Gods would provide some relief when the pain is being felt."

"He does," said Celia. "Look at all the crutches on the wall at the Oratory across the river. They were left by crippled people who walked."

"So you believe that miracles do happen?"

"There are cases of documented cures that bona fide medical experts have not been able to explain."

The religion debate between the two was on again, as it had been several times since they first met.

"It is easier for people with faith to believe in miracles," Langer continued. "For those who search and question and look for irrefutable proof, it is more difficult."

"Miracles provide a compass for life. Some direction for people. Some hope. Not just miracles, but religion as a whole. It provides direction and hope."

"Tremendous suffering also. Religious differences have caused some of the world's most horrible conflicts. Young Kateri here suffered tremendously because of her religion. She was an outcast among many of her people who believed in a spiritual world, but not the white man's religion. The difficulty with religion is that at its centre is an all-powerful, all-seeing God who supposedly punishes evil and rewards good, and of course sometimes punishes even the good. I can't believe that a God would interfere and make such decisions."

"I agree that religion can cause pain, but it is also creates healing. It provides comfort to many who without religion would know only despair."

"It would greater comfort to many more if so much of it was not based on a judgmental Deity who decides what is right and what is wrong. I don't believe in a God that is so judgmental. For instance, a soldier in war sees his fellow soldier cut almost in half by machine gun fire. The wounded man is screaming and bleeding out. His last few minutes of life will be agony, so his fellow soldier shoots him. Does God condemn that soldier to Hell because he has broken the Sixth Commandment: Thou Shalt Not Kill?"

Celia recalled Conrad's comment that his son had a hard time of it during the war and wondered whether the story of the wounded soldier was taken from real experience.

"So you believe there is a God who never lifts a finger and just lets us muddle through our lives?" Celia asked.

"If there is a God, surely he leaves people to make their own best decisions. Some will be right, some will be wrong. Surely what any God wants is for decisions be based on a striving to make things better. For instance, in your Catholic religion someone living in an abusive relationship commits a mortal sin if they divorce even though divorce makes life bearable, much better, for at least one of the parties."

Celia fell silent and reflected on that., but not for long. Nancy came running through the front doors of the church to announce that it was pouring rain and she wanted to return to the hotel.

Langer had hoped to see the community's little museum and old Fort St. Louis. However, it had been obvious from the beginning that Nancy's interest in the place was zero. Her mother had the interest, but Langer could see that she had other things on her mind, so he ushered them both out to the taxi and they returned to downtown Montreal.

CHAPTER 31

Police

"IT'S ABOUT TIME," Langer muttered at the abrupt rap on the thick oak door of his hotel room. He had telephoned down twenty minutes earlier to the bell captain asking for someone to take his luggage downstairs. Train departure was two forty-five. It was now one ten and he needed to settle his bill and get a cab to the rail station.

He opened the door to two tall gentlemen dressed in wool suits, topcoats and dirty gray fedoras. One pulled a hand from his topcoat pocket and produced a badge case.

"Sargeant Bouchier. RCMP," he said repocketing the badge. "We need to speak with you."

"What's this about? I'm in an awful hurry," Langer replied, pointing at his two leather valises at the side of the door. "I have a train to catch."

"We need to speak to you, at headquarters. You might have to miss that train."

"Ridiculous. I'm not about to miss a train because you need to speak to me."

Langer began to close the door. The second policeman jammed his foot into the door opening and put a hand on Langer's elbow.

"This is serious," said Sargeant Bouchier. "You need to come with us without a fuss."

"I am not going anywhere with you," Langer said motioning them to leave.

Bouchier produced a pair of handcuffs from his rear trouser pocket. "You can walk with us or be dragged in handcuffs."

Exasperated, Langer grabbed an overcoat from the closet and followed the two men without further protest, except to mutter: "Someone will hear about this."

The offices of the Royal Canadian Mounted Police were housed in an uninspiring ochre brick building with small rectangular windows equally spaced on both floors. Once through the double grey wooden doors the officers led Langer down a concrete block and terrazzo corridor and into a dim interview room that housed a grey metal table and three chairs, two on one side of the table, one on the other. There were no windows and a single light bulb that did little to brighten the greyness.

Sargeant Bouchier told Langer to sit in the single chair.

"We need to go over your passport and have you give us a summary of your travel for the last six months," he said.

"Before I give an account of anything, I want to know why I am here. Why are you making me miss my train and likely my Vancouver connection to Australia."

"It is war time and the government needs to check out all foreigners."

"That's rubbish," Langer snapped. "I am not a foreigner. I am British, which gives me the right to travel a Commonwealth country without harassment from the police."

"And being British you no doubt are well aware of the Nazi sympathies of many members of the British aristocracy, of which you are one, I believe."

Langer chose not to answer, throwing the sargeant a look of disgust. The look relayed more than any number of words Langer's opinion of the policeman's lack of information, and the level of his intelligence.

"There is a long list of British lords and ladies who are German sympathizers," Bouchier continued waving a piece of paper. "Lord Brocket. The Duke of Wellington, the Duke of Westminster. Lord Londonderry, who is Churchill's cousin. Then of course the Duke of Windsor, your former King."

Bouchier listed various exchanges between British aristocrats and German officials. Lord Brocket had invited various Nazi officials to his home before the war. Lord Londonderry had visited Germany regularly and had stayed with Joseph Goebbels, one of Hitler's closest associates, at his hunting lodge. Wallace Simpson, who before marrying abdicated Edward VIII and becoming the Duchess of Windsor, had well-known sympathies for the Nazis.

"There is speculation," said Bouchier, "that the Germans have a deal with the former king to place him back on the throne of England if they win the war."

Langer was not one to base his opinions on speculation. He was well aware that some British aristocrats, in fact a couple of his acquaintance, were sympathetic to the Germans. He understood why. The Russian Revolution left them with a fear of rising Communism. Some also feared there was a world conspiracy based on a union of Communism and the Jewish people, who some people saw as pushy and having too much control of world finances. Fascism, they believed, was a counter balance to Communism. Hitler was Fascism's anchor and appeasing him would help ensure a check on Communist plans for world domination.

"There are many people who believe this war could have been avoided by addressing German grievances. Grievances that go back to the First World War. Some of the world's most prominent economists, including John Maynard Keynes, have said German punishment for that war was far too excessive and would leave permanent resentment. So here we are."

That had little impact on the policemen, who had scant knowledge of, or interest in, international history. Langer, however, was correct. The 1919 Treaty of Versailles peace treaty at the end of the First World War forced Germany to disarm, pay billions in reparations and give up substantial territory.

The two officers were not well informed enough to debate Langer. They asked him where his sympathies rested, whether he ever belonged to a Fascist organization and why he was travelling in Canada, the latter being the only question he chose to answer.

"I told you before, I'm trying to reach Vancouver which is on the Pacific Ocean where there are ships that can take me back to Australia where I have family."

The two police officers took their time with the questioning. Langer believed they were stalling deliberately. He checked his watch and realized he likely would miss the train.

By the time the questioning ended, the train departure timed had passed. The officers told him he was free to go but that he should not leave Montreal for a couple of days while they checked his background. They could keep him in custody but would allow him to stay at his hotel.

There was no offer to drive him back to the hotel, so Langer left the police building, asked a passerby for directions and began the mile and half walk back. The sidewalks were full and animated as he walked, taking little note of the people around him. His concentration was on the police interview. It was so non-specific and unfocussed. The officers were not well versed for members of an intelligence service. He pondered making a fuss about it. Contacting a lawyer. Push them into explaining why they were detaining a Commonwealth citizen for no apparent reason except some speculation on German sympathizing.

He decided against that. He had more important activities to plan. The first being to figure how to catch up with the Coulson women and make that Vancouver sailing to Australia.

CHAPTER 32

Black Spruce

"Something has happened to him," Nancy cried, pushing her mother aside and stepping down onto the station platform. "He's been hit by a motorcar. You saw the maniacal motorcar drivers on the streets."

"Nonsense," said Celia. "He's been delayed. Or perhaps he's already on the train."

"He wouldn't be on the train without me knowing," Nancy snapped. "He said we would see each other in the waiting room."

They had sat in the cavernous stone waiting room at Montreal's main rail terminus for thirty minutes despite not having to. Their drawing room quarters allowed them direct boarding, while passengers with less expensive accommodations had to wait until a public address system called boarding. The hands on the huge wall clock moved closer to departure time, making Nancy increasingly agitated.

Finally Celia insisted they board. A porter had placed their travel luggage in their sleeping compartment and their two large trunks containing their less immediate things had been loaded into the mail-freight car.

The waiting room passengers filed up the steps to the departure platform as boarding was called.

"Nancy, it's almost train time. We must board now."

They climbed the stairs but Nancy did not want to step up into their car. She looked back hoping to see Langer come dashing for the train.

"All Aboard, Miss," said a trainman standing by the car steps.

"My friend isn't here yet. I'm waiting for him."

"Sorry, Miss. It's departure time. You'll have to board." He placed his hand on her elbow intending to help her onto the step-up. She shook it off.

The train's whistle sounded and down the platform the conductor's shouted a long and drawn out: "All Aboard!"

The trainman reached down for the step-up, signalling he didn't care whether Nancy stepped aboard or was left behind. Celia grabbed her daughter under the armpit and pulled her up as the train inched forward.

They stood in the corridor outside their drawing room and watched the backs of Montreal's buildings pass across the rail car windows. Nancy had insisted on watching the trackside from there, as if she expected to see Langer running beside the escalating train in hopes of jumping aboard. The door from the coupling deck wheezed open and the conductor appeared, one hand holding his ticket punch, the thumb of the other hand hooked into a pocket of the dark blue serge vest. The gold watch chain stretched across his tummy twinkled in the sunlight falling through the windows, as did the gold buttons on his jacket and the gold 'Conductor' lettering across his cap.

"Bit rocky out here," he said pushing the cap brim higher up on his forehead. "Much more comfortable in your compartment."

Nancy seemed not to hear him but turned and asked: "Is Mr. Langer, Niles Langer, on board?"

"Langer, Langer," the conductor mused putting his hand to his chin. "I don't recall the name."

"He's travelling with us and I haven't seen him. I'm worried that he has missed the train."

"There is an empty compartment on the car one back," said the conductor, pushing the peak of his cap higher on his forehead. "I'll know if anyone is missing when I complete my count."

Thirty minutes later Celia and Nancy were settled, staring out the drawing room windows and not speaking, when a tap on the compartment door broke the silence. It was the conductor who informed them that Mr. Langer had not made the train, and neither had his luggage showed.

"There, I knew it," Nancy wailed, flinging herself against the compartment door. "He's ill or has had an accident."

"You don't know that," said Celia. "Anything could have delayed him. Traffic. The same thing happened in London. He missed the ship but still got to Montreal."

Nancy tossed a look of deep disgust.

"Traffic! The station is walking distance from the hotel!"

She was winding herself into a rage. It was a rage fuelled by a thought that she had tried to block from her mind several times since the day on the hill overlooking Langer Manor. Niles was becoming distant and not paying her the attention she needed. First he had missed the boat, probably the result of hesitation about their future. Now the train.

She scowled at her mother.

"At least you must be feeling good about it."

"What do you mean by that?"

"You've wanted to break us apart from the beginning."

"What are you talking about?"

"You just couldn't handle me falling in love with an older man."

Celia saw a narcissistic rage building. Anything Nancy said now would not be rational. She was uncertain what to reply.

"You don't know what love is," she said.

"I certainly never knew it from you. You saved all yours for Neil! You still do, worshipping the memories of him. The perfect child!"

Celia picked up her purse and left the compartment without a word, slamming the door behind her.

Arguments sometimes could be cathartic, even useful in finding solutions, but not arguments with Nancy. Whatever the problem of the moment, it was Celia's fault. No number of words, however conciliatory, would change that. Even trying to end the argument by agreeing to be at fault would steer the fight off on another tangent. It was better to turn and walk.

Nancy juddered when the compartment door slammed shut, leaving her alone with her stormy thoughts. Thoughts that intensified with the click-clack-click-clack-click of the train's wheels spinning on the rails. The click-clack-click grew louder and faster, then morphed into: Bit by a snake. Bit by a snake. Bit by a snake.

She placed her fingers to her temples, then moved her hands across her ears, but that didn't block the rushing and rocking sounds of the train, and its wheels on the rails crying: Bit by a snake. Bit by a snake. Bit by a snake.

Bit by a snake. Among the last words she hurled at her brother before his fateful camping trip with three friends seven years earlier.

"I hope you get bit by a snake and die," she had screamed at Neil during dinner the evening before the trip.

"Nancy, that's an awful thing to say," Celia said sharply as she attempted to break up the sibling squabble.

Bertie was home for dinner that evening and took a sip of his wine to hide the smirk that Nancy's conduct had brought to his face. The verbal brawls between Nancy and Neil never bothered him like they did Celia. He appreciated Nancy's fighting spirit and wished Neil had some of it. He often thought that she should have been the son and he the daughter.

The squabble had started over a piece of lamb. It was the last piece on the platter and Nancy leaned over the table to snatch it with her fork. Celia took the platter before Nancy could reach it.

"We have to save that for Neil's lunch tomorrow. By the time we drop him off and they hike into where they are going he won't have had any time to make something to eat."

"I'm still hungry," Nancy pouted. "Why does he always get everything? Mommy's boy!"

That's when the squabble got heated, culminating with her wish that Neil would be bit by a snake and die.

The next morning the entire family had driven to the rendezvous point where the four boys shouldered their gear and stepped off on their weekend camping adventure. They were all school friends who enjoyed bush hiking, and despite being fourteen-year-olds were experienced and competent at being on their own in the bush.

Memories of that time often swept Nancy's mind like an incoming tide. Most often they flooded in after an argument with her mother. They brought small feelings of guilt, but never any shame.

Even in death, Neil was someone who deserved her contempt. Through their brief lives together she always had seen him as the white swan. In her mind, if he was the white swan, then surely she was the black swan. It was logical to her: he is, therefore I am not. It was the logic upon which her personality was built.

She would never go into his room, which her mother kept as if expecting him to return. She always hurried past its closed door as if afraid that it would swing open and draw her inside. More than once over the years she had passed it and heard her mother's sobs coming from behind it.

She could recall the room in detail. The pencil and paper sitting on the desk by the window overlooking the garden that he helped his mother with. He liked to sit and draw the flowers and the trees. On the wall beside the desk was the wide cork bulletin board with neatly arranged cut-outs from magazines and newspapers. Mostly they were photographs of places in the Outback, and pictures and stories about Aborigine life.

Stacked on the floor beside the desk were back issues of Boy's Own Paper, a popular monthly boys' magazine from Britain. It came in the mail monthly and was stuffed with stories related to science, natural history and adventure. It also had puzzles, personal reminiscences and essay competitions, which Neil often entered. He hoped to be a writer and dreamed of winning one of the competitions and having a story published in Boy's Own.

In a corner near his iron frame bed stood an unfinished hiking staff. He was carving into its top the head of a koala, the stocky little open woodland creature that people had incorrectly taken to calling Koala bear. He had chosen it as his totem for the hiking staff.

Nancy never did understand fully why she disliked her brother. Perhaps because others saw him as the perfect child, sandy hair, light brown eyes, a smile that melted hearts and a bearing that was non-aggressive and always made people feel comfortable. He never did anything apparent to attract attention, yet Nancy found she had to compete with him for her parents', and others, attention.

• • •

After slamming the compartment door, Celia walked two cars back to the observation-lounge car. It was one of the few rail luxuries left over from the days before the Depression. It had an observation section with large rectangular windows for panoramic viewing and separate men's and women's smoking lounges and a solarium with special glass that allowed in only healthful sun rays.

There was a small library in one corner, stocked with relatively recent American releases including *Gone with the Wind* and the heart-tugging *The Yearling*. She flipped the pages of a couple of the books, then decided she could not concentrate enough to read.

She sat in a deeply comfortable chair beside one of the large windows and watched the Quebec farmyards and fields flying by. A farmhouse with a broad front sun porch where a family sat and talked. A driveway with a red panel truck with gold lettering Chaisson et Fils, Épicerie. A greyed wood plank barn.

All scenes from people's lives, some clear, some blurred or obscured by passing trees and bushes. Much like my life, she thought. Quickly passing scenes, some happy, many blurred by disappointment and pain.

Nancy, she reflected, was the source of much of her own disappointment. She had worked to make her a more complete person, capable of loving, giving and helping other people. That was the way she had grown up.

One of Celia's father's favourite sayings, taken from Cicero's 'On Duty', was "We are not born, we do not live for ourselves alone."

Nancy was an anomaly. Outgoing and charming on the surface. Confident and assertive. Viewed by many who met her as someone who would break through the barriers to women. Amelia Earhart resurrected. But just below the skin someone hard and sharp, capable of bruising or cutting anyone who did not give her the attention she expected.

Few saw what Celia saw below the surface: Nancy was a façade screening a weak personality. Behind the façade lay a confidence problem sustained by envy of others. Envy compelling her to manipulate and undermine others to show them as lesser beings. When anyone penetrated that façade Nancy became arrogant, condescending, petulant.

"Everyone is always wrong because she is always right," Celia muttered, looking around to see if anyone was listening. The car was empty except for her.

To prove people were wrong Nancy resorted to lying, not only to others but to herself. If she ever saw the truth, she could not accept it.

Self-indulgence drew her into risky behaviour. By her early teens she was sexually provocative, teasing and twisting adolescent males into her playthings. Through those years Celia worried about Nancy getting pregnant, which of course Bertie would have had taken care of, while blaming her for not properly preparing Nancy with the facts of life. Later it was college boys, and some older men. Langer certainly was not the first seasoned veteran to walk into Nancy's web.

The barney that Celia had walked away from and brought her to the observation-lounge car was not a rare or exceptional incident in their relationship. They had clashed since Nancy was a child. Celia had come to accept long ago that they could never be friends.

She loved Nancy. Mothers were supposed to love their children, weren't they? More and more, however, she wished she could be free of her daughter. Did that mean she did not love her? It was all too confusing. She sometimes wondered if her conflicted thinking was so abnormal that it indicated flaws within herself.

She had mentioned this to the psychiatrist she saw after Neil's death. He wanted to explore this more with her but Celia stopped asking questions and offering any other thoughts on her feelings about Nancy. She stopped seeing the doctor when she read about the increasing use of electro-convulsive therapy and lobotomy operations on people with persistent troubling moods.

Besides, the problem was with Nancy, not with her. Nancy resisted the traditional pattern of girls growing up viewing their mothers as best examples of the person they want to be. The maturing process of young women included periods of resistance and natural anger, but almost always gave way to a natural friendship between daughter and mother. It did not happen that way in some mother-daughter relationships. The anger persisted, allowing other bad feelings to fester.

Cora had told her that some children considered deliberately difficult are simply strong willed by nature. They genuinely feel that their wholeness is compromised if they submit to another person's will.

It was fine for Cora to think that way. Her daughter was an example of what daughters should be. And, she did not have the burden of a dead child straining and complicating her family relationships.

Celia got up and began walking back to the compartment when she saw Nancy behind the glass of the women's smoking lounge where she had come to quiet the 'bit by a snake' clicking and clacking inside her head. Celia checked her step and started to push open the glass door. When Nancy turned her head away quickly, she removed her hand from the door and went directly to her compartment.

They ate at separate sittings in the dining car that evening, Nancy taking the late sitting. Celia was in bed, pretending to sleep, when she returned.

The next morning Celia found Nancy relaxed and pleasant, as if nothing had happened.

"I'm going to lie in a bit," Nancy yawned elaborately.

Every table in the dining car was occupied so Celia was seated with a pleasant young couple travelling to Edmonton to visit the husband's parents. They were curious about Australia and asked many questions, which Celia delighted in answering.

It was a joy to have a relaxed conversation with people acutely interested in what you had to say. Celia could have talked with them all morning but the next sitting had to be served. The couple returned to their car and Celia went to the comfort and quiet of the observation lounge to watch the passing scenery.

Morning sun splashed the grey granite outcroppings, but did not chase off the gloom of the stands of black spruce standing forlorn at the edges of the black bogs.

The young couple, who had made this trip before, had told her that once the rail line reached the Lake Superior shore the scenery would be less melancholy. She hoped so. The passing wilderness was dark and depressing. She shuddered when thinking about the train breaking down, stranding them in this dark mess of tall and skeletal trees that looked as if the black waters were drawing life's juices from them.

She had seen photos and films of what the Europeans and North Americans called Christmas trees. Evergreens with lush branches of soft needles. Shapely trees offering comfort and protection. So unlike these lean and desperate looking trees. The passing waves of them created a brooding atmosphere. Black spruce creating black thoughts.

Celia had enjoyed talking with the young couple and wished they were here to talk more. Talking helped to dispel black thoughts but it had been many years since Celia had someone to talk with.

Growing up she could always talk to the nuns at the mission in Waitara. As she matured, however, their views and advice seemed less relevant, less connected to the world's realities. There were nuns, for instance, who continued to take the immaculate conception literally: God, not a man, had impregnated the Virgin Mary.

When she entered womanhood she learned how it was impossible to become pregnant without being with a man. The immaculate conception, she learned, had nothing to do with sex. It was a theological concept in which Mary was born free of the original sin that banished Adam and Eve from the Garden of Eden.

She also could talk to her mother, until she passed away just before Celia's marriage. Bertie was not someone she could talk with. He didn't talk. He acted. He had little time for mulling over and debating life's complicated questions. Get on with it was his central philosophy about living. They were different in so many ways. Celia the giver, Bertie the taker.

Celia did not criticize him for that. She understood. He grew up differently. His father was a dock worker who clawed his way to prosperity. If you didn't take it someone else would. Get as much as you can before it is gone.

Celia grew up in an atmosphere of giving. Giving, comforting and making things better for others. That was life. It was the only life that the nuns knew as they nurtured and guided the wayward expectant mothers through their pregnancies, then looked after their babies and tried to set the mothers on a new course. Their work was double pronged: put the single mothers on the correct track for the rest of their lives, and arrange the lives of the babies either with their mothers, which was rare, or through adoption.

Her parents were immersed in that work; her mother supporting the nuns and the girls and their babies, her father maintaining the physical facilities.

Celia worked at the home after completing Year Four in the secondary school system. It was assumed she might enter the convent. Although she was much around the nuns, she had never given this any thought. In fact, she had given little thought to what she would do in life. She presumed that someday she would marry and look after a husband and family. She would follow the tradition of giving and comforting.

Nuns' life, although giving and comforting, seemed too severe. They followed aspects of religion that did not make sense to her. There was no discussion of the beliefs or the rules, so acceptance seemed the best course.

Life at the home became difficult when the flu took her father. Celia found hard accepting that he could be one of the victims. He was fit and healthy, a labourer and handyman who engaged in physical activity every day of his life. His hands were stone rough and thick with callouses earned from working with the hand tools necessary to keep the essentials of the home in working order.

His fingers split and filled with the rich brown earth from the garden which he turned and raked by hand at the start of each planting season. The garden, with a dozen or more varieties of vegetables, was a must for the home's survival because there was never enough money. He usually worked from first light until supper time but never complained.

"Aches and pain ain't for the working person," he would say whenever anyone mentioned the bruising labour of the foundling home.

After his death the nuns hired out for whatever work they could afford. Celia and her mother continued on, her mother doing administrative work plus any labour she could help with. Celia helped with all aspects of the operation including baby care and teaching some of the girls.

Most were from lower levels of society and had little schooling or even experience in domestic matters.

Working with the girls and their babies was a learning experience. Celia learned that children are children no matter their appearance or their status. No matter who they were or who they belonged to. All deserved an equal chance at living and being loved.

The home and Celia's dedication provided little opportunity for a social life. She had some friends from school but Waitara was a small family-oriented community where many activities were held within families.

Several months after John Dalby's death, Mother Superior approached Celia and asked her if she would go into Sydney to buy some needed supplies. Celia had been to Sydney only twice in her life, accompanying her father, who made the Sydney runs for items not available in Waitara. She had never been any great distance from the home on her own and the trip to Sydney was an adventure, and a recognition by the nuns that she was an adult now.

She caught the early train to Sydney. By time she found all items at various stores it was time for lunch and she found a lunch counter at one of burgeoning number of Greek cafes bringing American style soda bars and lunches to Sydney.

There was only one empty seat in the place, a stool at the counter. Next to her was an attractive young man enjoying the improbably combination of an ice cream soda and a mutton meat pie slathered with sauce.

"Try a soda," he said turning and holding her in his gaze. "It's ace!"

Celia intended to avoid talking to any strangers on her first solo trip to the big city. However, the young man on the next stool, who introduced himself simple as Bertie, was a compulsive conversationalist.

He was not hard to look at. He had a full face that easily accommodated a seductive smile that drew you close. Even then he had the eye corner crinkles that radiated friendliness. He had a big forehead made bigger by the hairline receding at the corners, leaving a peninsular-like tuft of chestnut brown hair with reddish gold undertones.

He was engaging and made it impossible for anyone to avoid talking with him. They talked mainly about Sydney and train travel but in the process he managed to extract information about her without her realizing it. He showed a genuine interest in the Waitara home for unwed mothers and her work there.

Lunch done, Celia said she had a 2:15 train to catch. He insisted on walking her to the station and waited until train time. When they parted he said he intended to come out to Waitara to see her and learn more about the home. He did and that visit led to others, and an engagement.

Jane Dalby was not totally happy with her daughter's engagement to Bertie, who she had met only a few times during his Waitara visits. There was something about him that did not seem right for Celia. He was pushy and bombastic, traits difficult to understand by a woman whose life had been patient service.

Jane died suddenly one month before the wedding.

Celia was now pretty much alone in the world except for Bertie. Their marriage took place and they lived for a year or two in Sydney before deciding mutually that the north shore was a good place to raise a family and a place that Bertie's successfully growing business activities could support. They bought the house in Wahroonga.

So much had happened in those twenty-five or so years just passed. Much of it seemed like a deep sleep dream from which she would awake soon and find herself in a new life.

CHAPTER 33

Hillcrest

T HE YOUNG COUPLE at breakfast had been right. The gloom of the black spruce forests and the melancholy they exhaled dissolved into golden sunshine and flashing blue waters when the train reached the Lake Superior shores. The train twisted and turned, rose and fell through mixed forests clinging to ancient granite outcroppings hugging the lake.

Autumn had coloured the trees then thinned their leaves, allowing wider views of the world's largest freshwater lake, which looked like a rumpled blue table spread sprinkled with silver sequins.

The bright weather, spectacular scenery and fresh news had relaxed the tautness between Celia and Nancy. They were speaking to each other civilly. Nancy was especially buoyed by a telegram waiting at one of the station stops. It was addressed to her alone and read:

UNAVOIDABLY DELAYED. ARRANGING AIR TRANSPORT VANCOUVER. NILES.

It was a relief to hear from him. She had not seriously thought about him missing the train because of an accident or any other physical catastrophe.

Her real worry was that he had lost interest in her and had decided to go his own way.

"Air transport," she said after reading the telegram. "I didn't know they had air transport in this part of the world."

"Brand new," said the telegraph counter clerk. "Trans-Canada Airlines started flying right across the country this year. Wouldn't catch me on one of them though."

"That means he should be there waiting for me when the train arrives," Nancy said to her mother.

Celia smiled and said nothing.

"I can't imagine what delayed him. We were so looking forward to seeing the mountains together."

Still Celia said nothing. She was thinking of her own telegram, this one from Bertie. It was addressed to her care of the Windsor Hotel, Montreal.

ARRIVING MONTREAL DAY AFTER TOMORROW. STAY PUT.

The hotel, owned by the railway company, had instructions to forward any messages to rail stops along the route to Vancouver. A porter, walking the station platform and calling out passenger names, had delivered that telegram a few minutes after the train pulled into the waterfront station at Port Arthur, a terminus town at the top of the Great Lakes.

Nancy was strolling the other end of the platform, smoking when Celia received it. She destroyed it immediately. She still had not told Nancy about her father's attempts to reach them and saw no need to tell her now.

The telegram contained only seven words but she could sense Bertie's anger in the spaces between the words. He would not have been amused when he arrived at the High Commission in London and received the note saying they had sailed for Canada. Now he would be furious when he arrived in Montreal and received the note saying they were travelling to Vancouver.

Not waiting in Ceylon was understandable. So was not waiting in England, where danger grew each day. But not staying in Montreal, which was not only safe but interesting, was incomprehensible.

The note she had left for him in England said she feared that North Atlantic passenger travel would be closed off as the war worsened. She wanted to get out of the war zone and back to Australia. She had made no further mention the Langer problem.

The Port Arthur stop was two hours to allow taking on coal and water and restocking of supplies for the next leg across Northwestern Ontario and into Winnipeg and the Prairies. Passengers were allowed to get off for shopping and sightseeing. The downtown heart was a two-minute walk up a slope from the lakefront. A trolley car took passengers farther up the hill to Hillcrest Park where they could sit on the mortared rock wall and take in a spectacular view of the city and the lake.

Celia rode the trolley to the top of the hill while Nancy jumped off in the centre of the shopping area. It was a short walk from the trolley stop to Hillcrest Park, which had a sunken garden of now fading summer flowers but remained alive and bright with autumn chrysanthemums.

The view from the rock wall was sweeping and spectacular. It took in the entire eastern horizon from the bush country on the left to Port Arthur's twin city of Fort William on the right. Celia looked out over the rooftops of houses on streets built into the hill, the downtown buildings, then the waterfront and the giant grain elevators standing sentry duty along the waterfront. The white concrete cylinders, one hundred feet tall, were silent soldiers shoulder-to-shoulder, hip-to-hip, in four fused rows stretching to the water's edge. Some people saw them as monuments to the breaking and taming of the Canadian West, now called the World's Bread Basket.

The lake wanted to stretch to infinity but was blocked by unusual pieces of geography. Nanabijou, the Sleeping Giant, filled most of the centre and left horizon. To the right Pie Island protruded from the deep waters, looking more like a tall round cake than a pie.

Celia stood at the rock wall erected to stop people from tumbling down the steep hillside and chatted with a few people before walking back to the trolley stop. The trolley, an open car painted cream and red, clattered back down the hill, stopping for passengers at an intersection marked Arthur and Algoma Streets.

One boarding passenger, a late middle age nun in white habit, struggled to lift a cloth valise up the trolley car steps. Celia jumped from her side seat, grabbed the valise with one hand, and the nun's elbow with the other.

"God bless you, my dear. Those steps grow an inch higher every year."

Celia laughed as the trolley inched forward and resumed its clattering slide into the downtown core.

"I'm Sister Alexis," the nun said, offering her hand, which Celia took and introduced herself. "I just walked over from the convent behind the church there and it took the breath from me. I hurried a bit too much because I don't want to be late for the train. You have a delightful accent. British?"

"No Sister, Australian."

"Good Lord, so far from home!"

They fell into easy conversation as the trolley rocked and swayed through downtown, stopping whenever passengers wanted off or on. One of the stops was in front of a modern looking Eaton's department store.

"My daughter probably is in there shopping," Celia said pointing to the three-storey building curved comfortably around a corner of the town's busiest intersection. Its flat concrete panels and wide street level display windows told of a new era coming to a main street of red brick neo-Gothic buildings. "If there's anything she loves, it's shopping."

"I've not been in there," said Sister Alexis. The Sisters of St. Joseph, she explained, occupied the old red brick convent squeezed between St. Andrew's Church and St. Joseph's Hospital and no longer shopped, ordering everything they needed by telephone.

The trolley's last stop before turning off the main street was atop the slope above the train station. Celia carried the nun's bag off, then helped her navigate the step to the sidewalk. They paused before starting down the hill and stood facing the lake and admiring the view. The air was crystal clear, allowing the Sleeping Giant to appear much closer than it really was.

"There was a story in the newspaper recently about the man who paddled out there in his canoe," said Sister Alexis, apparently an overflowing font of local knowledge. "He made it there and back. It's eighteen miles out, although it looks so much closer today."

"It certainly doesn't look eighteen miles off," said Celia.

"Have you heard the legend of the Sleeping Giant?" asked the nun.

Celia had not and asked what it was about.

"Well, that land form is the Indian giant called Nanabijou, an Ojibwe chief who lay down in the lake and turned to stone. You see, his tribe had a secret treasure of silver hidden beneath a small island called Silver Islet. When the white men came they heard about the treasure, went looking for it and decided to build a mine on the little island to get at it. So Nanabijou laid himself down in the water and turned himself to stone to guard the rich silver below. When anyone comes to try to steal the silver, Nanabijou roars his thunder and tosses lightning bolts to frighten them away.

"See," Alexis said pointing out to the lake, "there's Nanabijou's headdress, and his arms folded across his chest and his legs stretched out. You can hear the thunder and see the lightning from here whenever Nanabijou becomes angry."

"So did the white men get the silver?" Celia asked as they walked hill down to the railway station.

"Some of it. They built their mine but later Nanabijou threw a horrific storm over the lake which flooded the mine shafts and the remainder of the silver has been safe ever since."

They reached the rail station, an impressive railway red brick Gothic building with corbelled turrets and loophole windows, that buzzed with activity beyond what might be expected from a small city. Porters carried luggage, people scurried along the platforms. Cars and trucks came and went after depositing passengers or freight items for the soon-to-depart train.

Celia helped Sister Alexis settle into her coach seat and invited her later to the observation- lounge car to talk some more and have tea. On the way back to her drawing room she met Nancy trying to navigate the narrow corridor with an armful of awkward boxes all marked Eatons. She helped get the purchases into the drawing room and deposited on the couch and floor.

"It was a miserable walk back down that hill," Nancy complained. "With the boxes I couldn't see where I was going. I thought someone would help me carry them down to the station."

"You could have hired a taxi," said Celia.

"I didn't see one around," Nancy replied, beginning to take her purchases from the boxes. She had bought a couple of skirts, some sweaters and two pairs of shoes. Her mother looked at them skeptically, thinking that the last thing Nancy needed was one more item of clothing. The two trunks back in the baggage car were filled mainly with her clothing, some pieces yet to be worn and with the sales tags still attached to them. Nancy sensed her mother's lack of enthusiasm for the purchases.

"I don't understand why you must criticize everything I buy," she complained.

"I haven't criticized a thing, nor said a thing about your shopping," Celia replied.

"Well, I can see you are thinking of it."

"Really Nancy. Sometimes you are too much. You need to learn to deal with people in a more relaxed fashion."

"I deal with people just fine. I'll be happy when this trip is over and when I'm twenty-one and Niles and I can marry."

"That's assuming a lot. You keep saying that Niles is going to ask you to marry him but you don't have any proof of that. And, your father won't allow it."

"My father will allow whatever I say is good for me. And Niles is good for me."

"Time will tell," said Celia.

"What is that supposed to mean?

"Nothing. I'm going to the observation car to have tea."

• • •

"I'm not used to this luxury," Sister Alexis smiled as she joined Celia in the observation-lounge car. "Usually I just stay up front in the day coach and watch the wilderness pass by."

"You take this train often?" Celia asked.

"A couple of times a year," said Alexis looking about admiring the polished mahogany woodwork and the plush seats. "Whenever they need help at the home."

Celia cocked her head inquiringly and Alexis continued.

"I'm a nursing sister, which you probably figured out from the white habit. Sometimes the Indian residential school in Kenora is short their nurse and I go up as relief. Usually it's for a couple weeks. The rest of the time I work on the surgical ward at St. Joe's, that brick hospital behind the corner where the trolley stopped."

Alexis looked like a nurse. Her amber eyes were intelligent and compassionate. They were honest eyes that had seen much, but eyes that would never exaggerate or tell a lie. They were set in a choir boy face, totally free of wrinkles and framed by the starched white linen wimple from under her chin to her forehead where it rose to a Cornette that held her silk veil.

Her hands did not match the smoothness and gentle look of her face. They were rough, red and wrinkled from years of bandaging, massaging, washing and the other chores of helping people in need of nursing. Discounting her youthful face, Celia put her age at late fifties, perhaps early sixties, at any rate ten to fifteen years older than herself.

She asked about the residential school, which the nun said was one of dozens established across Canada, where Indian children were brought for cultural assimilation after being snatched from their homes. Celia assumed it was a system similar to Australia's, which the bureaucrats there termed 'civilizing' its aborigines.

"I don't relish going there," said Alexis. "Many of the children are ill. You can't be healthy when you are sad and lonely. You hear them crying in their beds at night. It is cruel to take them from their families and their homes."

The remark startled Celia. It was unexpected coming from a nun. Back in Australia at the home for unwed mothers and orphans many of the girls were aborigine. The sisters who operated the home all were of the view that the only salvation for the girls was religion and assimilation into white culture.

Alexis continued:

"These people had remarkable, self-sufficient lives until we decided to push them aside. Here in Canada our governments want to round them up, take them out of their communities and force them to integrate into our cities. The residential schools are a step in all this. Our politicians believe what they call the savage Indian cultures can be dissolved through integration into our cities."

She stopped after noticing the incredulous look on Celia's face. It was obvious she had shocked the Australian visitor and needed to explain.

"I'm an unconventional nun. I don't believe or follow closely some of the harder beliefs of our governments, or of my order for that matter."

"I wasn't thinking so much of that," said Celia. "It was just so unexpected to hear a religious speak out against what I also believe are wrong-headed policies. Our government in Australia is much the same, wanting to make the aborigines like the rest of us by destroying their culture. Even my husband believes aborigines are wild people who need to be tamed. What we have done to them is cruel and destructive."

The conversation then moved on to convent life, which of course Celia knew demanded communal thinking. Novitiates left their individualism and contrary views at the convent door.

"In our convents back home there is little room for the unconventional," said Celia. She left unspoken the question of how any sister who did not fully accept communal views could last three-plus decades in a convent.

"My views developed over years of what I observed," said Alexis. "They are not the same views of the sixteen-year-old girl who left my mother and father at the convent doors in Chapleau. Perhaps over the years my thinking became too contrarian to be in the order. But convent life is what I know. There is no other place for me. I am a nurse. That is why I am here on earth. Everything else, including convent life, is secondary."

Alexis stared out at the passing landscape, then continued. "Probably convent life is the best for someone like me. It dictates that I keep my views to myself. If I was on the outside I would become a social crusader and get myself kicked out of nursing."

They both laughed.

"Thank God we can laugh at ourselves and our world," Alexis continued. "That's what my father always said. 'Laugh at the world because people and their situations are not what they appear to be.'"

"That's interesting," Celia said quietly. "There was someone on our ship from Australia who said that a lot – things are not what they appear to be."

"My father had a funny little story to illustrate that. I shouldn't tell it. It's sacrilegious. They would all faint at the convent if they heard it."

"Oh, go ahead," Celia urged. "No one here will hear. And I won't tell on you."

"Well one day Jesus was bored in Heaven," Alexis began in a quiet serious voice. "There wasn't much to do that day so he walked out to the pearly gates to talk with Saint Peter. While he was standing there he noticed far down the line of people waiting to be checked in an old man who looked familiar.

"Jesus walked down the line to get a closer look at the man. He had wispy white hair and rough hands marked by old scars. When Jesus got closer to him he became excited and began questioning him.

"'Say old fellow, when you were down on earth did you work as a carpenter?'

"'Well yes I did, sonny,' said the old man. 'And a good one I was.'

"Jesus became even more animated.

"'Did you have a son that used to help you in the carpentry shop?' asked Jesus, his voice rising with excitement.

"'Yes, an only son and a good boy he was,' replied the man.

"Jesus danced about and blurted: 'And did he die tragically as a young man?'

"'Ah yes,' answered the old man. 'It was a sad time it was.'

"Jesus, tears now rolling down his cheeks, throws open his arms to embrace the man and shouts:

"'Daddy! Daddy!'

"The old man, tears in his eyes now, throws open his arms and embraces Jesus, crying: 'Pinocchio!'"

Celia laughed so hard she drew stares from a couple at the other end of the car. She laughed while wiping the laughter tears from her eyes.

"Where is your daughter? I thought I would get to meet her here."

"Probably in the bar car," said Celia. "We're not exactly best of friends these days."

She immediately regretted saying that and wondered why she had. She was not one to share details of her life with anyone.

Sister Alexis picked up the regret instantly and wondered why a mother and daughter were not friends.

"But that's a story for another time," Celia smiled.

The pair chatted more, mainly about Celia's upbringing around the nuns and the home for unwed mothers and foundlings. They finished their tea and said their goodbyes, Alexis returning to her coach seat while Celia stayed behind, still smiling at the Jesus joke.

CHAPTER 34

Kenora

T HE TRAIN DECELERATED, chuffing wearily to a stop beside the canopied platform of a Tudor style rough brick and granite building. Black and white lettering on the overhanging platform canopy identified the station as Kenora, the last stop before the Northern Ontario bush country gave way to the open Prairie lands of the Canadian West.

Passengers stepped from the train onto the wood plank platform then hurried into the station, hands clutching their jackets at their throats. A sharp north wind blew across the platform, pushing blotches of hard white snow. The sky above was a battlefield on which a weak sun wrestled cold grey clouds for possession of wind-whipped chunks of blue. Celia paused to pull a scarf around her chin when she heard a voice behind her.

"The last battle between autumn and winter. No question which will win."

It was Sister Alexis, lugging her cloth bag while looking up at the angry sky. Her white habit was incongruent in the cold wind but at least she had her shoulders and much of her upper body wrapped in a thickly knitted black wool shawl.

Celia helped her carry the bag through the station door and into the waiting room where passengers blew into their hands and rubbed them together. They were anxious to hear more news of a delay announced twenty minutes earlier by the conductor and trainman walking car to car.

"There will be an unexpected delay in Kenora," the conductor had barked unhappily before arrival. "Please check with the station master for more information."

The waiting room, large and airy at most times, was close and overly warm. Every foot of floor space was occupied by passengers anxious for news. They mingled impatiently, speculating about how serious the delay might be.

The stationmaster appeared on the steps leading down from the offices above the waiting room. His news brought sighs and groans. A grain train headed for the elevators in Port Arthur had left the track ten miles west of the station. It would be two days before the line could be reopened. Passengers could remain aboard the train. Extra food and other supplies were being brought in.

"For those who might want a bit more comfort and space, there are some rooms available downtown," said the stationmaster, an officious looking fellow with close-cropped grey hair, wire-rim spectacles and a pointed salt and pepper goatee. "However, they are limited. The Kenricia Hotel has only a few available because of the influx of hunters at this time of year."

Celia sighed and turned to the nun.

"At least you have reached your destination. Is someone here to pick you up?"

239

"I have to ring the school and one of the maintenance men will drive over for me. Derailments happen a lot out here when trains hit moose. Fool animals sometimes charge the train headlight. I hope no one was injured."

"Let's grab one of those rooms," came a voice from behind Celia. "I'm not going to spend two more days locked up in that train." It was Nancy, who Celia had last seen pacing and smoking on the cold station platform.

"There's always room at the school," said Sister Alexis. "You're welcome there and it's much cheaper than the Kenricia."

Nancy looked the nun up and down, her facial expression clearly asking: Who are you and why are you butting in to our conversation?

"Nancy, this is Sister Alexis," said Celia. "Sister, my daughter Nancy. Sister is a nurse who has come here to help at a residential school for Indians."

Nancy ignored the nun and watched a couple of people heading hurriedly to the waiting room door.

"I'm going to that hotel," she said and pushed her way toward the entrance.

The Kenricia was five blocks from the station and Nancy half fast walked, half sprinted along the street, arriving just as a few other train passengers got out of a taxi and hurried up the steps and across the hotel's wide porch that stretched the lengths of the hotel's two wings. The hotel was not large by European standards and stood like an 'L' on the corner of Main and Second Streets.

It did have six storeys, if you counted the top floor of the blockhouse-like structure perched in the L's corner. It was a modified Beau-Arts design adored by American architects but was more frontier-like than gracious except for its second-floor balconies. Its red Wisconsin brick and grey Manitoba limestone were symbols of the region's dual heritage, developed from Kenora's closeness to the U.S. border.

It was the most comfortable hotel in the wild vastness called Northwestern Ontario. It had been built almost thirty years earlier as part of the town's efforts to become a tourist destination.

Kenora sat on the northern edge of Lake of the Woods, a giant, sparkling jewel that overlapped the Canada-U.S. boundary. Its estimated fourteen thousand islands and more than one hundred thousand kilometers of shoreline attracted hunters, fishermen, all sorts of outdoors folks and others wanting to experience the northern wilderness.

Despite her dash, Nancy found herself out of luck when she reached the reception desk. All rooms were taken.

"I'm really sorry," said the desk clerk, a pleasant and handsome young man who eyed Nancy appreciatively.

"Is there absolutely nothing?" Nancy asked in a distraught voice. She twisted a handkerchief nervously with her fingers then touched the corners of her eyes with it. The clerk, who wore a gold-plated name tag with PAUL in black letters, looked around to see if anyone was in earshot.

"We do have staff quarters," he said. "If you are really in a jam I could let you use my room and perhaps I could bunk in with one of the other guys."

"That would be so wonderful, Paul. I just could not bear another night on that train."

"You'll want to collect a bag, I expect," said Paul. "When you come back I'll show you the room. I'm done my shift at one and I can show you some of the sights if you like."

"That's so nice you," Nancy said demurely. "I'll collect my things and see you soon."

She returned to the station to find her mother and the nun sitting and chatting in the waiting room. Most of the other passengers had cleared out.

"I got the last room," said Nancy. "But it's so tiny. One person only. Barely room to swing a cat. I thought I would take it and you would be more comfortable just staying on the train."

"That's fine," Celia said, showing no visible reaction. Alexis stared, dumbfounded. In her world, someone else's comfort took priority over your own. She quickly renewed her offer for Celia to stay at the residential school.

"The accommodations are modest but the food is home cooked and excellent. It will be a good break for you from the train."

• • •

Half an hour later Celia and Alexis crammed onto the bench seat of the residential school's 1926 Model T pickup truck. The truck cab, enclosed with a decaying canvass top, was not designed to carry three people. Fortunately, the two women and the young Indian driver were of slight builds and managed to squeeze in, leaving the driver scant space to move the floor mount gear shift.

The old truck did have a windscreen but the chilly air blew through tears in the canvass.

"Thank God for the bouncing," Alexis said as they turned into the stony driveway that snaked through patches of dark forest. "The jostling creates some warmth."

Off to the right Celia saw a line of boys carrying spades and hoes. She guessed they ranged in age from seven or eight to early teens.

"The boys do some of the gardening," Alexis explained. "Probably just been putting the gardens to bed for the winter. The girls have chores in the laundry and the kitchen."

St. Mary's Indian Residential School was a broad three-storey brick building atop a rocky slope overlooking Lake of the Woods. It was a bold but pleasant setting carved out of a forest hillside.

The building appeared well organized and maintained. The first floor contained the services such as laundry, kitchen, furnace room. Above that was a straight line of rectangular windows allowing southern light into the classrooms. The third storey with its row of distinctive dormitory windows was where the children slept in rows of brown metal frame single beds.

"This school accommodates ninety students," Alexis said as the truck dropped them at the staff residence, a separate new building with unpainted wood siding. "The previous sisters' quarters burned. And this one is not quite finished."

Alexis had explained the residential school system during their chats on the train ride from Port Arthur. There were eighty such schools across the country, all part of an Indian re-socialization program overseen by the federal government.

"As I said before, we Canadians don't consider Indians civilized," Alexis had said, arching her eyebrows as sarcasm. "So, we round up the kids from the reserves and bring them to these places to learn how to become like the rest of us."

"Attendance is mandatory," she explained. "Anyone resisting sending a child to one of the schools could be arrested. Children regularly are taken screaming from their families. There is much pain and sorrow but the government line is that we are better without an Indian society believed to have done nothing to advance the growth of the new nation."

She added that the government selected religious groups to operate the Indian schools. It provided funding to Roman Catholic, Anglican, Methodist, United and Presbyterian churches to carry out the work of re-socializing Indian children. Re-socializing meant learning to speak

English and the schools administered punishment for any child caught speaking his or her native tongue.

Inside the sisters' residence they were greeted by Mother Superior who Alexis had telephoned from the rail station to get permission for Celia to stay at the residence.

"Your room is ready," said Mother Superior, a female version of Ichabod Crane with deep forehead worry lines that contradicted her pleasant personality. "Everything is plain and simple here but we welcome you and hope you are comfortable."

The interior of the single-storey house was similar to the nuns' residence in Waitara. There was a small prayer room, a kitchen-eating area and a hallway punctuated by narrow doors that opened into cubicle sleeping rooms. Each had a single metal bed with a portmanteau at its foot, a small square table and a wooden high-back chair.

"Barely room to turn sideways," Alexis laughed as she showed Celia her room. "But it's comfortable and quiet."

It was suppertime and they joined a half dozen nuns in the eating area. These were the teaching nuns. The others, who cooked, cleaned and organized, ate with the children in the school's dining hall. Talking was not allowed during the meal but later they adjourned to a sitting area where Celia learned more details of the school.

It was operated by the Oblate order of priests and the Grey nuns of Montreal. All were French speakers but had a good command of English, and a few had learned some Ojibwe and Cree.

They took pride in the self-sufficient efforts of the school: it had fifteen acres of garden that produced heaps of potatoes and some other vegetables. It also had a few cows, goats, dozens of laying hens, turkeys, geese and six pigs.

The nuns questioned Celia on Australia and she told some stories from her childhood at the Waitara home. The after-dinner conversations didn't last long and the nuns retired to their prayers and bed. Alexis did not join them. She seemed different and apart from the cloister although she wore the nun's habit and was expected to follow the rules of the convent. She walked Celia walked down the sleeping wing hallway and stopped at Celia's door.

"Do you want to come in to talk a bit more?" Celia asked. "Sitting and napping on the train I'm not tired." Alexis sensed more than a simple invitation in the voice. Intuition told her that her new friend was a burdened soul who needed to talk.

Inside the tiny room, Celia offered the nun the chair and she sat on the portmanteau. They talked more about the school, Alexis eagerly telling of a supposed curse that hung over the place.

"Years ago, I guess it was about fifteen years ago, two hired hands were in the barn, milking and preparing to bring milk buckets up to the school kitchen. One of the men, Francois Selou, grabbed a bucket in each hand and turned to leave the barn. His working partner, Yves Bernicott, continued his chores then turned around to see Selou holding a gun on him. Can you believe!"

"Selou pulled the trigger, shooting him in the face. But he didn't die. Bernicott ran up the hill to the school, chased by Selou. Inside, Selou encountered Brother Apolinaire D'Amour and shot him dead before running off into the woods and shooting himself."

"Some of the children have been told by their grandparents that the killing was ordered by a Great Spirit to demonstrate the evil of this place."

"But why did this Selou do the shooting?" asked Celia.

"No one ever knew," said Alexis. "There apparently were no signs. The two men got along. He just snapped. There are enough tensions here to make a person snap."

"You sound as if you believe the Indian superstitions."

"I don't believe this is an evil place, but it is a wrong place. The priests and nuns here mostly are kind, God-following people. They believe they are doing the right thing; doing good for these children. And, yes while they are doing good in educating them for a changing world, they are damaging them by removing them from their homes and culture. They should not have their culture wrung out of them. It is wrong, and cruel. No one culture is better than another."

Celia thought on that, then returned the conversation to the school's murder mystery.

"No one knows what goes on in another's mind. Sometimes even those closest to them."

"True," Alexis agreed, pausing and looking at her hands while contemplating how to open the subject she suspected was crowding Celia's mind.

"I hope your daughter will not be lonely in town. It would have been nice if she had come out to see the place. There's always room for one more."

"Nancy has no interest in a place like this. She has no interest in much . . . except herself."

"I sensed that you two might be travelling over troubled waters. That happens sometimes between mothers and daughters. Travelling in close quarters sometimes makes it worse."

"I wish it was that simple." Celia got up from her seat on the portmanteau, looked at the closed door and seemed hesitant. "Would you take a sip of sherry, Sister? I carry it sometimes to help me sleep."

Alexis smiled.

"It's usually forbidden except for medicinal purposes. But I have been known to have a dram, if offered."

Celia opened the portmanteau and removed a bottle of sherry. She took a small corkscrew from her purse. There were two glasses on the table. She poured a couple of ounces of sherry into each and handed one to the nun.

"Cheers," she said raising her glass.

"Passages!" Alexis offered.

"Safe passages" said Celia.

"Just passages. They aren't always safe, but some must be taken."

They sipped their sherry and talked about their lives. Alexis came from a large family. Six boys and four girls. Two of the girls became nuns, one boy a Jesuit priest. There all were raised in the Northeastern Ontario railway town of Chapleau, where Celia's train had stopped earlier. Life there was hardscrabble, but always filled with adventure and laughter.

Alexis told of the Christmases when the men took a bucket and a brace and bit to the rail yards. They would crawl beneath a boxcar and drill through the floor and into a whiskey keg, then catch the whiskey in the bucket.

"They all worked for the railway so knew which cars were carrying the best whiskey," smiled Alexis. "There were lots of us, and we were all close. We still are even though we are spread across the country."

"I've never had that type of closeness in family," said Celia.

She explained that neither of her parents' had close relatives in Australia and so much of their family life blended with mission life.

The sherry, the talk and the quiet surroundings spread mellowness throughout the tiny bedroom. Celia poured them each another glass. Alexis protested mildly, then allowed Celia to continue pouring.

"But you have your own family and you can age happily surrounded by grandchildren," said the nun.

"I wish," Celia sighed, swirling the sherry and watching the smooth arcs rise and fall slowly against the side of the glass.

"It's something for you and your husband to look forward to."

"There is nothing that we look forward to together these days," Celia replied quickly. The sherry was loosening her reserve, and her tongue. She continued, saying out loud what she was thinking.

"It didn't used to be that way. We shared everything. Thoughts and dreams. Our passion. Bertie drew me out of a restricted world much like this one."

Alexis listened as Celia told how as an only child her world centred on the mission at Waitara. She went to school at the Catholic primary school next to the foundling home, then to a middle school nearby. When she finished the middle grades she attended tutoring classes offered to the older girls still at the home. Between tutoring sessions she worked at the mission and there was no time left for a social life beyond the mission.

The meeting of Bertie in Sydney led to a brief courtship, too brief for Celia to properly bridge her Waitara world with the new world that stretched before her. They married without having had time to get to know each other. Their lives moved to rhythms acquired from cultures and communities close in distance but worlds apart.

Bertie was a young entrepreneur with some inherited family money, huge charm and an ego to match. He knew a wider world that was foreign to Celia and he opened it to her. They loved each other and laughed when they made love. Then the realities of married life arrived. The house in Wahroonga. A son Neil, followed two years later by Nancy, then increasingly separate lives.

Celia's life was the home and the babies. The fondling home was close by and remained an important part of Celia's life. She donated her spare time to volunteering there, sometimes taking the babies with her. For Bertie life was more business deals, more business trips and more excuses for staying in downtown Sydney.

Neither seemed to notice nor mind the growing separateness of their lives. Any marital tensions were soothed by their increasing affluence. Bertie's enterprises flourished and the Wahroonga house lacked none of the most modern innovations and conveniences. Celia learned to drive and had her own auto. There was a maintenance man to look after the house and gardens, which had become one of Celia's passions, and a maid who did the housework.

"Ah yes, the routine of life," said Alexis. "It's not much different in anyone's life. Here in convent life the excitement of novitiate life becomes absorbed into routine, and questioning. Everyone questions the life they have chosen, or the life they have been given. We all accumulate knowledge as we live and with knowledge comes questions, some of which we are told we must never try to answer."

"Like why God does what he does?" Celia asked, reaching for the sherry bottle. "Like how he can be so giving, yet so cruel."

"Cruel?"

Celia's face crumpled under a weight of sadness. She put down her glass, dropped her face into her hands and began to cry.

"It's so unfair," she murmured. "Everything changed . . . ."

Alexis rose from her seat, put her arms around Celia and pulled her close to her and felt the sobs erupting from a pit of sorrow seemingly miles below..

"Tell me about it. Release what you have been holding in for so long. Purge it."

Celia clung to Alexis and told the story.

Theirs was a family of two distinct parts, Celia related. Bertie and Nancy did their things, which usually involved the city and its entertainments, notably the beaches. Celia and Neil did not like the hustle of the city, preferring the calm beauty of the outdoors. Some of their most pleasant times were spent bushwalking and picnicking in the abundant bushland hills and valleys south of Wahroonga.

"Nancy and her father were never ones for the adventures of the bush," said Celia. "In many ways they detested the outdoors, except for golf. Neil loved the outdoors. He dreamed of having a cabin in the bush one day and I encouraged his dream and hoped it would come true for him."

The morning following the dinnertime argument in which Nancy said she hoped Neil would be bit by a snake, Celia, Bertie and the two children had driven out to the meeting point where the four boys would begin their bush outing. Some of the other parents and children were there to see to boys off on their adventure. They were to return two days later to pick up the boys.

They watched the boys shoulder their packs, then waved and blew kisses as they left on a trail into a field of high green ferns and blue gum eucalyptus. Neil brought up the rear and before he was out of sight turned, smiled broadly and blew his mother a kiss. That was her last view of him.

The boys were headed down to Berowra Creek where they planned to explore for traces of early Aborigine occupation. They had heard that there were rock carvings and paintings to be found.

Berowra could be a cold place at the start of the Australian winter. The average overnight temperature in July was five degrees Celsius and often went down to freezing. They boys knew of an abandoned cabin in the creek valley and found it before dark. They would sleep there because it had an old metal woodstove that could be fired up to keep off the night cold.

They had trouble lighting the stove, which was filled with damp ashes. One of the boys had a can of kero and splashed some on the damp stove bed to boost the fire. The kero hit an ember and exploded into flame that reached up the boy's arm and into the can. He dropped the flaming can and when it hit the floor, the place exploded in flames.

Neil and one of the other boys had been outside gathering wood for the fire. They heard yelling and turned to see the cabin ablaze. The doorway was a wall of flame but Neil rushed through it intending to help the two boys inside. He never re-emerged.

The one boy not in the cabin hiked out for help. When rescue teams arrived there was nothing but ashes and smoke curling up through the treetops. What charred fragments of the boys that could be found were buried following a joint funeral at which Neil Coulson's bravery was honoured.

"Everything changed then," Celia sobbed while accepting the tissues offered by the nun. "Bertie blamed me for . . . whatever. Nancy grew distant and difficult accusing me of being unloving and disappointed because she wasn't Neil."

Bertie began spending more time in Sydney, supposedly managing the business but more likely in the nightclubs and with other women. Their marriage never had the strong foundation needed to support a bridge over the chasm left by Neil's death. It settled into a convenience arrangement best left undisturbed to anyone looking on from the outside. Their marriage became just another business arrangement.

"I'm sorry, you deserve better," Alexis whispered, hugging Celia more tightly. "You are a loving person who has been denied love. I pray to God for him to help you find it."

Alexis helped her onto the narrow bed, tossed a blanket over her and dimmed the room's single light before slipping quietly out the door.

Celia sensed the room darken and heard the door latch click shut. Her eyes never opened before she slipped back into sleep and a dream in which Niles Langer pulled her body into hers and kissed her.

CHAPTER 35

Dancing Through Hoops

THE SHOUTS OF children playing in the school yard woke Celia. She looked at her watch and was astonished she had slept so long. It was almost eight o'clock and the children had an hour of outside play before a nun appeared on the school doorstep to shake the heavy brass hand bell commanding them to line up for classes inside.

Celia washed, dressed and got coffee in the kitchen. Alexis was at the school doing her morning sick call, so she wandered out into the schoolyard to watch the children. There was a skiff of snow on the ground and the waning autumn sun did little to warm a cool breeze coming off Lake of the Woods. The children, boys dressed in denim pants and light checked shirts, the girls in cotton blouses and skirts, didn't seem to mind.

She noticed one girl, perhaps nine or ten, sitting alone on a stump and staring into a picture book. She was a sweet but sad looking child with hair as glossy black as a crow's wing and round dark eyes that were much older and experienced than her years.

"Hi," said Celia as she approached the stump. "What are you reading?"

The girl held out the book to show its cover on which a spotted fawn frolicked with butterflies in a forest meadow. Celia recognized it immediately. It was a children's version of 'Bambi: A Life in the Woods' by the Austrian writer Felix Salten.

"Sister Marie gave it to me," said the girl. "She said I should read it to learn about life. But I can't read too well."

"I can read to you a little before the bell rings," said Celia.

The girl smiled shyly and held out the book for Celia to take. She took it and glanced at the pages where the girl had it open. On the left page was a drawing of a majestic old stag looking sternly down at a tiny fawn who had tears running down its snout. She read out the words on the opposite page, not realizing how they might affect the little girl.

"What are you crying about? the old stag asked severely. Bambi trembled in awe and did not dare answer.

"Your mother has no time for you now," the old stag continued. Bambi was overwhelmed by his commanding voice. "Can't you stay by yourself? Shame on you!"

The bell clanged. The little girl snatched the book back and ran off to where the children lined up in a double row by the school's side door.

Soon after the children were settled in their classrooms, Alexis came outside and joined Celia. They walked to the lake's edge where the water licked the smooth granite slope.

"Everyone healthy today," Alexis smiled. "Visitation Day is in a couple of days so the children are excited. For now. There'll be a lot of sad faces and crying after."

She explained that only some parents from the reserves closest by came for Visitation Days. The number would be fewer than usual at this time of year because many families were away hunting.

"That's sad," said Celia. "I remember the same sadness and the tears of the orphans at Waitara."

She paused then added: "By the way, I'm sorry about last evening."

"What part of it?" Alexis asked. "We . . . ."

Celia coloured with embarrassment. "I'm sorry to have burdened you with my troubles."

"Sometimes troubles are best shared. Someone else will never solve them but talking often creates the clarity necessary to figure out how to get through them."

"Life has changed so much," said Celia. "I don't seem to be living in the same world I always knew. My thoughts have become all mixed up."

Alexis looked over the lake and thought about their talk in Celia's room. Even after decades of nursing experience she found it difficult what to say to a parent who had lost a child. Deaths of children at St. Mary's and other residential schools were not rare. Pneumonia and a variety of fevers took them. Then there were drownings, disappearances in the woods and a variety of accidents. And yes, some kids Alexis believed simply died of hearts broken by being removed from their families. Children who died often had siblings at the school and Alexis had seen how the loss affected them. She saw and understood the damage but never had found a prescription to remedy it.

"These people, the Indians, live every day with the troubles resulting from their changing world," Alexis said. "They turn to their spiritual sides to deal with them. They even have a dance to help them deal with troubles."

"A dance?"

"Yes, the Hoop Dance. It starts with drummers beating their drums as a dancer carrying a handful of willow hoops dances into the dance circle.

The drum beats intensify as the dancer slips into the hoops, placing them around her legs, neck, arms until she is dancing inside a tangle of hoops."

Alexis held her arms in the air, widened her stance and twisted and turned to demonstrate.

"The hoops represent life's problems, and the more hoops the dancer uses, the more her problems multiply. The dancer calls for help by putting the hoops into shapes symbolizing animals such as the eagle, the snake, the bear. The animals are the manitous who the dancer wants to take away her problems. The dancer twists and turns, pleading with the manitous for help. Finally she realizes that the manitous cannot help and that the only way to get free of the hoops is to dance her way out of them.

"The message is that everyone has problems but asking for someone else to make them go away is not the answer. The only way to get rid of your problems is to face them and solve them – to dance out of them - yourself."

Celia pondered that. "Interesting. But what if some solutions to your problems mean doing something wrong in society's eyes, or God's eyes."

"God does not judge anyone for using their intellect," said Alexis. "Free will is his greatest gift to us. God expects us to use our conscience to guide choices. God does not praise nor punish us for our decisions."

"That is not what we hear in church. The church says we can burn in Hell for some decisions."

"That is religion practised through doctrine. True religious belief is the enduring values that make us better people. Not doctrines designed to keep people on a straight and narrow path by having them stop thinking. These values are presented to us in parables, not real happenings. God did not appear through the clouds on the mountaintop and present Moses with the Ten Commandments carved in stone. It is simply a story that helps us guide our lives."

"You are not anything like the nuns I've known, Alexis," said Celia.

"I wear the habit, but it's important to have an independent mind no matter what the outward symbols. I refuse to be tied to the dogmas of my order or its religion. I believe in God but not the God of radically organized religion. Just because organized religion says something is bad does not mean you are bad."

Celia stared out across the water and sighed.

"I wonder about my faith. There are times when I have doubts."

"There is no faith without doubt," Alexis replied. She paused as if gathering courage to say something that can be thought but should not be spoken.

"Sometimes I think we might be better off without any organized religion. Look at these people. We see them as ignorant and try to force on them our values and religious practises but perhaps it should be the other way around. We have much to learn from them."

"How can you possibly continue to exist within the convent?"

"It's not easy. I am a maverick but I try to keep my views to myself and follow the rules so as not to upset others who are firm adherents. It is difficult knowing that I can never change anything within the convent or within the church. I cannot be a bishop. I cannot be pope. I am a woman."

"Would it be so difficult to break away for a new life?"

"Where would I go? This is who I am. And before anything else, I am a nurse. I help people. That is my first reason for being. Speaking of which, I must get back."

Alexis hiked her skirts to halfway up her shins, revealing her white socked ankles and clunky white leather walking shoes, then strode up the smooth rock slope. Within a couple minutes Celia saw she was up on the flats, her skirts and veil flowing behind her as she made for the school's side entrance.

Such a contradictory character, Celia thought. She reminded her of her mother, who had chosen a religious vocation, then left it. She left it for love, not because her thinking sometimes opposed that of the order, although her thinking often did not run parallel to the order, or even that of the Catholic church.

Her mother said that service must be put before belief in any organized group. To her the Sisters of Mercy and the Catholic Church were what she knew and lived with. She could have been born into any religion and become associated with any religious group and still have served those who needed help.

Sister Alexis was much the same. She was who she was. The church, the nuns and their rules and beliefs were what they were. Her purpose was not to change them. It was to change the lives of people through helping them. Alexis was an independent thinker, but she was dependent on the life structure in which she existed. Was it courage that kept her within a religious order that she questioned and sometimes challenged? Or cowardice – maybe fear was a better word - that kept her from leaving the safety and comfort of an established life?

Celia imagined her mother sitting beside her here gazing out onto the lake. brow furrowed, eyes sad. She had faithfully raised Celia to be immune to situations faced by 'other' people. Despite all that effort her daughter now found herself questioning her faith, her marriage, and her life while yearning for something different. And, questioning whether she could continue to have any relationship with her own daughter.

Celia absent-mindedly ran a hand over the smooth rock and watched the morning breeze tickle the sleepy lake surface. The lake gave a rippled smile. Farther along the shore the rock slope angled upwards until it became a rocky cliff.

Alexis had said that the Indian children sometimes sneaked up there seeking solace. More than one child over the years found the ultimate solace by leaping off the cliff into the dark, deep waters below. It was a place to go when dancing through life's hoops no longer was possible.

Celia saw herself on the cliff's edge. She was struggling to break free of a tangle of hoops. So many hoops to dance through. Her head ached with the drumbeat pounding of her heart. The harder it pounded the more the hoops seemed to tighten around her. The more they tightened, the more the water below called to her.

• • •

Later that morning word reached the school that the rail line blockage had been cleared and the Vancouver train would resume its journey by mid-afternoon. Celia packed the overnight bag she had brought, stuffing the sherry bottle among the clothes. It was empty but she would take it with her so it would not be found in the residence trash.

She said her thank yous and goodbyes to the sisters working in the kitchen and to Mother Superior. The old pickup truck was waiting at the front door, Alexis standing beside it.

"Thank you for your kindness," Celia said drawing the nun close in a hug.

"Don't let the hoops overwhelm you," Alexis smiled. "Remember God wants us to make our own decisions. That's why he gave us free will. He doesn't judge or punish when we do."

Twenty minutes later the truck skidded into the station platform curb then groaned as the engine died. It had snowed overnight. Just a couple inches but enough to make driving and walking difficult.

A jalopy banged into the parking curb nearby. The driver's door flew open and Paul, the desk clerk from the Kenricia, slid out, followed by

Nancy. He tossed her bag up onto the platform, then grabbed her in his arms and kissed her. He lifted her onto the platform. When she regained her feet she turned, blew him a kiss and shouted: "Don't forget to write."

The train whistle blew, the conductor shouted "All 'board" and within a few minutes the transcontinental train had moved into the dark forest path leading to the open Prairie, the majestic Rocky Mountains and finally the West Coast and the waiting ship at Vancouver.

CHAPTER 36

TCA

BERTIE COULSON JOG-WALKED across the tarmac to the waiting aircraft. As much as he dreaded flying, he hurried to get inside 'the soup can with wings' to hide from the sharp November air. The stewardess, flashing a smile and welcoming eyes despite the cold, checked his ticket and guided him up the two steps into the Lockheed Electra's tail entrance. The icy breeze licked at gossamer strands of blonde hair trying to escape from under her cap.

Bertie thought her enticing in her dark blue gabardine uniform. She was slim and the jacket, skirt and white blouse were tailored not to hide her well-proportioned curves.

She should make this marathon of flying more bearable, he thought. It had been a long trip – Australia to Ceylon to England and now Canada – and with some, but not enough female comfort. There had been Molly, the tea man's wife, on the sailing from Ceylon but nothing since.

He settled into a window seat at the front of the plane. All seats were window seats. The passenger cabin had seats for ten passengers, five along each side of the plane, but only six were filled. The cabin air was uncomfortably close and smelled of hot engine oil, polished metal and aviation fuel. Bertie also whiffed a hint of vomit but that might have been produced by his imagination after seeing the air sickness bag in the seat pocket in front of him.

For distraction he pulled Celia's note from his suit jacket pocket. She had left if for him at the Windsor Hotel in Montreal. She had booked passage for her and Nancy on a transcontinental train to Vancouver and would wait at the Hotel Vancouver before the sailing to Australia. Nancy's 'older friend' had followed them to Canada from England and the 'friendship' continued to blossom.

He folded the note and jammed it back into his pocket. Why couldn't she just stay put? It was stupid to have left England. The country was in no grave danger of a German invasion. However, the end of this world excursion was in sight. He would meet them in Vancouver, settle whatever problems needed to be settled and be on their way back home.

It wasn't as if he didn't have things to attend to. His businesses were booming thanks to the war. He and his colleagues had picked up properties, goods and businesses left in the wreckage of the Depression and were turning them over for profits as the economy improved. Now there was a boom in selling war supplies and services to the Australian government. He had a good team and could keep himself involved through telegraph but really needed to be in Sydney.

He hoped the man apparently pursuing them was out of the picture now. Hopefully Celia's reports had been exaggerations, fuelled by her inability to handle their daughter. To be sure, Nancy was impulsive to the point of being reckless but Celia's concern and attempts to redirect her only made Nancy worse. The cattiness that had developed between the daughter and mother at times drove him wild enough to be ropeable.

Give her what she wants and let her go her own way, was his approach. She would grow out of it.

Bertie admired Celia's innocence and her desire to always do the right thing. She was virtuous, the result of her sheltered upbringing, but she was naïve. The world was changing and you had to drop much old-fashioned baggage and run hard to keep up.

He wanted to expand his world. The businesses were producing the wealth to make that possible. Why drink plonk when you could afford the delicate flavours of a twenty-dollar bottle of wine?

They had argued about the possibility of moving into one of Sydney's fashionable areas. There were magnificent houses by the ocean. He wanted a yacht and the social mingling that the yacht club provided. Celia seemed to want to diminish her life.

Passing years often draw couples together. Two distinct creatures gradually meld into one another, becoming one. Twenty years of marriage had left them as two individuals still drifting separately in their own worlds. Perhaps it would have been different, Bertie thought, if Neil had not died. That tragedy more than anything had changed their lives. They had blamed each other.

Losing a child changes a family. Forever. Life after the child is taken can never be the same. Like someone losing a leg, or eyesight. A vital part is gone for always. The body must learn to cope, to do things differently. With death of a child some families adjust more smoothly and naturally than others.

Neil's death affected each of the Coulsons differently. Bertie elbowed himself forward with even more bombast. Celia retrenched, glancing back at her earlier Waitara life as a refuge from a dangerous world.

For Nancy, her parents' grieving was upsetting and increased her craving for attention. She awoke at night crying and calling for her father to chase away her fears. If this could happen to the chosen one, the first born, the son and heir, it could easily happen to her.

Seven years had passed since Neil's death. The wounds were scar tissue that swelled and turned red and painful from time to time. Bertie's patience thinned. He drank more, and stayed around home less. His interests narrowed to business, female companionship in Sydney and mentoring Nancy on becoming the leader he had hoped Neil could be.

Drinking was good for business. Drinking with business associates built camaraderie and trust. Lunches, dinners and parties were where deals were made. It wasn't good for personal life. Celia drank little so was a reluctant companion and confidant over a good bottle of Scotch.

The booze had allowed Bertie to say some things to Celia that never should have been said. They were things that he might have passed through his head but they were things he didn't really mean, and could not be taken back. Booze short-circuits the brain's trip wire that warns a person that their actions will have consequences. It allows a person to say things that might not otherwise have been said. Things that hurt but cannot be pulled back.

Worse than the things he said were the things that he did when charged with too much drink. He stared out into the airplane window and saw his reflection – a face filled with regret and contrition.

"I never should have slapped her that week before they left," he said to himself.

It had started with the typical argument about Nancy. He had come home late from the office having stopped with some colleagues at a drink house. Celia had told him she and Nancy had argued about her going off with a pub crowd of boys who were of legal age. Nancy had told her to 'piss off' and left the house.

"Let her run," he had shouted flinging a glass across the room. "Quit trying to rope her in."

"Let her run like you!" Celia, flushed with anger, shot back. "Let her run like you – a grog hound who never saw a skirt he did not want to sniff!"

He stepped forward and slapped her cleanly across the cheek, sending her hair swirling as her head went sideways. He had never struck her before, and the slap shocked both of them. He felt shame and embarrassment. She felt the stinging warmth of the blood rising to the surface of her pale left cheek. A tear tracked down the cheek and hesitated before dropping off her chin and falling slowly to the rug below where it left a mark that would dry but would be visible forever.

Their life together was a rain barrel filling slowly over the years since Neil's death. When the water reached the brim it sat there placid and patient waiting for the final drop. The falling tear was the final drop that began the overflow. Their lives never could be the same.

How had things gone wrong between them? Two good people whose different lives had come together at a lunch counter in Sydney. How different each of their lives would have been if that meeting had not occurred. It had occurred and brought a brought a union that promised a future of happiness, prosperity and love.

Tragedy smashed the dreams, but it could not be blamed for everything happening between them. Relationships are shaken and cracked by tragedy but the strong relationships endure, and often are made stronger, life's unexpected calamities.

His reflection was interrupted by the banging close of the rear door, then a whining and growling from the left engine. Out his window he saw fire explode from the exhaust port of right engine as it sparked to life. The stewardess walked forward to the cockpit door, poked her head in, said something to the pilots, then closed it. She picked up a microphone that fed into a scratchy intercom system needed in the small space only to lift her words over the roar of the engines.

"Please buckle your belts. The pilots are ready for takeoff. Store books, magazines and anything else that might fly about. I'll have details on the route and service after we are at cruising altitude."

Bertie could feel the aircraft's power rumbling in the bottom of his seat. He looked about at the other five passengers, all men. The aircraft seldom left the ground with all seats full. Commercial flying was only a couple of years old in Canada. It had been only six months earlier that Trans-Canada Airlines had started this cross-country service, a fact that did not lessen Bertie's nervousness.

The aircraft swayed and bumped along the taxiway, then made a sharp turn to the left and braked. The engines ran up to high speed, then subsided. When they ran up again, Bertie could feel the brakes release and the plane bound forward. Runway markers and airport buildings flashed by outside the window. The plane's tail raised, the cabin shook and rocked then steadied as the plane freed itself from earth's grip, then clawed its way upward, passing through a thin cloud layer before levelling out.

"Please keep your seatbelts fastened in case of turbulence. And welcome aboard for the first leg of our cross-country journey. Our first stop on the way will be North Bay in roughly two hours. My name is Lucile and I'm here to make your journey more comfortable."

Flying to Vancouver was arduous, usually taking fifteen hours without any weather or mechanical delays. The route followed rail lines, which helped the pilots know where they were and whether they were on course. There were emergency air fields built between the main stops of North Bay, Winnipeg, Regina and Lethbridge. The most scenic, and the most dangerous, part of the journey would be over the mountains between Lethbridge and Vancouver. The little Electra could not fly above fifteen thousand feet and cloud cover might mean having to fly through the passes between mountain peaks.

Bertie was feeling a bit woozy and had closed his eyes. He felt a light touch on his shoulder then the delicate smell of perfume.

"Can I get you anything? A drink perhaps."

"A drink would be lovely. Scotch preferred."

Bertie turned and watched the shapely form float to the aircraft's rear service area. She sorted through the well-organized shelves filled with liquor bottles, soft drinks, crackers, Alka-Seltzer and aspirin. The motto of the stewardess, a fledgling trade, was 'Be Prepared.' Lucile, like all stewardesses was a registered nurse prepared to handle anything from air sickness, to air accidents to serving snacks and drinks, and lighting passenger's cigarettes.

Lucile returned with a good bolt of Scotch in wide-bowled whiskey glass, then turned to the gentleman in the seat across the aisle.

"And you, sir?"

"Ah," said Niles Langer, leaning forward and peering around her at Bertie. "I'll have what that gentleman is having. Looks enticing."

After she delivered his drink, Langer looked at Bertie and raised his glass: "Soft landings!"

"Cheers, mate," Bertie replied.

"You are Australian?" said Langer.

"Yes. And you? English?"

"Yes, we're both far from home."

"Hmmm." Bertie sipped the Scotch. "It will be good to get the feet planted back in the bulldust."

Langer felt a twinge of alarm. The Australian accent. An obvious love affair with Scotch. Heading home through Vancouver. So what? All of that could apply to any Australian traveller. Activity toward the rear of the airplane interrupted his thoughts. One of the passengers was not handling the flight well.

"The mate's throwing up buckets," Bertie said to Langer.

"I hope it's not contagious," returned Langer.

They settled back into their Scotch and chatted casually about flying, Canada and the reputed beauty of Vancouver.

"I'm meeting my wife and daughter there," said Bertie. "They've been in England and decided to leave because of the war."

Langer's twinge became a sharp pang. He felt warm and began to perspire. He knew it was not the Scotch. Was it at all possible?

"What about yourself?"

"Oh, I'm off to visit my sister in Victoria," Langer lied. "She emigrated some years ago. Good time to visit and get away from the fireworks back home. Looks like it's going to be a bad show."

"Oh, I think it will all blow over quickly," said Bertie. "However, it has ruined the grand tour of Europe for my daughter."

"You were not travelling with them?"

"No, my wife is a panicky sort and wired me to come and escort them home. Hell of a mess. I got stranded in Ceylon and have been trying to catch up with them since. I don't know why they just couldn't have waited for me in Ceylon or London."

"By the way," he added extending his hand across the aisle, "I'm Havard. Havard Coulson. People call me Bertie."

Langer summoned his warmest smile to wipe the shock from his face, and shook the extended hand. "I'm Nelson. Nelson Langford."

He wondered how he had managed to blurt out the phoney name. It had just happened and thank God it had. His bags carried the initials NL.

It was possible that Coulson had not even heard of the name Niles Langer. Would Celia or Nancy have mentioned it in any communication with him? If either had, would he even have remembered it? That didn't matter now. He had introduced himself as Langford in case the man did know the name. The problem now would be the stewardess, who knew the name of each passenger and who now was coming down the aisle to speak to them.

"Gentlemen. More drinks. How about you Mr. Lan. . . ."

Langer cut her off quickly.

"Nelson. Just call me Nelson. No need for any formalities on such a relaxed trip."

"Okay, Nelson. Will you have another Scotch?"

Langer said yes and so did Bertie and they spent the next hour in pleasant conversation about world affairs.

The stop in North Bay was brief and the leg to Winnipeg uneventful. The conversation petered and Bertie dozed as the plane bored through the cloudless blue sky above the flat Prairie landscape west of Winnipeg. He awoke when the wheels rubbed the runway at Lethbridge.

CHAPTER 37

The Plan

JOHN RICHARDSON CHEWED the end of his yellow wooden pencil then pushed his chair back from a scuffed and bruised oak desk that looked old and battered enough to have been discarded by Captain Cooke during his exploration of the Vancouver shoreline. He stared up thoughtfully at the pressed tin ceiling, now cracked and flaking after a poorly applied paint job.

"We need a workable plan," he said. "An executable plan that has the full co-operation of our friends at immigration. If we work it right we can get rid of your persistent Mr. Langer."

Celia smiled demurely.

Richardson was an intent man in his early thirties, neatly bearded. This was a unique and important case. Opportunities to assist a prestigious eastern law firm did not come every day for a small legal firm perched on Canada's western edge. Resolving the matter to everyone's satisfaction would establish a reputation with the Montreal legal firm, which was important because of the increasing business connections between the distant and isolated Canadian West and the eastern establishment.

As instructed by the Mr. Paquette in Montreal, Celia had telephoned him soon after her train arrived in Vancouver. He had been expecting her call earlier in the week and when he didn't hear from her became concerned. Through telephone calls to Montreal, then the rail company, he learned of the delay at Kenora.

Celia had left Nancy at the Hotel Vancouver, saying she had to go to the steamship ticket office to confirm their already booked passage to Australia. She found the lawyer's office in a three-storey stone building on a side street just off Granville Avenue. Richardson and a partner occupied the offices. The reception area was by no means shabby, but certainly not opulent.

Much of the furniture was dated; likely collected from a previous law firm but the accessories and pictures on the walls were modern. Entering the office Celia got the sense of younger lawyers trying to break through into loftier circles.

After the usual introduction and pleasantries, Richardson leaned back and listened while she told the entire story of her trip and Langer's pursuit. He listened carefully despite already knowing much of the story, which had been contained in the letter from Charles Paquette K.C., Helene's father.

Paquette, no doubt thinking of what it would be like to have his daughter pursued by a man twenty-five years her senior, had been quite direct. His letter to Richardson openly suggested ways, not becoming a member of the Bar, of handling the Langer problem.

"We are convinced," Paquette wrote, "that he is a coward and it is possible he can be persuaded from pursuing the girl if interviewed by some forceful constable or private detective. "What he needs, of course, is a thrashing."

Richardson stared at Celia, wondering about her thoughts on a thrashing for the man chasing her daughter. He had no intention of suggesting a vigilante type plan, but was interested in her thinking. She offered no hints. The fashionable slouch fedora casting a shadow over her stonily attractive face gave her an enigmatic look. Maybe he had been seeing too many Marlene Dietrich films, he thought. Yet she was the mysterious, silent type, her face and body language giving away little.

"He is clever," Celia offered. "So any plan must take that into consideration. He takes great care never to board a ship or train unless he is certain we are on board. And he never disembarks unless he knows that we have disembarked."

"I have made an initial contact with immigration here," said Richardson. "They already had heard from Mr. Paquette, whose firm has some influence in Ottawa. They are agreeable to help. They are particularly interested in this fellow's Nazi connections. They are anxious to have him in for questioning which could take long enough to make him miss your sailing."

A ripple of concern ran across Celia's face, which up to that point had been unreadable.

"He's not a Nazi," she said, which Richardson thought was a bit too quickly. "He has a better understanding of why the Germans feel the way they do and people interpret that to be pro-Hitler."

She was about to say more but checked herself. "At any rate, I suppose it doesn't matter if the authorities think he is a Nazi. It will play into our hands."

"Absolutely," said Richardson. "It gives immigration a reason to help us put a plan into place."

He then outlined his idea. Celia and Nancy would arrive at the ship terminal and go through the immigration checkpoint for departing international ship passengers. An officer would order them into a side office for questioning about their travels with a man named Niles Langer. When Langer arrived he would be pulled aside and directed to a separate room and questioned about his Nazi sympathies. Celia and Nancy would be escorted onto the ship minutes before it sailed while Langer would be held long enough to miss the sailing.

"Of course, there will be no legal reason to hold him very long and no guarantee that he won't try to another sailing to catch up with your ship. But I think the police and immigration officials will be able to talk to him in a way that will discourage his further pursuit of you."

"My daughter has said she will not board the ship without him. She must see him on the ship or she will not leave."

"Well, she is a minor, not a Canadian citizen and we can have her deported, placed on the ship forcibly."

"Do we really want that kind of a scene? Officials dragging her kicking and screaming onto the ship."

Richardson's face lighted up with an idea.

"What if we arranged to have her talk to the shipping company. She wants to know Langer is aboard so immigration rings the shipping company and we have arranged for the office manager to stand by, answer the call and confirm that Langer is aboard."

"That is excellent," Celia smiled. "Helene Paquette's father made a good choice in recommending you. Here's something that might help the immigration people."

She pulled a photograph from her purse and handed it across the desk.

"I think it's important for them to identify him from this photograph because I believe he sometimes uses a fake identity."

"Bit of a hard looking fellow," said the lawyer. "I don't know what your daughter would see in him. I'll give it to the immigration people and they will have it at the departure gate when he arrives. I'll set this up and call you at your hotel to confirm the plan is in place."

Richardson was charged up and anxious to get moving on the plan. They shook hands, said goodbye and Celia descended the stairs and out into the autumn sunshine. She was pleased with the plan and anxious to prepare Nancy.

• • •

At the hotel Celia found Nancy pitching a fit on the telephone.

"I hope your pilots are brighter than the rest of you," she was yelling. "If not, God help your passengers." She slammed the telephone in to its cradle. "They don't even know who is travelling on their own airline," she said, face screwed into disgust. "Or, they just won't say."

While she had ben unpacking a bellboy had brought a telegram to the room. It was from Langer and the desk clerk had forgotten to give it to her at check-in. It read simply:

FLYING VCR. SEE YOU THERE. NILES.

No details but Nancy had launched a mission to get them. She had telephoned the airline office to find out when Langer had left Montreal and when he was expected to arrive. The airline clerk on the telephone said it was not possible to know where a passenger might be if she did not know on what day he left. If she had a departure time and destination she still would have to contact Montreal to get that information.

"He should arrive tomorrow in time to catch the ship," said Celia.

Nancy's head snapped upward and she stared at her mother in disbelief.

"How do you know when he is coming? I just got this telegram saying he is flying."

Celia opened her suitcase and began arranging some clothes. "Let's go to the dining room for a drink and dinner. I'm tired and hungry. I'll explain it all there."

"Forget dinner. I want to know how you know when he is arriving," Nancy sputtered.

"Nancy, relax dear. Let's wash, change, dress and have a nice dinner and talk. It's about time we did. The dining room - it's the Panorama Room on the fifteenth floor - is said to be excellent. The King and Queen ate there earlier this year when they opened this hotel."

Nancy jumped to her feet to demand to know now but her mother already had gone into the bathroom and closed the door. She had been acting strangely, especially on the latter part of this journey. Obviously she had something on her mind and had picked dinner tonight to reveal what it was. Nancy began changing for dinner.

The Panorama Room was crowded with women in gossamer dance frocks and men in business suits. Celia had made a reservation upon returning from the lawyer's office. It was a large room with mirrored square pillars and a band stage and a mahogany-coloured hardwood dance floor at one end. Tonight was dance night. A waiter guided them to a table offering a southern view of the city, which included the swish Point Grey residential neighbourhood and a sweeping view of the Strait of Georgia.

Celia ordered her favourite cocktail, a Negroni with its odd mixture of gin, vermouth rosso and Compari. Nancy, in a hurry to pry from her mother details of the conversation with Langer, ordered a beer.

"Now are you going to tell me about how you know when Niles is arriving," she said, a sour look emphasizing her impatience.

"'There was a telegram from him waiting for me at the Kenora station. He asked me to telephone him in Montreal."

"Why did you not tell me? Why would he telegraph you and not me?"

"You shot off to that hotel in such a flash. Then of course we didn't see each other for two days. I gather you had made a new friend in that young man who worked at the hotel."

Nancy began to protest, but Celia held up her hand.

"So I telephoned Montreal from the residential school. I left the nuns money. The telephone rates here are atrocious . . . ."

Nancy was impatient. "Tell me what he said!"

"Be patient. I want to explain myself clearly and calmly. This trip has been a disaster from the beginning." Celia went on to say how distressing it had been to see her daughter pursuing a man twice her age.

"Mother, I . . ." Nancy tried to argue but her mother hushed her and continued on.

"At any rate, Mr. Langer obviously knows my feelings. We had talked about this at various times on the trip from home and in England. He said he wanted to apologize for any distress I might have suffered, made clear his honourable intentions and hoped that we could all be friends."

"But . . . ."

Celia held up her hand again. "I would like to finish. I've decided that there is no use fighting this. I'm tired of swimming against the tide. Mr. Langer said he is flying to Vancouver and has booked passage on the Niagara, our ship. We will travel home and your father can sort it out from there."

Nancy studied her mother. It was difficult to know whether to believe her. She was rabidly opposed to Nancy seeing Langer from the beginning and had not softened at any point during the trip. Until now. Something was different about her. There was some change that told Nancy she was not telling the entire story, and therefore probably not the truth.

"When is he arriving?"

"I don't know. He said he would see us on the ship."

"I don't intend to step onto that ship unless he is with me."

"That's fine. We'll wait for him and all board together."

"I find it odd that you have decided not to oppose this."

"I didn't say I am not opposed. I said I am tired of fighting. Tired of fighting with you. I have done everything I can for you. You no longer have any need of me."

"There would be no fighting if you didn't keep trying to change me. All my life you wanted me to be someone else. Someone else like . . . Neil."

Celia glanced about the room to see if anyone was staring in their direction. Nancy was becoming emotional, her voice rising. Celia motioned for her to be calm.

"That's untrue. I always wanted you to be just you. I have tried to direct you away from habits and attitudes that will hurt you in future."

"You always loved Neil more," Nancy said, lowering her voice. "After he was gone you hated me for not being him."

The waiter's appearance with their dinners stopped a heating conversation from breaking into flames. Celia had ordered West Coast native style salmon cooked over alder wood. The waiter smiled and made a fuss of presenting Nancy with her steak.

"This looks lovely," said Celia. "I understand they cook it on a wooden plank and glaze it with their maple syrup."

Nancy tried to resume the discussion about their relationship and feelings for each other but her mother hushed her.

"This is our last night. Let's enjoy this. I can't hear any more of this. I don't have the time or energy for you anymore. I have made a good life for you and your father. Perhaps it's time I found my own."

The rest of the dinner was pleasant enough, Nancy sulking and saying little while her mother enthused about the salmon and the view.

The band exploded into dance music as they finished their coffee and desserts.

"Tomorrow is a big day," said Celia. "We should get to bed early. I want to be able to leave in plenty of time to get through immigration at the ship dock."

They readied themselves for bed without conversation. When the lights were out Nancy lay on her back staring into the darkness and wondering was going on in her mother's head. The mention of perhaps finding her own life. The sudden acceptance of Niles. Sometimes she wondered about her mother's mental health.

Nancy was confused, but inside the confusion was a deep suspicion. Her mother had a plan, Nancy had convinced herself. And, it likely had something to do with keeping Niles Langer off the Niagara. She had to be alert to make sure that did not happen.

CHAPTER 38

Terra Firma

"Terra firma!" Bertie exclaimed stepping through the Electra's rear door and down the two steps onto the black asphalt tarmac at the Lethbridge airport. "Steaming across the Pacific will be like floating on a bowl of cream compared to this. If we ever get to the ocean."

He was talking to no one in particular as the passengers exited the plane and milled about, trying to steady rubbery legs and clear woozy heads. Some looked peaked and the stewardess held one by the elbow to keep him from keeling over. He was the one that Bertie had mentioned as throwing up buckets in the rear of the plane.

It had been a rocky ride across the Prairies. The flight was delayed by strong headwinds that tossed the Electra about like a tin can even though the skies were totally clear.

The pilot reported that the clear but rough skies ended just inside the Rocky Mountains and they would have to overnight in Lethbridge. The ceiling over the mountains between Lethbridge and the coast was low with thunderstorms forecast. The Electra did not have the high ceiling capability to get over them. They would continue on early the next day when the weather was less threatening.

When the group entered the terminal an airline employee intercepted the crew and asked if they knew a Montreal-Vancouver passenger name Mr. Coulson.

"That's him there just picking up his bag," said the stewardess.

The employee, a young man barely beyond pubescence with a face rioting with pimple eruptions, approached Bertie and handed him a telegram. It had been sent from Vancouver and was from Celia.

NIAGARA DEPARTS 5 PM. MEET US PORT OF VANCOUVER IMMIGRATION 4 P.M. OFFICERS KNOW WHO YOU ARE. CELIA.

So, finally an end in sight to this around-the-world chase, Bertie muttered as he stuffed the telegram in his suit jacket pocket. He wondered what the plan was and whether he would have the chance to meet and confront this pervert. Beyond that he had to think about how to handle Nancy.

He did not know what to expect but settled himself by thinking that perhaps Celia had exaggerated the situation.

Taxis were waiting to take the passengers and crew into downtown. Bertie rode in one taxi with Langer and two other passengers. He had tried to get into the other taxi with the two pilots and the stewardess but another passenger beat him to it.

"Have you ever seen such a dismal landscape," Bertie remarked as he stared at the unbroken prairie rolling by.

"Bleak but a lot of history here," said one of the passengers who had a front seat.

"How so?" asked Langer who was squeezed between Bertie and another man.

"Right near here was Fort Whoop-Up, the most notorious whiskey trading forts in the West. It was so wild out here that the government got fed up and formed the North West Mounted Police and sent them out to restore order. Today they are called the Royal Canadian Mounted Police."

"Ah yes," Langer said in his most sarcastic British tone. "Better that they had left them chasing whiskey runners."

The other passengers looked at him, waiting for an explanation but the taxi pulled up to a three-story brick hotel on the corner of a downtown street.

The outside entrance to the Alexandra Hotel did not impress. From the sidewalk it looked like it had once been a storefront, which it had. A butcher shop had occupied part of the front floor level. Inside was not less unusual. The lobby also served as the terminal for the Greyhound Bus Lines.

It was empty now, with no buses scheduled until the next day. During the check-in Bertie heard the pilots talking about going to a Chinese restaurant for dinner.

"There's an idea," he interjected. "Let's make it a party. I'll stand drinks for the whole group."

The crew accepted happily as did two of the other passengers. Langer begged off.

"I'm afraid the flight did me in," he explained. "I'm not sure dinner would sit well. Thanks for the generous offer and we'll see you all in the morning."

It was a fun evening at the restaurant. The crew members were relaxed and obviously trying to please the passengers. It was critical for the airline to build a reputation of safe, comfortable cross-country service. One satisfied customer told three other potential flyers but an unhappy passenger passed along a negative service experience to three times that number.

The crew did not drink but that did not deter Bertie and the other passengers. There was much alcohol-fuelled joviality by the time the dinner ended. However, Bertie's not-so-subtle attempts to cut the stewardess out of the herd and take her off with him were not successful. She joked and laughed a lot but kept him at a distance.

CHAPTER 39

Vancouver

THE ELECTRA ROARED off Lethbridge Runway 27 early the next morning into the strong westerlies riding the long tail of overnight thunderstorms. It was seat belts and no service as the plane pitched and rolled through peaks and troughs of rough air. The plane seemed to make little headway against the winds, and passengers peering through the porthole windows saw what appeared to be a never-ending array of mountain peaks and forested valleys.

It seemed that the aircraft would be up there forever, but the crew announced that they would make Vancouver within fifteen minutes of scheduled arrival. Enough time for Bertie to get a taxi into the city and reach the ship docks by four p.m.

The mountains peaks eventually gave way, revealing a broad valley and plains stretching out to a thin line of blue – the Pacific Ocean. The plane descended, making a couple of steep turns before flattening its glide over the water, worrying passengers about when, and if, land would show beneath them.

A bump and the screech of tires on pavement announced touchdown on a runway that appeared to extend into the ocean. The plane taxied to a stop at the terminal and the passengers spilled out of the rear door, once again seeking their land legs and sucking in the fresh ocean air.

"Shall we share a taxi to downtown?" Bertie asked Langer, who hesitated, then agreed. "I'm going direct to the ship terminal," Bertie said. "Are you going directly over to Victoria?"

"Yes," Langer lied. "At six o'clock so I have some time."

Their conversation during the cab ride was limited to the beauty of the Vancouver area. Bertie remarked it was similar to Sydney but not quite as picturesque. He had little interest in his fellow passenger; where he lived, or what he did.

When the taxi arrived at Ballantyne Pier on the Vancouver waterfront, the men exchanged pleasantries, shook hands and parted at the main entrance. Bertie followed the international departures sign while Langer hesitated, appearing to look for the dock where ferry passengers embarked for Victoria.

Odd fellow, thought Bertie as he walked the concourse. Not talkative. Moody Brit. They were all like that. He would be glad to get back home to normal company.

He stopped at a bench in front of and just off to one side of the immigration checkpoint. He was anxious, not knowing what exactly to expect. He assumed his wife and daughter would be here waiting for him. He did not notice the two immigration officers with their heads together looking at a photograph. One of the officers approached him.

"Excuse me sir. Are you bound for Australia on the Niagara?"

"Yes, I am. I'm just waiting for my wife and daughter."

The officer looked at the photo again, did not ask to see a passport and took him by the elbow, guiding him to a doorway off the concourse.

"Come along with me, sir."

Bertie, remembering Celia's note, followed without protest.

"We are going to join my wife and daughter?" he asked.

"There are some people here who want to speak with you," the officer said curtly, heightening Bertie's anxiety. Some people? Had something happened to Nancy and Celia?

As the officer and Bertie disappeared through a side doorway, Langer appeared on the concourse. He walked smartly up the immigration desk where the lone officer was watching his partner take Bertie away and presented his passport.

"British, eh," said the officer. "Off to Australia are you?"

"Yes, sailing on the Niagara," Langer smiled broadly. "Going to visit my sister."

"Have a safe passage," said the officer stamping the passport and handing it back while he turned to see if his partner had had any problems with the man he was escorting to the immigration shed.

CHAPTER 40

Interrogation

Celia and Nancy sat in hard back chairs and stared up at the swirled pattern in the white plaster interrogation room ceiling. They had been brought there when Nancy, as Celia had planned, refused to go through the immigration checkpoint without seeing Langer. The immigration checkpoint officers had been briefed that this was expected and took the two women off to the immigration shed.

There was a furtive tap on the door soon after they were seated. The deputy director of immigration for the Port of Vancouver stepped in. He was a burly man with hard, no-nonsense eyes and a bald spot beyond his forehead that reflected the harsh lighting from above.

"I understand there is a problem here," he said firmly.

"I told my mother earlier that I will not board the ship without my friend. She wants to separate me from him. He is supposed to be here now."

"That may be," the deputy director said clasping his hands behind his back and circling the stained wooden table where the women sat.

"However, you have no right to remain in Canada. We can order you on board the ship."

A flicker of alarm showed in Nancy's eyes but was quickly replaced by defiance. "I am not leaving without him."

"Perhaps he's already on board ship, Nancy," her mother said, making an effort to conciliate the situation.

"That's a possibility," said the deputy director. "And easily enough confirmed or denied. You are sailing on the Niagara?" When Celia nodded, he stepped back and lifted the wall phone earpiece off its cradle. "We'll call Canadian-Australiasian Line and find out."

Nancy looked surprised and somewhat pleased.

"Hello, it's Donaldson at immigration," the deputy said loudly and with authority. "Let me speak to the general manager. Yes, Donaldson at immigration here. Can you quickly check whether you have a Vancouver-Sydney passenger by the name of . . . "He looked toward Nancy. "What is the gentleman's name again?"

She told him. "Yes. Langer, Mr. Niles Langer." There was a long pause, then "He has! That's fine." He was about to hang up when he saw the suspicion on Nancy's face. "Hold on. Can you confirm that for someone else?"

Donaldson motioned Nancy to the phone and handed her the earpiece. "Hello," said the voice at the other end. This is Mr. Radford. Mr. Langer has a first-class cabin Vancouver to Sydney. He apparently called from the airport to leave a message for his travelling companions that he will see them at the terminal or on board."

Nancy thanked the man on the other end of the line and hung up.

"That's settled," said Donaldson. "Here are your passports. You are cleared to leave. Feel free to wait here if you wish. Have a good trip."

He left the room and headed for his office to telephone that lawyer to tell him the plan worked well. The Langer fellow was being questioned in a nearby room. Maybe a couple of kidney punches were changing his mind about chasing young girls. Everyone should be satisfied, especially whoever managed to get the brass in Ottawa on the case.

"Let's go," said Nancy. "I'll wait at the top of the boarding ramp for Niles."

"We should wait here for him," said Celia. "You had said you refused to board without him so I suggested that he meet us at immigration. The checkpoint officers will direct him here. It's near sailing time and if there is a mix-up he might miss the ship."

That made sense. Nancy remained seated, pleased with how her persistence had won this battle of wills against her mother.

It wasn't that she hated her mother. It was just that she was always trying to break her spirit. If her mother had had her way, she would have been raised to become a nun. Niles initially would be a problem for her father, but she could work on that.

"I'm going to the washroom." Celia said. "When he arrives wait here for me and we can all board together."

Fifteen minutes passed and her mother had not returned. Nancy wondered what was taking her so long. She got up from her chair when there was a quick rap on the door and it opened. She expected to see Niles, but the person who entered was an immigration officer.

"We need you to identity someone down the hall. Can you come along please?"

• • •

"Have you Canadians all gone mad," Bertie shouted at the two RCMP officers who had been waiting for him when he was escorted into the interrogation room. "Christ, can no one in this country think for themselves!"

"Calm down buddy," said one of the officers, the tall slick-looking one with the pencil thin 1920s movie star moustache. He was doing most of the talking while the other, a fellow who looked like a retired football player leaned against the wall and watched. The immigration officer who had brought Bertie to the room was leaning against an opposite wall.

"The country is at war. We have information about you expressing Nazi sympathies on several different occasions. We need to find out what you are about."

"I am not a Nazi sympathizer," Bertie shouted slamming his fist so hard against the table that it rocked.

"That's what a lot of you British upper class say," snorted the bigger cop who pushed himself off the wall crossed the floor and pushed his oversized pocked face to within a couple of inches of Bertie's.

"What are you talking about? I am not British, you fool. I am Australian. Are you too stupid to distinguish accents?"

"Call me a fool again and I'll make your face a part of this table." The big cop grabbed Bertie by the hair and appeared ready to drive his face into the tabletop. "Then the young girls you chase won't find you so interesting."

Bertie became frightened. These people were mental cases. They obviously had him mixed up with someone else, someone who they intended to do some damage to. He pointed at his two bags that accompanied him to the room and which the immigration people had tossed into a corner.

"Please. I am not British. I am from Sydney, Australia. Can't you tell the accent. Look in my bag. I have my travel documents there."

The moustachioed cop walked over and poked the bags with a scuffed black loafer. Then he bent over and began pawing through them. He pulled out a leather passport case and brought it to the table where he emptied its contents including an Australian passport.

"Is this yours or did you steal it?" sneered the cop.

"It's mine. Open it and you'll see my photo. That's what you normally do with passports. Or did they not teach you that in police kindergarten."

The big cop grabbed Bertie's elbow with a huge meaty hand and twisted it until Bertie howled.

"It's his photo," said the other cop. "Havard Coulson, Sydney, Australia." He motioned the other to let go of the elbow and to back away.

"Have you any other way of proving who you are?"

"A passport is recognized as proof by most governments," Bertie sneered. "However, my wife and daughter are here somewhere. I was supposed to meet them at 4 p.m. but your goons prevented that."

The slick cop turned to the immigration officer and nodded toward the door. "Go down the hall and see if the women are still there. Bring them here."

Minutes later the door opened and Nancy entered with the immigration officer at her elbow. She looked across the room dumfounded.

"Daddy! What are you doing here? Where did you come from?"

She ran across the room as Bertie rose and clutched her to his chest.

The officer who Bertie had mentally named Slick stepped forward with a look of grave concern.

"Is this your father?" he asked.

"Of course it is. What are you doing with him? He's supposed to be at home in Sydney."

Bertie held her by the shoulders and stared at her.

"Did your mother not tell you?"

"Tell me what?"

Slick looked at the pair then put his fingers to his forehead and stared at the floor. He had a deep empty feeling that someone had made any incredible screw-up. Despite information given them it appeared that the girl and the man were daughter and father, not the infatuated girl and the Nazi pervert.

"Everyone just relax and stay put," he said. "I've got to find out what's going on here." He slammed the door on his way and headed for the main immigration offices.

"I have friends in the Australian government and they are going to hold someone in this backward country accountable for this," Bertie told the two remaining officers.

"Our government is too busy at the moment preparing our young guys to go out and face your Nazi bullets," said the meaty RCMP officer.

Nancy and Bertie, both totally confused, huddled in a corner muttering and asking questions of each other, no longer aware of their surroundings or the passing minutes. Half an hour later, Slick, looking sickly pale, returned with Donaldson, the immigration deputy director, who was obviously distressed and fumbled his words.

"I'm sorry, there's been a dreadful mix-up," Donaldson said, trying to focus his thoughts on the telephone calls he had made to the lawyer Richardson and the meeting with his director. The entire mess was too confused to even begin sorting out now. He was sweating profusely and motioned one of the officers to open a window.

"I'm not sure what to . . . ."

A long blast from a ship's horn drowned the rest of his sentence. He stepped to the interrogation room window overlooking the harbour and saw the ship's blast came from the Niagara as it signalled a portside turn and passage under the Lion's Gate Bridge and out to sea.

CHAPTER 41

Open Sea

CELIA LEANED OVER the Niagara's starboard rail and let the breeze wash her face and play with her hair. The light ocean breeze, stiffened by Niagara's forward thrust, seemed to penetrate her skin, massaging taut muscles and nerves in her neck and shoulders. She drew in a lungful of cool air and felt it evaporate the tension.

She stared up at the Lion's Gate Bridge spanning the First Narrows entrance to Vancouver harbour. So spidery, its steel members and cables much more delicate than Sydney's Coathanger. Perhaps because it was longer and lankier and placed in a much prettier setting, which was unusually bright and sparkling under a cloudless sky. The mountains behind the north shore were almost overbearing and from sea level below the bridge. Vancouver's urban sprawl was hidden from view.

Beyond the bridge, open ocean appeared but really it was only the Strait of Georgia and its cluster of large and small islands. The Niagara would turn south to avoid the Gulf Islands, cross the United States border and set a southern course for San Francisco where there were various choices of connections to ships that would pass through the Panama Canal and steam across to Europe, or sail west to Hawaii and Australia.

Celia was at peace with herself. Weeks of careful thought went into her decision to be here. She did not consider her actions impulsive. Her statement to Nancy the night before that she no longer had the time nor energy for her was not an impetuous comment that slipped out in the heat of argument. She had reflected upon it and chose the words carefully. That's what the old stag in *Bambi* had said, wasn't it?

Children reach a point where their parents owe them nothing. A parent provided a child with life, protection and all the tools and advice for living a constructive life. How the child used these in adulthood was up to he or she.

The whole purpose of relinquishing parental control was for the adolescent to develop self-control. Some parents never understood that their purpose was to equip and prepare a child for adulthood, not to be a guardian angel directing every step through life. Their motives for not letting go were selfish. They resented letting go, thinking "this is what I get for investing so much in their lives?"

As for Bertie, they both realized that they never belonged together. He was basically a good man. Self centred but generous. Life was easy for him because he never gave it much thought. It was full speed ahead and deal later with the consequences.

Celia pushed the hair away from her face and walked the deck to her cabin to unpack. There was not as much luggage because she had arranged for a porter to remove Nancy's trunk and bags at last minute, saying her daughter had decided to stay on in Vancouver to be with her father.

She opened the double doors to the bedroom section of the stateroom and smiled when she saw the long-stemmed red rose on the white satin bed pillow. She lifted it gently and breathed in its fragrance. It was a cool, wet fragrance with only a hint of sweetness. It reminded her of a spring garden in Wahroonga.

She picked up the note set beside the rose. She unfolded it and read: "Things are not always what they appear to be."

There was a light tap on the cabin door. Celia opened it and embraced the visitor. He took the rose from her fingers and set it down on the side table that held a small bottle of champagne and two glasses. He uncorked the wine, poured it into the glasses and handed one to Celia. Their glasses clinked to his toast:

"Trouble free passage!" he smiled.

Celia returned the smile and raised her glass.

"No passage is ever trouble free, Niles. But there are passages that must be taken."

EPILOGUE

Twilight slid across her face like the shadow of butterfly wings descending for the night. Soft twilight smoothing the puckers and pleats of age and caressing the heavy eyelids, encouraging her to sleep.

Celia resisted. Sleeping would deprive her of the garden's splendor.

The twilight signaled the English daisies to fold their petals and hide their bright smiling faces for the night. The day lilies stood sturdily against the rising evening breeze, their delicate appearance belying their toughness and tenacity.

The evening air was thick with blossom scent. Lavender and lilac and roses. Yes, the roses, the vibrant stars of any garden.

She sensed that this was much like a garden in another time. She wanted to remember that other garden, but her mind resisted going back.

Going back was like turning a ship around into its wake. Once the ship has turned, two wakes blend into one, mixing present and past. Confusing the real and the imagined.

The magnificence of the garden in which her wheelchair sat was real. Roses, heady, bold, rebellious. Metaphors for life. Symbols of freedom, of independence gained. But roses came with thorns in the form of doubts and questions that prick the conscience. Once you understand who you are, should you be free to be that person? Does it matter that knowing who you truly are and being that person can drastically change the lives of others?

The answers did not exist here and now. They would be found only when the eyelids closed for a final time, allowing her to slip inevitably toward that brightly-lighted door behind which all answers are said to be found.

The cooling air chilled her, and as she reached for the blanket covering her legs, she felt a touch on her shoulder.

It must be him, she thought. Bringing my shawl. She heard a voice but could not grasp its words. Then the hand moved away.

She forced her eyes to open wider, but the twilight dulled her vision. Off to one side, blurred by shadows, were two figures, one with long, dark hair. The other appeared brighter with a white dress and white veil. They spoke to each other quietly and Celia could not catch the words. She was confused about why they were here in her garden and why they whispered, so she shut her eyes again and tried to hear them better.

"She loves being out in the garden but we worry about her catching a chill," said the one that was a white blur.

The figures moved further away.

"She always loved her garden," said Nancy. "It was the best in Wahroonga. My father tried to keep it up for her but he got sick and passed more than a year ago."

"Your father, Havard Coulson? They were quite close I understand," said Sister Alexis.

"They adored each other," said Nancy. "It was difficult for dad once her mind started to go. She began inventing things, accusing him of drinking and cheating on her. It was heartbreaking, especially considering he was a lifelong teetotaler. And, in more than fifty years of marriage I doubt he ever looked at another woman."

She smiled, then added: "He was too busy working. The only days off he took were for their tea dances."

Sister Alexis cocked her head and glanced quizzically at Nancy.

"Every Sunday for years," Nancy explained. "They never missed the Sunday tea dance. They were excellent dancers. She loved to tango but my father was a waltz man. I used to call him the waltz king. If I recall correctly they won a few competitions. Her dream was to go to the Waldorf's Palm Court tea dances in London."

"They never got to go?"

"My father had plans but it was too difficult to travel after the dementia started. We thought it was just forgetfulness but then she began to invent all those crazy stories."

"It's the disease, dear," Sister Alexis said, placing her hand on Nancy's. "You can't blame her. Someday medicine will find a cure."

"They say that psychological trauma can cause it," Nancy offered. "She certainly had her share. We all did. My brother Neil died tragically as a teenager. Neither mom nor dad were quite the same. I don't think I was either, but fortunately I met Niles when we were both college freshies."

Alex nodded. "Yes. I've read in medical journals that parents who lose a child prior to midlife have a much high risk of developing dementia when they get older. The best we can do now is keep her comfortable."

She walked over to the wheelchair and spoke gently into Celia's ear.

"It is getting quite chilly and we are going to go in now, Mrs. Coulson. I promise we'll bring you out first thing in the morning."

"And Sunday Niles and the boys and I will come, mom," said Nancy. "We'll all have lunch together and you can tell the boys how to identify the flowers."

Alexis settled Celia in her room and turned on the television.

"She seems to enjoy that," Alexis said after Nancy had kissed her mother and stepped into the hallway.

"I have to get back and make supper. I'll be back tomorrow and we'll all come Sunday.

"Your family is so dedicated and kind. I wish they were all like that. Some of these people don't see family from one month to the next."

"Well, Niles has always loved my mother. And she him. I think he reminds her of Neil. They would be the same age. Neil was two years younger than I, so I robbed the cradle," Nancy laughed.

"God bless you dear. We'll see you tomorrow."

• • •

Inside the darkened room, Celia opened her eyes. Outside, the twilight had succumbed to darkness. The air held a coolness and she pulled her blanket higher.

Somewhere off in the distance she could hear music. It was a tango tune, with a bright and lively beat. She closed her eyes again and began to hum the tune.

I'm with you once more under the stars
And down by the shore an orchestra's playing

And even the palms seem to be swaying
When they begin the Beguine

She couldn't remember when or where she had heard the tune before. She felt warmer as she hummed it, although her shoulders still felt cool.

No matter, he would come soon with her shawl.

Niles would come. Or was it Neil? It was difficult remembering everything these days.

###